Purr M for Murder

A CAT RESCUE MYSTERY

T. C. LoTempio

CROOKED
LANE

NEW YORK

Published in the United States by Crooked Lane Books, an imprint of The Quick Brown Fox & Company LLC.

Crooked Lane Books and its logo are trademarks of The Quick Brown Fox & Company LLC.

Library of Congress Catalog-in-Publication data available upon request.

ISBN (hardcover): 978-1-68331-092-1
ISBN (ePub): 978-1-68331-093-8
ISBN (Kindle): 978-1-68331-094-5
ISBN (ePDF): 978-1-68331-095-2

Cover design by Louis Malcangi.
Cover illustration by Rob Fiore.
Book design by Jennifer Canzone.

Printed in the United States.

www.crookedlanebooks.com

Crooked Lane Books
34 West 27th St., 10th Floor
New York, NY 10001

First Edition: March 2017

10 9 8 7 6 5 4 3 2 1

To all my furbabies past over the years: Phyllis, Misty, Trixie, Gata, and Zee . . . and to my current boys, ROCCO and Maxx! You are my inspiration!

Chapter One

"Sir Walter Scott said it best—cats are mysterious kind of folk."

I reached out a hand as I spoke to stroke the head of the silver-and-black-striped tabby that lay in my sister's arms. My sister Katherine (Kat for short) and I have always been confirmed animal lovers, which is why the job of director of Friendly Paws, the animal shelter located in our hometown of Deer Park, North Carolina, suited her to a T. Kat grinned at me and shifted the tabby so that its head was cradled against her chest, then reached over and squeezed my hand. "Oh, Sydney, I knew bringing you on board as a publicity consultant was a stroke of genius."

I held up my hand. "Better save all that praise until we see how the event turns out. Who knows, I might end up making lattes at Dayna's."

Kat shook her head vehemently, causing her blonde hair to fall across one shoulder. "Not a chance. Once the shelter's finances are back on track, I'm sure the mayor will make room in the budget to bring you on full time. Especially since advertising and publicity are your areas of expertise."

"Let's hope so." Up until a few weeks ago, I'd been the director of marketing at Reid and Renshaw, a prestigious New York ad agency. The agency had been exceptionally busy, and I'd just finished a grueling ad campaign and was looking forward to a quiet weekend getaway with my fiancé . . . until I walked in on him and my secretary in—ahem—a very compromising position. It didn't help matters either that my fiancé was Preston Renshaw the Third—the boss's son. I turned in my resignation that same afternoon, packed up my things, and moved out of the apartment we'd shared and into a hotel. One good thing Preston had done for me was share the name of his financial advisor; as a result, I had quite a tidy little nest egg saved up. I was mulling over my career options when my sister called. "If you haven't found another job yet, I've a proposition for you, Syd," she'd said. "The shelter's in trouble. Some of our donors didn't come through with expected donations, and our last two fundraisers have been duds. If this keeps up, we'll have to cut back on accepting homeless animals, and we might have to transfer some of the ones who've been here over six months. We need help. What do you say?"

What could I say? Kat was the one who'd stayed behind in Deer Park after high school, giving up college to take care of our ailing parents and run the family business so I could get the fancy education. One thing my sister and I had always shared was a deep love for animals. The thought of the shelter having to turn away helpless animals or turn some of their existing ones over to other shelters, many of which didn't have a no-kill policy like Friendly Paws, made me sick to my stomach.

And so I'd returned home to my roots, to Deer Park, to the sleepy town I'd once been so eager to escape. Its southern charm seemed a welcome respite now, after living with the hustle and bustle of New York City the past few years. And even though it might take a bit of getting used to, I had to admit, slow and sleepy sounded good after fast and frantic.

I leaned back in the leather chair. Kat and I were seated at a long table in the room abreast of the cattery that served as a playroom, which smelled of kitty litter, kibble, and pine-scented air freshener. I took a minute to study my sister. Two years my senior, she's tall and slender, a natural blonde with the kind of good looks that turn heads. Me, I'm the opposite. Petite, a bit on the curvy side, what most would call average looking. My only distinctive feature is my mane of long, wavy dark-brown hair that I try to soften by adding gold highlights. Right now, said hair was pulled into a chignon at the nape of my neck, a tribute to the superhot, humid North Carolina weather. "I'm so glad Dayna wanted to be a part of this," I said. "I mean, it's not like we gave her a lot of notice."

"True." Kat laced her fingers behind her neck and leaned back in her chair. "Dayna loves animals, and she thought it was a great idea—not only for the shelter but for her business as well. I'd like to see her succeed. After all, when you get down to it, the coffee shop was originally *McCall's*."

I nodded. When my father had passed away two years ago, Dayna Harper had bought the family business, McCall's Sweet Shoppe, after both Kat and I had declined wanting to try to make a go of it. She'd changed the name to Dayna's Sweets and Treats and had done pretty well. Of course, acquiring my dad's built-in clientele hadn't hurt, but lately it seemed business had been slacking off. Dayna attributed it to people veering away to buy coffee at kiosks and specialty shops, courtesy of the recently renovated supermall on the highway. Excited to revitalize the business, she'd been more than eager to give our idea a try.

"Honestly, I don't see how it can miss. Cat cafés are all the rage in Europe," I said. "Patrons who are interested in the interaction pay a cover fee that is split between the café and the shelter providing the animals. Think of it as a sort of supervised indoor pet rental. It's been a big success abroad, providing hundreds of otherwise homeless cats with loving humans and good homes."

The little tabby let out a plaintive *merow*, and my sister shifted the cat in her arms just as the door to the cattery opened and Maggie Shayne, Kat's assistant and general right-hand person around the shelter, stuck her head in. "Hello, McCall sisters. Look what just came," she cried, holding up a large pasteboard sign. "Deer Park's First Cat Café Event—Where Cats and Humans Meet and Greet" was emblazoned across the top of the sign in large black letters. Underneath were photos of some of the shelter cats in different poses, playing with each other and with some of the shelter volunteers.

"Ooh, that came out great!" Kat squealed.

I bobbed my head up and down and shot Maggie a big grin. "Those photos you donated add a nice touch, Maggie. They make the posters seem more personal. Good job."

Maggie blushed right to the roots of her henna-tinted hair. "Thanks. I'm glad I could help."

I leaned in for a closer look at the poster and then pointed to the photo at the top of a large gold-and-white cat. "All the cats are adorable, but I have to say, I'm kind of partial to this one."

Maggie peered at the picture over the rims of her violet-framed glasses. "Ah, that's Toby. He's been here for a while." She shot Kat a quick look. "Sort of our unofficial mascot, right?"

Kat gently disengaged the tabby's claws from her blouse and passed the cat across to Maggie. "Put Sheila back in her cage, won't you? And yes, I guess you could call Toby that—sort of."

I felt a pang of disappointment. "Oh, so he's not available for adoption then? I thought all the cats in the photos were."

"Oh, no, no." Maggie shook her head. "Every cat here at Friendly Paws is available for adoption. Toby's just . . . fussy." She made a shooing motion with her free hand. "I don't know how else to describe it. He's had plenty of people interested in him, but . . . he always manages to do something to discourage them. As a matter of fact . . ." She leaned forward and said in a conspiratorial tone, "We call him the Wanderer."

The lyrics of the popular Dion song from the fifties floated through my brain. "The Wanderer? Why, does he roam around a lot?"

Maggie walked across the hall to the cattery. I saw her pause before a large cage, open the door, and gently deposit Sheila inside. She moved over to another cage, opened that door, and scooped its occupant, a pretty brown-and-white-striped tabby, into her arms. She walked back into the play-room and said, "Oh, yes. And not only inside the shelter. Every now and then, he manages to sneak outside. We're not quite sure how he does it. Once, he was gone two days. But he always comes back."

I touched the cat's picture lightly with my forefinger. "He looks like he's got wanderlust in his soul," I murmured. "I wonder what he's searching for?"

"Some say the perfect mouse, but I like to think he's searching for the perfect human, the one who will make his life complete," Maggie said. "One day, he'll find just the right one. I checked his cage before. He's out wandering now, or I'd introduce you."

I dragged my eyes reluctantly away from Toby's photo and tapped a nail against the poster. "Getting back to the event . . . our full-page ad will run in the Deer Park Her-ald on Thursday and Friday, and I also placed smaller ones in the surrounding towns' papers. That should attract cat lovers here. Plus, I've arranged to have a reporter from the *Herald* cover the event."

Kat chuckled. "This reporter wouldn't happen to be your roommate, now would she?"

I flashed her a wide smile. "None other. Leila said she'd be thrilled to do it. It beat the garden show that her editor wanted her to cover." Leila Addams had been my best friend all through grammar and high school. We'd lost touch after graduation, when I went to NYU and she went off to study journalism at East Carolina University in Greenville. We'd managed to reconnect in recent years, and she was the first one I called after discovering Preston's infidelity. "I never liked him," she'd declared in her slow southern accent. "I never trusted him. Spoiled rich playboy. Don't you dare waste a minute crying over him. Men!" When I called her a few days later to tell her about my decision to move back to Deer Park, she immediately insisted I move in with her. "Grandad's house is way too big for me," she'd insisted when I demurred. "Honestly, I'm tired of rattling around there all by my lonesome. You'd be doing me a favor, Syd."

In the end I acquiesced. Kat and I had sold the family house along with the business, and Kat's three-room apartment was way too small for a roomie. The idea of living alone after cohabitating with Preston for the last two years didn't thrill me, and I had to admit I was looking forward to being with my best bud again. Although, between Leila's erratic hours and the time I put in at the shelter, we'd seen precious little of each other. I was hopeful, though, that once the shelter was back on track, that would change.

Maggie snuggled her face into the cat's fur. "Delilah is especially looking forward to Saturday. She's been at the shelter for almost two years now. She needs—no, she *deserves*—a chance at a good home."

I bit back a grin. "The cat's looking forward to Saturday, huh? Did she tell you that?"

Maggie chuckled and adjusted the hem of her bright-pink T-shirt that read, "Friendly Paws Animal Shelter." "She didn't have to. Body language, Syd, body language. She used to skitter to the back of the cage when I went to pick her up. Now she comes right into my arms. Plus, she's purring like a race car."

I leaned forward. The cat was indeed purring loudly and had a look of kitty contentment on her pretty face.

I glanced at my watch and motioned to Kat. "We should get going. We promised Dayna we'd stop by the café so she could give us samples of the goodies she's making for Saturday, remember?"

Kat grinned as she pushed back her chair. "How could I forget? I hope those deluxe brownies of hers are on the menu. They're always a crowd pleaser." My sister has a sweet tooth the size of Texas; one would never guess to look at her, because she's thin as a rail. I, on the other hand, only have to look at a brownie and I gain ten pounds.

"Ooh," Maggie squealed as we headed for the door, "this is all so exciting. This fundraiser is going to be the biggest event that Deer Park has seen in a long time. If this doesn't pull Friendly Paws out of the red, nothing will."

I touched two fingers to my forehead in a salute as I followed Kat out the door. "Let's hope so."

*　　*　　*

Twenty minutes later, Kat and I entered Dayna's Sweets and Treats. Aside from changing the name, Dayna had kept the shop pretty much as my father had left it: The wide counter took up most of one wall, with high-backed stools in front of it. The glass case next to it showcased dozens of mouthwatering treats, all baked by Dayna and Louise, her niece-slash-assistant. The tables were still covered with the familiar red-and-white-checked tablecloths I remembered from my childhood. Dayna, an attractive African American woman, was behind the counter, ringing up a brownie and a coffee for a tall gentleman, and as soon as he paid and shuffled off to a table in the rear of the store, she came out from behind the counter and bustled over to us.

"The sisters McCall. Let me guess. You're here to check on the pop-up's progress?" she asked in her melodic voice. Dayna was about five foot seven, slight build, with straight black hair that she wore in a bob that framed her heart-shaped face. No one on this planet would have ever taken her for fifty-seven years old; I'd almost fallen over when she whispered her age to me. Her face was clear and unlined, her skin dewier than a twenty-year-old's. She parted her thick red lips in a smile, revealing straight white teeth any movie starlet would envy. "I think you'll be pleased. McGee's Hardware really came through."

"Eddie McGee said all that was left was the carpeting," Kat remarked. She held out one of the signs. "We brought this for you."

Dayna took the sign with a wide smile. "I'll put it up in the window. It came out great. I'll eat my hat if every one of those cats doesn't get adopted."

Kat grinned. "That's the point, right? To make a profit to benefit both businesses and to find the kitties good homes."

"Absolutely. Now about the pop-up." Dayna spread her arms wide and motioned us toward her back room. "Come see the transformation for yourself. Eddie finished laying the carpet down last night, and we brought some of those cat towers and scratching posts in. Pet Palace donated three boxes of squeaky toys."

I wasn't prepared for the sight that met my eyes as I stepped over the threshold, and judging from my sister's sharp intake of breath, she hadn't been either. "My gosh," I said. "This is amazing."

It really was. Eddie McGee, the proprietor of McGee's Hardware, had always been a loyal customer of McCall's and now Dayna's. He'd volunteered his own time and managed to turn the room that Dayna had been using as a sort of second-office-slash-coffee-storeroom into a gigantic playroom for cats and humans. There were some folding chairs and tables set up so that people could bring their goodies into the room. Scattered throughout were cat climbers, cat trees, scratching posts, and boxes with various toys designed to appeal to feline sensibilities. The rug was a soft rose color that went perfectly with the soft eggshell-white walls. It looked just perfect, and I told Dayna so.

"I'll pass your praise on," she grinned. "It sure was nice of Eddie to donate his time to this project."

"He said he wouldn't trust anyone else to do a good job. When you get right down to it, everyone wants to help animals in need," I said.

"Either that or he just wanted free coffee and doughnuts," Dayna said with a chuckle.

I grinned back at her. "Probably a little of both."

We walked back out into the main part of the café and took seats at the counter. "Did you finalize the menu for Saturday?" Kat asked Dayna.

"Sure did." Dayna reached beneath the counter and whipped out a sheet of paper. "Look that over and tell me what you think. And while you're doing that, how about some coffee? I just finished brewing a pot of Kona Royal . . ."

Dayna stopped speaking abruptly, her gaze fastened on the front door. A look of annoyance flashed across her face. I turned my head slightly, and the source of Dayna's discomfiture became quite clear.

Trowbridge Littleton.

Littleton was one of Deer Park's most influential citizens, if not *the* most. He was what southerners like to refer to as "old money." His father had made a pile of it in various investments, and upon his death, the entire fortune passed to Trowbridge as the sole heir. Kat had always said he was "richer than King Midas, with the personality of

Ebenezer Scrooge." The stories I'd heard through the years certainly bore that out. Littleton was also the proprietor of The Brush and Canvas, an art gallery located just down the street. There had always been speculation about just why he'd entered into that venture when he didn't need the money. Some said it was because he had a passion for art; others thought it was more likely a tax write-off. I was inclined to agree with the latter observation.

As he stood framed in the doorway, I took a minute to study him. He was tall and thin, with a pinched face, a beak nose, and a shock of unruly red-gold hair that he combed low to hide his receding hairline. Today he was dressed impeccably in a three-piece suit with shoes polished so bright, you could almost see your reflection. Littleton stepped inside the shop, shut the door behind him, and strode imperiously over to the counter where he stood, surveying us over his wire-rimmed spectacles. His lips thinned as he gave Kat a curt nod. "Ms. McCall," he said stiffly. His gaze shifted to me, and he raised a brow inquiringly.

"Mr. Littleton," Kat said stiffly. She laid a hand on my arm. "This is my sister, Sydney. She's recently relocated here from New York."

"Oh?" Interest flickered briefly in his beady eyes, and he fastened his gaze on me. "New York, eh? What happened? Big-city life too much for you?"

"Not at all," I answered, making sure to keep my tone cool. Arrogant people like Littleton tended to get on my nerves rather quickly. "You might say I felt a yen to return to my southern roots."

"Hmpf." His gaze shifted briefly to Kat, then flickered away. "I'm surprised to find you here, Ms. McCall," he said. "Shouldn't you be out saving raccoons, or whatever the animal in peril is at the moment, or something?"

Beside me, I felt Kat stiffen. Whereas I've been known to get overpassionate on a subject, my sister is usually calm, cool, and level-headed—that is, unless something happens to trigger her temper. Then, trust me, all bets are off. Nothing, I knew, could get a rise out of Kat faster than a slur on her beloved shelter. I reached out, grabbed her hand, and gave it a gentle squeeze. She let out a breath, and her shoulders relaxed. I did note her clenched jaw, though, as she answered, "Not today, Mr. Littleton."

Dayna, apparently sensing the tension, stepped forward. "So nice of you to drop by my shop, Mr. Littleton," she said. Her voice sounded even more syrupy than the sweet tea she loved to serve on a particularly hot day. "Can I get you something? Hot coffee? Iced coffee? Cappuccino?"

Some hot sauce in your coffee? I thought but didn't voice aloud.

He drew himself up to his full height, probably somewhere around five foot seven, only about three inches taller than me in my stocking feet. "Thanks but no thanks," he said stiffly. "I am not here for liquid refreshment."

Dayna arched a brow. "No? Then perhaps you'd like a fresh-baked muffin or brownie?"

He glanced over at the display case, shook his head. "I'm not hungry, either." He fixed Dana with a hawkish stare before pointing to the cat café sign on the counter. "I cannot believe that you are actually going to do this."

Dayna's rigid posture relaxed, and she faced him, unblinking. "Why not? It's really a very humane undertaking."

"Humph," he sniffed. "It would have been more humane to just let the animals find homes on their own. Why, this project is little more than a glorified petting zoo—much like the shelter itself."

Kat drew herself up to her full height. "We're much more than that, Mr. Littleton. Which you would know if you ever bothered to visit us."

"Visit you? Hah. That'll be the day." He tossed Kat a scornful look. "I did send you a letter detailing my concerns, Ms. McCall, which I notice you have summarily ignored."

Kat's shoulders squared, and her jaw thrust forward. I squeezed her hand—hard—and then turned my head so that I could look him straight in the eye. "I'm curious. Just what are your concerns, Mr. Littleton?"

His eyes narrowed. Dayna cut in quickly with, "Sydney's working at the shelter too. She's the new publicity director. I'm sure she can address your . . . concerns."

"Publicity director?" Littleton let out a snort. "I imagine the shelter needs all the help it can get. Okay then." He leaned an elbow on the counter and looked me up and down. "Well, for one thing—how are these animals to be presented? Are they just to be set free to roam about this establishment?"

"Of course not." I swept my arm in the direction of the storeroom turned playroom. "The cats are all set up in what we refer to as a 'pop-up' area, an area specifically designated for humans and cats to mingle. We realize that not everyone has an affinity for cats, or for sharing their coffee time with animals. So, for a modest fee, you can take your coffee and snack into our play area, where the cats are allowed to roam out of the cages. The customer is allowed to pet them, interact with them—although we do advise against feeding them any of the baked goods or coffees. There are treats provided if one wishes to feed the kitties."

"Oh." Littleton seemed a little taken aback by my statement. Apparently he'd envisioned walking into Sweets and Treats and seeing it overflowing with roaming felines. "So if someone were allergic, let's say . . ."

"The cats are in a confined area, so it shouldn't be a problem." I fixed him with a baleful stare. "Why, are you allergic?"

"Me? Most certainly not." He shifted his position, and for the first time, I noticed the clipboard tucked under his arm. "I'm merely thinking of the welfare of the customers. It seems to me that serving food in such an atmosphere wouldn't be the healthiest."

I thought about all the times my mother had made supper with old Ginger, the family calico, either meowing at her feet or watching closely from a nearby counter for scraps. "As I said, the cats are confined to one area, so . . . not a problem."

He pulled a handkerchief from his jacket pocket and swiped at a bead of perspiration on his forehead, then pointed an accusing finger at Kat. "You are so fixated on your quest to get revenue for that shelter that you can't grasp the simple point I was trying to make."

Kat's brows drew together, etching a deep line in the center of her forehead. "And that is?"

"That this little project of yours could adversely affect the retail community! The kinds of people who would stop to drink coffee and play with kittens might not be the types of people who'd be interested in purchasing fine art. Or jewelry or antiques, for that matter! You're so fixated on your shelter, you're not even considering how this event will affect the shopkeepers on this block."

Dayna, who'd been standing off to the side listening quietly, now let out a sound that sounded very much like a snarl. "I beg your pardon, but . . . you're crazy. I don't see how my partnering with Friendly Paws can be anything but a positive influence on our little retail community."

His tongue darted out like a snake, licked at his painfully thin lips. "I disagree," he rumbled. "And I'm sure I'm not the only one."

Dayna frowned. "No one else has an issue," she said.

He snorted. "That you know of. But mark my words, once they think about it . . ."

Dayna crossed her arms over her chest. "I think I've heard just about enough. So unless you want to order something, I'd like you to leave. Now."

Littleton shook his clipboard in the air and fixed Kat with a burning stare, which she returned unflinchingly. "Oh, I'll leave . . . for now. But this isn't over, not by a long shot. Trust me, even if you manage to pull this . . . this event off, your shelter still isn't in the clear."

I narrowed my gaze at him. "Is that a threat, Mr. Littleton?"

His lips twisted in a sneer. "Oh, it's much more than that, Ms. McCall. It's a promise. You and your shelter haven't seen the last of me."

Littleton tucked his clipboard back under his arm, turned on his heel, and stomped toward the door. He whipped it open just as a young girl pushed past him at the speed of light. The force sent Littleton tumbling backward. He managed to keep his balance, but his clipboard clattered to the floor.

"Oh my gosh! I'm so sorry!" squeaked the girl. I recognized her as Sissy Arledge. She was a high school junior who volunteered at the shelter two nights a week. She also worked for Dayna part time. She started to bend over to retrieve the clipboard, but Littleton beat her to it. He whipped it out from under her fingers, straightened, tucked it back under his arm, and regarded her with fire in his eyes.

"Don't you watch where you're going, you impertinent young thing?" he cried.

Sissy's face crumpled. "I said I was sorry," she murmured.

"Sorry, hah!" Littleton tugged at his jacket, reached up a hand to straighten his tie. "I greatly doubt that. You're like most of the youth today. You only care about yourself.

You're not even cognizant of the people around you. Your parents should have done a better job of teaching you manners, missy."

Out of the corner of my eye, I saw a red flush start to creep up Kat's neck. Sissy was a shelter volunteer and therefore fell under the umbrella of one of Kat's employees. One thing I knew—my sister was extremely protective of people who worked for her, like a mother lion protecting her cub. She whirled to face Littleton, her hands on her hips.

"Sissy's manners are just fine," she said in an even tone. "And I'll thank you not to insult my employee."

Littleton stared down his nose at her, no easy feat, since Kat was only about an inch shorter than him. "I beg your pardon. She knocked into me." He paused. "Wait. Did you say *your* employee?"

"That's right," Kat responded, her tone smug. "Sissy volunteers at the shelter, therefore she's also my employee. As for bumping into you, she didn't do it on purpose. It was an accident."

Dayna reached out and touched Sissy's arm. "Sissy, get yourself a cup of coffee before you start your shift."

"You don't have to tell me twice," muttered the teen. She scurried off without a backward glance.

Kat turned back to Littleton. "I didn't appreciate your comments in your letter, and I didn't appreciate your behavior here today. You are welcome to your opinion on the shelter, but please bear in mind that it is *your* opinion and not reflective of the entire retail community."

Littleton's eyes narrowed to slits. "That's what you think, Ms. McCall." He wiggled his fingers. "Money talks, you know. I'm rather influential in this community."

"And you seem to overlook the fact that most people here possess basic humanity," Kat said hotly. "You can complain all you want, Mr. Littleton, about both this event and the shelter. I don't care how much money you have, or how you wave it under people's noses, but I assure you that this time it will get you nowhere. This event is happening on Saturday."

Littleton's lips drew back in a snarl. "Over my dead body."

Kat turned her back on him. "Don't tempt me," she flung over her shoulder. Her next words came out with a snarl. "Mess with my shelter, Littleton, and it'll be the last thing you ever do."

Chapter Two

For a minute after Littleton charged out the door, we all just sat in stunned silence. Then Dayna let out a slow breath.

"Well that was . . . exciting?"

We all started to laugh. "Frankly, excitement like that, I can do without," I said.

"I think after Littleton, we all need to get the bad taste out of our mouths. I've got some cherry scones coming out of the oven. How about a scone and a big mug of that Kona coffee?" Dayna turned toward Kat and winked broadly. "The way you stood up to that man, you deserve some sort of reward."

We both flashed Dayna a grateful smile. "Sounds good," said Kat.

We made our way to a table while Dayna bustled off to the kitchen. I noted that the man who'd been sitting at the rear table had vanished, most likely scared off by Littleton, and we settled into the table next to the one that had been formerly occupied. I leaned forward and placed my hand on my sister's arm. "I had a feeling there was a bit more to all this. Why didn't you tell me he sent you a letter?"

She sighed. "I was going to tell you, I really was, but the right moment never came up. To be perfectly honest, I can't see how anyone, no matter how influential they think they are, would want to put a stop to something that could benefit so many defenseless animals. Although after this display today, I can't help but wonder."

"Well . . ." I leaned back in my chair and stretched my legs out in front of me. "I think Littleton's got the market cornered on selfish. He makes Ebenezer Scrooge look like a saint."

I saw Kat's lips twitch. "Yes, he does, doesn't he? Well, I guess I lost my cool with him, but I just couldn't take any more after he was so rude to Sissy."

"Could he make trouble for us?" I asked.

Kat reached up to tug absently at a blonde curl. "He'd certainly try. I know he was a large contributor to the mayor's campaign." She let out a long sigh. "He was never a fan of the shelter, but his attitude toward it has gotten worse recently."

"Yeah, it's like he's obsessed." I stroked at my chin. "Remember what Nana used to say."

"Never trust someone who doesn't like animals." Kat rubbed at the sensitive spot above her nose with her fingers, a sign she was getting a headache. "I hope he doesn't turn the other shopkeepers against the idea. I was hoping you might work your PR magic and get some of them interested in sponsoring similar events."

"Let's not overreact," I advised. I nodded toward Dayna, who was coming toward us with a tray laden with coffee and scones. "Let's just enjoy our break. But when we get back to the shelter, I want you to show me that letter."

"Okay," my sister said, but she avoided my gaze. I remembered her doing pretty much the same thing when we were kids, when she used to hold something back from me. I sincerely hoped that wasn't the case now.

*　　*　　*

We returned to the shelter, but we didn't get to peruse Littleton's letter right away. An abandoned cat was getting ready to deliver a litter of kittens, and that occupied the next few hours. At last, once the mama cat had delivered a healthy brood of three newborns, we left Maggie and another volunteer, Viola Kizis, to the task of tending to mother and children and retreated back to Kat's office just shortly before six PM. She opened the middle drawer of her desk, pulled out a piece of heavy, cream-colored stationery, and passed it across to me. I sat in silence for several minutes, deciphering the flowery handwriting and getting madder by the minute as I did. Finally, I looked up at my sister.

"Oh my God. He can't be serious."

"That's what I thought—at first. But now I'm not so sure."

I shook the letter in the air. "The man's a menace," I cried. "He actually thinks the shelter is a detriment to the town!"

Kat nodded, her lips drawn downward. "Oh, yes. I especially liked the part where he says the mayor should concentrate on areas that will help people, not animals. I hate to say this, but it almost sounds as if he's lobbying to get the shelter closed down."

"He wouldn't dare," I cried. "He'd make more enemies than friends if he spearheaded a campaign like that."

"Maybe," Kat mumbled. "I'm sure he'd find some way to do it, though, so he wouldn't appear to be too much of a bad guy."

"Any way would make him look like a bad guy, if you ask me," I said staunchly as I tossed the letter onto the desk. "The man's a lunatic, pure and simple."

"Hey, hey, who are you calling a lunatic? Not me, I hope?"

We both glanced up. We'd been so absorbed in Littleton's letter, we never even noticed the office door opening until the woman standing in the doorway spoke.

"I hope you girls haven't eaten, because I've got pizza and a nice pinot grigio."

I jumped up out of my chair and hurried to divest the newcomer of the large pizza box she balanced in one hand. "Leila. Oh my God. This is great. I was just wishing for a slice of Bella's Pizza." I gave her a quizzical look. "I thought you had to work late tonight?"

"It started out that way, but then old Parker got Mina Drayton to cover the Heritage Society tea, so I'm free as a bird tonight. I hope you two like pepperoni, onion, and mushroom, by the way."

"Our favorites." Kat pushed back her chair and crossed over to the large file cabinet against the far wall. "Unless I'm mistaken, there should be some paper plates and cups in one of these drawers."

While Kat rummaged through the file cabinet, I set the pizza box down on the small table by the window. Leila set her tote and the brown bag that read "Lambert's Liquors" down next to the pizza box, then stripped off her light French terry jacket and tossed it over the back of one of the chairs. I gave my friend's outfit—a slim black pencil skirt with a stunning, soft-looking petal-pink sweater—an appraising glance. With her mane of perfectly coiffed dark-red hair, high cheekbones, and almond-shaped eyes, one might take her for a runway model rather than a fashion-and-society reporter. Leila caught me looking and grinned. She placed her hands on her hips and swayed them in an exaggerated pirouette. "Not bad for thirty-five, eh?"

"No one would take you for a day over thirty. But honestly, you didn't have to dress up just for us," I said teasingly.

"Don't worry, I didn't. I just never went home to change." Leila flopped down on one of the hard-backed chairs and kicked off one of the killer heels she wore. "I swear that Paul Mastin is an expert at thinking up things to keep me in that office later than I should be."

I looked my friend up and down. "That's because he's got a major crush on you."

"Humph." Leila snorted. "Then he'd better tell his girlfriend. He's been going out with Dorrie Cavanaugh for six months now."

Kat's eyebrows bounced upward. "Dorrie Cavanaugh? The judo instructor at Gold's Gym?"

Leila's green eyes sparkled. "The very one, so he'd best behave."

I frowned as I surveyed the wine bottle. "Oho, you bought the good stuff. But it's got a cork. I don't think we have a corkscrew here."

Leila reached into her tote bag and pulled out a corkscrew, which she waggled in the air. "So how are the plans for the cat café event coming along? I'm really looking forward to covering it."

I handed her the wine bottle. "We're looking forward to it too—unless Trowbridge Littleton has something to say about it, that is."

Leila shot me a startled glance. "Trowbridge Littleton? King Midas's evil twin? What does he have to do with it?"

"We're not sure yet. We were at Dayna's café this afternoon, going over the menu, and he came in and tried to make trouble over us having the shelter cats there."

"Now why am I not surprised? That man will do anything to cause a scene." She maneuvered the corkscrew, and we heard a soft pop as the cork came loose. Leila filled the glasses and passed them around. Kat lifted the glass to her lips, tipped her head back, and downed half of the contents in one large gulp. Then she held the glass out to Leila for a refill. "That's good stuff," she said, wiping the back of her hand across her lips. "Plus, it's been a very long day, made longer with this Littleton drama."

"Doesn't surprise me. He probably tied tin cans to cat's tails when he was a kid." Leila lifted the lid of the pizza box, and we all inhaled the enticing aroma of sauce, pepperoni, and mozzarella. "He's always writing to Ed Mortimer, the owner of the Deer Park Herald, about one thing or another. Last week, I believe he was complaining about Buck's eatery. The aroma from Buck's garbage was assaulting his senses, or some such nonsense. And the week before, he had it in for Grace Topping."

I took a sip of wine and reached for one of the paper plates Kat had set on the table. "Grace Topping? Isn't she the sweet woman who runs the hat shop?"

Leila nodded. "Yeah. I saw them last week at the mall. I was waiting in line at the sticky bun place at the food court, and I just happened to glance up. They were over in the far corner, right behind the fountain. Littleton was red as a beet. He had poor Grace pressed up against the far wall by the fountain, and it looked to me as if he was haranguing her about something."

Kat frowned. "Are you certain it was Grace? I can't see her arguing with anyone, let alone Littleton."

"Well, I was all the way across the court, but I'm pretty positive it was her. She had on that coral sweater she always wears." She shook her head. "Grace's problem is she's too nice. She just sat there and took whatever he was dishing out. I'd have dumped my lunch all over his head and stormed out."

Both Kat and I rolled our eyes, and Kat nudged me. "Remind you of anyone?"

I wrinkled my nose. "Yeah. Littleton's a jerk just like Preston."

"Wow." Leila waved her slice of pizza in the air. "I do believe that's the first time you've mentioned your ex's name since you've come back to Deer Park."

I bit off a piece and chewed rapidly. "That's because he's really not worth mentioning," I mumbled.

Kat eyed me. "Honey, you're not the first girl to be taken in by a smooth-talking guy. It's just unfortunate that in this instance, he happened to be the son of your boss." She wiggled a finger at me. "That's why it doesn't pay to date coworkers. Or get engaged to 'em."

"Ouch," I said. "It's my own fault. I should have known better, but—honestly, we seemed so perfect together. We liked the same books, the same movies, the same plays . . . I had absolutely no idea that he was dating my secretary at the same time, until . . ." I left the sentence unfinished, because they both knew full well what had transpired.

Leila and Kat exchanged a glance, and then Kat cleared her throat. "Well, they're together now, and I've got my sister back, so as far as I'm concerned, everything's hunky-dory." She slid her arm around my shoulders. "You know, just because you had one bad apple doesn't mean the whole barrel's bad. Who knows? Maybe once the shelter's back in the black, we can both start having more of a social life?"

I set the glass down. "Preston hadn't been supportive of me and my job for a while, and I knew we were drifting apart. I was just too lazy—and scared—to do anything about it. He found someone who suits him better, and I've got a whole new life." I snagged another slice of pizza and decided to change the subject. "You know, I never got a good look at that clipboard Littleton had tucked so carefully under his arm. I wonder what was on it."

"A petition to picket the shelter event, no doubt," Kat said, not even bothering to hide the bitterness in her tone.

"Maybe," said Leila.

I saw the expression on my friend's face and said, "You're hiding something, Leels. What is it you're afraid to tell us?"

Leila stretched her long legs out in front of her. "I don't know anything for certain," she said slowly, "but I heard Lola Whittier at the information desk talking to someone on the phone. I'm pretty sure it was Littleton. She was advising him on the correct way to file a petition."

Kat snapped her fingers in the air. "I knew it. He's trying to stop that event."

Leila squirmed in her chair. "It might be more than that. I've heard rumors—mind you, just rumors—that Littleton wants to get the shelter closed down permanently."

Kat and I exchanged a swift glance. "Maybe it's not the ravings of a lunatic after all," I murmured.

Leila shot me a sharp glance. "What on earth are you talking about?"

I plucked the letter from the desk and handed it to her. She read it through once, and then a second time, before handing it back to me with a scowl marring her lovely features. "He doesn't come right out and say it," she said, "but the implication is there. He thinks Deer Park would be better off without the shelter."

I took the letter and threw it on the coffee table. "Well, he can imply that all he wants, but he'd never get away with closing us down. He wouldn't get any signatures . . ." I paused as I caught sight of the stricken look on Kat's face. "Would he?"

Kat worried her lower lip. Once again, her gaze skittered away from mine. "You wouldn't think so, but Littleton's a bully. He browbeats people until they bend to his will, like he tried to do to us today. And some of these people are easily led."

"Say he did succeed. What would happen to the animals that are there now?"

"They'd be farmed out to other shelters." Kat ran a hand through her hair. "The big problem with that, though, is most shelters are overcrowded. Also, most of them don't have a no-kill policy like we do."

"So what you're saying, basically, is that if other shelters are too crowded to take our animals, they'll get put down?"

Kat hesitated, then gave a curt nod. "Unfortunately, that's exactly what I'm saying."

Leila reached for another slice of pizza. "What sort of person wants to close a place where defenseless animals can have a home until some kind human adopts them? Or deliberately make it so innocent ones are killed? Looks to me like Littleton is giving the Grinch a real run for his money." She paused. "Speaking of cute animals, I saw a real handsome cat nosing around outside when I came in."

"Big fellow? Orange and white?" Kat asked.

Leila nodded. "Is he one of yours?"

Kat nodded. "That would be Toby. Maybe he's wandering back in." She glanced over at me. "You'd like to meet him, wouldn't you, Syd? I'll be right back." She turned and hurried across the hall to the cattery.

I nudged Leila with my elbow. "Kat seems to think Toby and I would make the perfect couple."

Leila let out a laugh. "Well, maybe you would. He's got to be a damn sight better than Preston."

I leaned back and laced my hands behind my neck. "No arguments there."

"You know, if you want to get a cat, Syd, I really don't mind. Cats are a lot easier to have as pets than dogs, especially for a working gal. They pretty much take care of themselves."

I looked pointedly at my friend's outfit. "They also shed. Sometimes a lot."

Leila brushed at the hem of her skirt. "As long as you vacuum up the pet hair, I can buy a lint brush."

I placed my hand over my heart in an exaggerated gesture. "Awww . . . you'd do that for me?"

"Of course. What are besties for? Besides, when I have to cover something, I usually take my good clothes to the office to change."

I chuckled. "Your generosity overwhelms me, but I haven't even met the cat yet. Maybe I won't like him or he won't like me."

Leila snorted. "Who are you kidding? You love all animals. Remember the chameleon you had in fifth grade?"

My lips twisted into a grin. "Kammy the chameleon. I sure do. He was a great pet."

"Remember when your cousin Fred tried to flush him down the toilet?"

"Oh yeah. He might have succeeded if Kat hadn't caught him. Boy, did she give him what for! Even back then, she was a champion for animals."

We were still enjoying a chuckle over my first foray as a pet owner when Kat came back into the room. She shook her head. "Well, if it was Toby, he's apparently not ready to return. His cage is still empty." She sat down and picked up her wineglass. "Where were we?"

Leila shot her a mischievous grin. "Just discussing pets, past and present. I told Syd she could get a cat if she wanted." She held up her hand and made a crossing motion over her heart. "I promise not to flush it down the toilet."

"Down the toilet? What brought that—oh, right. Kammy!"

We all laughed, and then I picked up my glass and raised it high in the air. "I've made an executive decision. Littleton isn't going to get away with ruining our event or closing us down. Tomorrow I'm going to go over to his store and try to reason with the man."

Kat reached out and plucked at my sleeve. "Oh no. That would be a mistake. Just . . . just let it go."

"I can't do that. You just said some of these people are easily maneuvered. What if he manages to convince them the event is a bad idea or, worse yet, that Deer Park would be better off without an animal shelter?" I gave my head a toss, causing wisps of brown hair to fly into my eyes. I brushed them back with the tips of my fingers. "This venture could be the break we're looking for. I'm not about to let him ruin it."

"Say," Leila interrupted. "You all might be panicking for nothing. After all, I'm not 100 percent certain that it was Littleton Lola was talking to."

I arched a brow. "Maybe, but having a talk with him certainly can't hurt. Sometimes it pays to be proactive."

"You really think you can reason with him?"

I swallowed. "I'm certainly going to try. I mean, it's not as if I haven't had to plead my case with a difficult client before. I did lots of that back in New York, and I usually won."

Kat and Leila looked at each other. Leila shrugged, and Kat let out a long sigh. "I still don't think it's a good idea, but I know you once you get your mind set on something. Just promise me that if he starts to get ugly or insulting, you'll walk away."

I knew how my sister hated confrontation. "Sure," I said, deliberately crossing my fingers behind my back. "Promise."

Kat eyed me. "I know you've got your fingers crossed."

I stuck my tongue out at her. "What, you've got Superman's X-ray vision now?"

"That's something that would certainly come in handy," chuckled Leila, "especially when Bobby Warren delivers something from UPS. Doesn't he look hot in those shorts?"

Kat's cheeks flushed a delicate shade of pink. "I wouldn't know," she murmured. She turned her gaze back to me. "If you're determined to go through with this, then I'm going with you," she announced.

I frowned. "That's not necessary."

"Oh yes it is. I don't feel like getting a call from the police that you've been arrested for disturbing the peace or, worse yet, assault."

"Oh, puh-leaze!" I rolled my eyes. "What do you think I'm going to do, go over there and beat the guy to a pulp?"

"No, but I wouldn't put it past him to try to have you arrested."

"Uh, excuse me. I'm not the one who went toe to toe with him this afternoon—you were."

"True. He ticked off my temper when he started berating Sissy."

"Right. So what makes you think he won't say something to tick you off tomorrow?"

"He probably will," Kat admitted. "But losing it won't get us anywhere with him." She raised her hand and laid it across her heart. "I promise that tomorrow I will be calm and cool as a cucumber—the voice of reason."

"Uh-huh. I still don't think the two of us should go. He might think we're ganging up on him."

"Maybe, but he might listen more to me. He wrote me that letter, remember? I'm the one who's in charge of the shelter, not you."

I threw up both hands. "Fine. But I want to get to him early—before anyone has a chance to put him in a worse mood than he's usually in."

Kat's jaw thrust forward stubbornly. "We'll have to get up uber-early, then. I understand Littleton usually gets to his store around six AM."

I wrinkled my nose. "So early? People buy art at six AM? I thought his shop opened at eleven."

"He probably wants to get away from his wife," offered Leila. "She's always in the gym by seven AM."

I looked at her. "He's married?"

"Yeah. And Petra is a real stunner. She's around our age, a former actress and model."

"Really? An actress? Was she in anything I'd know?"

"Doubtful," Kat laughed, "although I think she did have some minor role on a soap a few years ago. She did mostly modeling—he met her at some sort of show, I think."

I twisted my wineglass in my hand. "I wonder what she saw in him."

"Isn't it obvious?" Leila laughed. "His checkbook. Petra's quite the fashion plate. Only last month, she showed up at the Lamplighter benefit in a Galliano ivory lace sheath that cost over two thousand dollars. A waiter jostled her arm and got red wine all over the front. Fortunately, it was toward the end of the evening." She let out a low whistle. "Can you imagine that dry cleaning bill?"

Kat leaned forward a bit in her chair. "She was in Devon McIntyre's jewelry shop, looking over that new collection of estate jewelry last month. She bought a large yellow diamond ring and put a deposit on matching ear-rings. I don't know the exact amount, but it was close to five figures."

"No wonder he's so miserable . . . and cheap." I gave my sister a sharp look. "How did you find all this out, anyway? You and I don't run in the same circles as this Petra."

"I can guess." Leila leaned forward eagerly, her eyes twinkling. "Diane Ryan? The girl who replaced Betty Campbell as admin at the police station, right?"

Kat grinned. "The very same. Diane is Sissy's next door neighbor, and she's a big animal lover. Her landlord won't let her have pets, so she volunteers here two nights a week. And just like Betty before her, she loves a good gossip session." She leaned forward a bit and dropped her voice to a whisper. "She also told me that Petra's been rumored to be pretty hot and heavy with one of the trainers at the gym."

I drained my glass. "And Littleton's not jealous?"

Kat shrugged. "From what I understand, Littleton's got a roving eye as well. Sounds as if they've got—what do they call that again?"

"An open marriage," Leila supplied.

I let out a little snort of disgust. "I've never understood that term. Why get married in the first place if you're not going to be true to one another?"

"Probably because staying married is cheaper than a divorce, or at least it'd be that way for him," Leila said matter-of-factly. "Petra negotiated a whopper of a premarital agreement for herself. Married or divorced, *she* makes out like a bandit."

"That's a surprise. Littleton didn't impress me as the starry-eyed type."

"Just goes to show you, you never know. He had blinders on where she was concerned in the beginning. Starry-eyed, like a teenager. And since she didn't exactly coerce him into signing, he's got no recourse."

"See," I said, "this is what I missed about Deer Park—the gossip chain."

"Why?" Leila said, giving me a look of mock horror. "You mean New York has nothing like that? I find that hard to believe."

"Oh, New York had plenty of gossip. But it's different. I don't know how to explain it."

"I can," Leila said brightly. "Gossip's more personalized here—fewer people. It's a lot easier to know who you're talking about in a town the size of Deer Park. Our population is forty thousand, and what's New York City? Six million?"

"Closer to ten, but who's counting?"

"Not me." Leila reached for the bottle of wine, shook it, and made a face. "Damn, all out. I knew I should have bought two."

"Hmm, there might be something in the storeroom," Kat said. Leila and I both turned to look at her, and she blushed. "Well, once we found out that we could hire Syd as a consultant, we had a little celebration. I'm pretty sure there was at least one bottle left over."

"You shelter people will use any excuse to par-tay!" grinned Leila.

Kat started to rise, but I could see how fatigued she was. I held up my hand. "Hang on. I've got it."

She flashed me a grateful smile. "Thanks. It should be in the big storage cabinet, top shelf."

I walked into the hall and down two doors to the storeroom. I saw the storage cabinet, tucked into the corner right next to the picture window, and made my way over to it. Just as I was about to open the cabinet, I happened to glance over at the window—and I let out a gasp as I saw a gold, furry face pressed there. "Toby?" I murmured. I reached out to touch the window, and as quick as that, the feline face vanished. I reached out, pulled up the window, and leaned out just in time to see a gold-and-white tail disappear into the shrubbery that surrounded the shelter. "Well, Maggie did say they call you the Wanderer," I murmured.

I couldn't help it—Maggie's words came flooding back to me. *"I like to think he's searching for the perfect human, the one who will make his life complete."* I stood staring out the window a few minutes more, but the cat—if it had indeed been Toby—did not return. I closed the window and went back to the storage cabinet. I found the bottle of wine tucked far back on the top shelf. As I tucked it under my arm, I couldn't shake the feeling that the feline form I'd seen had been Toby or the little thrill of anticipation at the idea that I might indeed be Toby's special human.

Chapter Three

After a good night's sleep, which included a dream of chasing a gold-and-white cat around my apartment, I awoke feeling refreshed and ready to take on any challenges the day might offer—including a confrontation with Trowbridge Littleton. What I wasn't ready for, though, was my sister tagging along. Even though she'd made a couple of good points last night, I still felt it might be better if I faced him down alone. I'd dealt with people of his ilk back at Reid and Renshaw in my day, and more often than not, I'd come out the victor. I had no reason to think this instance would be any different.

I'd set my alarm for four AM. Now I swung my legs out of bed and tiptoed quietly down the hall to the bathroom so I wouldn't disturb Leila, although there really wasn't any danger of that. My friend drops off and sleeps like a stone—I do believe she'd sleep through Armageddon. I showered quickly, dressed quickly in a crisp white blouse and tan slacks, then sat down at my dressing table and pulled out a small notebook. Whenever I'd had to prepare for a particularly grueling presentation at my former job, I'd always found that marshaling my thoughts into a cohesive state helped enormously. I had the feeling that I'd make out far better if I had an idea of what to say to Littleton. Going in unprepared with a type A personality like his would definitely be a mistake. I scribbled down all the points I'd thought about last night and in the shower this morning to plead my case, read them through, then crossed them all out and started over again. By the time I was satisfied, the clock read five thirty. I'd told Kat that I'd meet her at Littleton's shop at six thirty, but I'd always intended to get there first. I shoved my notes into my oversized tote, slipped on thick-soled sneakers, and padded softly down the hall and out the front door into my Jeep. Saying a silent prayer for success, I threw the car into reverse and backed out of the driveway as fast as I dared.

Once on the street, I drove slowly, taking in the early morning ambiance: birds chittering in the trees, the first wisps of sunrise peeping through the branches. At this hour of the morning, traffic was practically nonexistent. I drove along the residential district, admiring the neat rows of houses, most of which had been designed with a colonial feel. I passed a large redbrick edifice, an apartment complex for over-fifty-five seniors that had been erected a few years ago, as I made the left onto Main Street and the start of what was Deer Park's commercial district. Wide sidewalks provided ample room for pedestrians who wanted to peruse the myriad of stores and restaurants that lined the streets. I turned toward the middle of Main Street, where it intersected with Park Place to cut through the park that stood in the center of town. Well-tended flower beds surrounded a large, gurgling fountain. A large pagoda-style gazebo graced the fountain's left, and behind that stood a large flagpole from which flew the American flag and the state flag. Soon these streets would be bustling with activity, with pedestrians marching to and fro about their daily errands. But for now, all was still.

I made a left just beyond the gazebo and onto Elm Street. This route would take me around the back of the cluster of retail stores where Littleton's gallery was located. As I drove, I mentally went over my speech in my head. First, I'd bring up the fact that the shelter was one of the finest in the state of North Carolina, and a no-kill to boot. Second, I'd mention that several of its canine residents had gone on to become service dogs—dogs that served as companions in many hospitals and nursing homes. The shelter also had an impeccable record for adoptions, and its animals had all been given a clean bill of health by Donna Blondell, our local veterinarian. Lastly, I figured I'd appeal to the things Littleton valued most—sales and profits. I'd surfed the web before going to bed last night and had printed out several stories of successful cat cafés in Europe and other states as a sort of "product model." All the cafés and shelters had enjoyed boosts in businesses, and some had even turned healthy profits. And to my mind, a healthy profit in one area of business couldn't help but spill over. But was Littleton broad-minded enough to see my point of view?

I doubted it, but I was going to give it the old college try.

My plan was to park as close to the rear of The Brush and Canvas, where Littleton's office was located, as I could, to facilitate a quick getaway in case I needed to make one. I rounded the corner, frowning as I noticed all the cars— then I realized that they must be spillover from the popular Gold's Gym, which was just a block away. I was just about to give up and go back to park by the café when I spied a narrow parking space right at the very end of the block, between the curb and a gleaming white Lincoln Continental. It took me four tries, but I finally maneuvered my convertible into the spot without banging the Lincoln. I glowered at the car as I opened my door and squeezed out. As I rounded the car, my eye fell on the license plate—TLITTLE—and I sucked in my breath. This had to be Trowbridge Littleton's car. It figured. Well, at least this meant he was in his store.

I could see the rear entrance to The Brush and Canvas at the end of the alleyway, just a few yards away. Now that I was so close, the butterflies were starting to fly around in my stomach. I squared my shoulders and lifted my chin. It reminded me of the time I'd faced down the CEO of a popular jeans company who wasn't entirely on board with the ad campaign I'd designed. I'd gone toe to toe, presented my arguments, and in the end, we'd reached an agreeable compromise. I was hoping for a repeat performance today.

I hoisted my tote onto my shoulder and moved forward past the rear entrances of the other shops. City Jewel, Devon McIntyre's jewelry store; Hats Off, Grace Topping's establishment; The Fin and Claw, Buck Noble's eatery; to

name a few. My heart started to beat faster as I approached
The Brush and Canvas. As much as I hated to admit it, I
didn't have a good feeling about confronting Littleton.

*Oh, for heaven's sake, Sydney. Littleton's nothing more than
a bully. You've faced lots worse than him. Just get it over with.*

A few more steps, and I was at the back entrance. I cupped
my hand over my eyes and peered through the glass portion
of the glass-and-wood door. The interior was dark, but I
could make out a small entryway with a corridor beyond. A
faint glow emanated from somewhere in the store's rear—
the office, no doubt. Well, if a light was on, Littleton must
be in there. I glanced around for a bell but saw none. Great.
I raised my hand, rapped sharply on the glass.

Nothing.

I frowned. Maybe he wasn't here after all. Maybe he'd
had car trouble and had to leave the vehicle overnight. My
hand rested lightly on the door handle, and I gave it a tug.
Much to my surprise, it turned easily, and the door swung
inward on rusty hinges. I stepped over the threshold cautiously. "Mr. Littleton," I called out in a hoarse voice. "Are
you here? It's Sydney McCall."

No answer.

I closed the door softly behind me and let my gaze skim
over the room. I saw boxes stacked to one corner, a few
frames, empty of canvas, pushed up against one wall. There
was a small desk shoved in one corner, its middle drawer
yawning open. Several low-hung shelves boasted minia-
tures, pewter figurines encrusted with semiprecious stones,
a few odd plaster pieces of sculpture. The light glistening

at the end of the narrow corridor beckoned to me, but still I hesitated. "Mr. Littleton?" I called again. "Are you here? It's Sydney McCall, you know, from Friendly Paws Animal Shelter?"

Still no response.

I drummed my fingers on the side of my tote. Okay, I had a few options. I could retrace my steps, go back the way I'd come like I'd never been there, and return later with Kat, or I could just march down that corridor into Littleton's office and have it out with him. Neither was particularly appealing. If I had to tell the truth, I was losing my zest for this whole undertaking. Maybe Kat's original assessment had been correct: leave it alone and let it die a natural death. I cast a wary eye down the corridor, then jumped as something brushed my elbow. I whirled around, hand at my throat, and relaxed slightly when I saw my sister standing there. "God, Kat," I cried, "what are you trying to do? Give me a heart attack?"

"You were so deep in thought, you didn't hear that door creak." Kat gestured toward the half-open door.

I frowned. "What are you doing here?"

Her eyebrows rose. "I knew darn well you'd pull something like this."

I feigned innocence. "Like what?"

"Like confronting him without me. I've been hanging around across the street since five forty-five, waiting for you to show up."

I gave her shoulder a little shove. "Well, sorry you got up so early and made the trip for nothing. You can go on back home or over to the shelter, I don't care which. I can take care of Littleton."

Kat shrugged my hand away. "You didn't hear a word I said yesterday, did you? I'm the one who should take care of him. I'm the shelter director and the one who should be settling things, not you."

"Maybe so, but showing the shelter cats was my idea."

"Our idea," she amended. "I agreed to it, remember?"

Kat's gaze dropped to the floor. I touched her arm. "Is there anything else you want to tell me? Something else I should know about Littleton?"

Kat's shoulders squared, and this time she did meet my gaze. "I think you know all you need to," she said. A low sound emitted from her throat, a cross between a groan and a laugh. "Is he even here? You'd think he'd have come out by now."

My gaze skittered toward a closed door over on the left. "Maybe he's stuck on the toilet and his legs fell asleep and he can't get up." Voicing it aloud made me break out in a wave of giggles, and Kat joined in.

"That's a depressing visual," she gasped when our laughter subsided. She peered down the corridor. "A light's on down there."

"Yes, but it's pretty faint. I think it's just a night-light, or he was working back there and forgot to turn it off or something. If he were here, he'd surely have come out by now."

"Oh, I don't know about that," said Kat, starting to push past me. "He's good at ignoring people he doesn't want to talk to, and after yesterday, I'm sure we're number one on

44

that list." She reached into the bag on her shoulder and whipped out her phone. It only took a few minutes for her to call up her flashlight app. "It puts a strain on the battery, but it sure beats those little minilights I used to carry," she chuckled. She aimed the beam at the hallway. "Shall we?"

I hesitated. "You know, now that I think about it, I—I'm having second thoughts. Maybe this wasn't such a good idea."

Kat chuckled. "That's usually my line, Syd."

"Yeah, but think about it. If Littleton's in a particularly vindictive mood, he could accuse us of breaking and entering."

"How is it breaking and entering? The door was open, was it not?"

I paused. "Yes it was," I admitted. "But this isn't our property, and technically the store isn't open for business yet. He could have us arrested for trespassing."

Kat shrugged. "I think we could probably argue that point. I spent a lot of last night tossing and turning, and this morning I decided that he's just not worth all that energy. I refuse to be bullied by him any longer, and I know you feel the same. So let's just find him and have our say before we lose our nerve." And with that, Kat called out Littleton's name.

And got no answer.

I touched my sister's arm. "Maybe we should go and come back later," I murmured. "We might have a better perspective on things after a good breakfast."

Kat gave her head a firm shake. "Nope. I'm here now, and I'm going to see this through." She raised her voice and called, "Ready or not, Mr. Littleton, here we come. We want to talk to you calmly and rationally about the shelter issue."

"I think we're wasting our time. He's probably not even back there. Maybe he stepped out for something?"

Kat snorted. "The only other place open this early is the gym. I doubt he'd even set foot in there, unless he was desperate for a drink. I understand they have a very nice juice bar. Besides, he wouldn't want to run into his wife. She's always one of the first ones there every morning."

I stopped and shot her a quizzical look. "How do you know all this? Oh, wait, let me guess. Diane Ryan, right?"

"Right." She started down the hall. "Come on. If he just left the light on, then we'll shut it off for him—save him a few dollars on his electric bill. We ought to earn some brownie points with him for that."

I sighed. Well, it had been my idea in the first place. In spite of the trepidation I felt, I had to agree. Might as well see it through.

We moved down the corridor and after a few minutes spied an open doorway from which pale light spilled. The office, no doubt. As we started forward, I reached out and grabbed Kat's arm.

"Shine your light over there," I hissed. "I thought I saw something move."

Kat turned the flashlight in the direction I indicated, and we both jumped at the sight of two gold eyes caught in the beam. Kat dropped the flashlight, and it clicked off. A loud *merow* echoed in the darkness.

"A cat," Kat breathed. "What do you know? Littleton has a cat!"

"Maybe," I muttered. I'd only had a quick glimpse, but I could have sworn that not only was the cat large and yellow, but its face was the same one that had peered through the kitchen window at me last night—Toby? Heck, anything was possible. "It might have been a stray. He could have gotten in the back door, same as us."

"You're probably right. I can't picture Littleton being a pet owner." Kat had retrieved the flashlight and switched it back on. She played the beam around, but the cat was nowhere to be found. "Hmm, well, we seem to have scared him off. Come on, let's see what's in there." Kat moved forward, and as she moved the beam of light, I caught a flash of white on the floor in the spot where I'd seen the cat.

"Wait a sec," I said. I bent down to have a closer look. It was a small square of paper, dirty around the edges. I picked it up gingerly. It was damp around the side, and I could see teeth marks—apparently Toby, if it had been him, had been having a nosh on it when we'd startled him. I turned the paper over. The words were cramped together, but they looked like *Kahn Lee*. Reflexively, I shoved the paper into the pocket of the light jacket I wore and motioned for Kat to continue walking. As we approached the open doorway, I called out again.

"Mr. Littleton, it's the McCall sisters. We need to speak with you." When silence greeted us once again, I said to

Kat, "Is it my imagination, or is this starting to seem like a bad episode of *Murder, She Wrote*?"

We were in the doorway now. A large desk was at the far end of what appeared to be an office. The light was coming from a small lamp perched on the edge of the desk, and as we crossed the threshold, it flickered and then went out. Kat shone the pencil-thin beam of the flashlight around the room, letting out a sharp cry as it hit the wall nearest us. "Light switch," she squealed, and a minute later, the room was filled with a harsh fluorescent light.

I glanced around. Yes, this was definitely an office, and not a very tidy one at that. There were several file cabinets pushed up against the far wall, and two of the drawers in the one on the left were half-open. Papers were strewn across the desk, and some file folders had dropped onto the floor and were scattered across the Oriental rug. I crossed over to the desk to take a closer look, pausing as I caught sight of something glinting just to the left of the desk. I bent down and saw a few slivers of dark-blue glass scattered there.

"Good Lord," my sister exclaimed. "For someone always so fastidious about his appearance, he certainly likes to work in a mess."

I frowned, looking around for something that might be broken but seeing nothing. "It looks more to me like it's been ransacked. Someone was searching for something. What do you think, Kat? Kat?"

My sister had moved over to the far corner of the room and was standing before a large wardrobe. "Wow, this is beautiful," she said, lifting a hand to run it over the smooth exterior. She balled her hand into a fist and rapped it against the wood. "Solid oak. I saw a picture of one like this in a catalog. French. Dates back to the late 1800s. I wonder what it's doing in his office."

"Who knows? Maybe he keeps his suit jackets in it," I said. "Why do you care, anyway?"

"It's such a beautiful piece," my sister murmured. "It seems out of place in this office. I wouldn't mind having something like this," Kat said, running her hand once again across the smooth wood.

She gave the handle a tug. "Hmm. The doors seem to be stuck."

I waved my hand impatiently. "Oh, for goodness' sake, leave it alone. Must you examine it now?"

She shot me an appealing look. "Give me a hand, won't you? You're strong. Maybe if we both pull on the handle at the same time, it'll open."

I knew my sister. Once Kat made up her mind about something, she was like a pit bull with a bone. I knew when it was futile to argue with her. "Okay, fine. But if we get this open, one quick look and then we're out of here."

She nodded, and I placed my hand on top of hers. "On the count of three, give it all you've got. One, two—three."

We both tugged at the same time, and suddenly the door flew open. We went staggering backward at the same time the body of Trowbridge Littleton, his eyes bulging almost out of their sockets, tongue lolling to the side, hit the floor at our feet.

Chapter Four

Kat let out an earsplitting shriek and threw her hands across her face. I, on the other hand, leaned down for a closer look at the body, an action that elicited a horrified gasp from my sister. "Syd! What in God's name are you doing?"

"What does it look like I'm doing?" I knelt down. I'd never been particularly squeamish, as evidenced by my love of horror movies, and I was always glued to the screen when *Autopsy* was on. Preston used to get up and leave the room, shaking his head every time as I sat, eating popcorn, caught up in the adventure of a real-life forensic pathologist. Before I decided to major in business and marketing, I'd toyed with the idea of becoming a homicide detective. Actually, I'd more than toyed with it. I'd actually filled out an application for the police academy. Only my mother's impassioned plea for my safety (*"I can't spend the rest of my life worrying about you getting shot, Syd!"*) had dissuaded me. I felt now, though, as if I were finally fulfilling a life-long ambition as I looked at the body.

Littleton hadn't been that great-looking in life, and he was even worse in death. In addition to the bulging eyes and lolling tongue, Littleton's skin had a slightly bluish cast to it. I touched two fingers to his neck, but I couldn't feel a pulse.

Kat, who could get queasy at the sight of a mere drop of blood, tugged at my arm. "Get away from him! He's dead—isn't he?"

"Certainly looks that way." I looked the corpse up and down. I didn't see any bullet wounds, or stab wounds, or any blood, for that matter. I looked up at my sister. "What makes the skin turn blue?"

Kat stared at me as if I had two heads. "What?"

"What makes someone's skin turn blue?" I pressed a hand to my head, struggling to recall old episodes of *Murder, She Wrote* or *CSI*. "Cyanosis!" I cried suddenly, snapping my fingers.

Kat frowned. "Cya-what?"

"Cyanosis. It's caused by a low oxygen level in the blood or by poor circulation. I remember reading about it in one of my mystery novels."

Kat peered fearfully down at Littleton's body. "You think that's what killed him—poor circulation?"

"It's possible. Poor circulation could cause a pulmonary embolism or a heart attack. But if that were the case—what was he doing in that armoire?" I straightened and started to walk slowly around the office, glancing around as I did so.

Kat was at my elbow almost at once. "What are you doing?"

"Just looking around—trying to see if maybe there might be a clue here as to what happened." I paused, ran my hand through my hair. I'd forgotten to tie it back, and the humidity already hung in the air, making my curls even curlier and stickier. Quite a contrast to my sister's hair, which, of course, lay straight and perfect across her slim shoulders. "No sign of any sort of weapon," I mumbled. "No defensive wounds, either. His guard was down. I'll bet he knew whoever did this to him."

"Wow, Nancy Drew, you're in rare form," my sister cried.

"I read enough of 'em as a kid. And we've both watched enough crime shows to know what comes next."

I whipped out my cell and flopped into the leather chair behind the desk as my fingers punched in 9-1-1. "May as well get comfortable. We're probably going to be here awhile."

*   *   *

Within ten minutes, an ambulance had double parked near the back alley, and two female paramedics—one blonde and thin as a rail, the other slightly stouter with hints of silver in her brown hair—had barreled up to the back door. I met them and led them back to the office, where they wordlessly knelt down beside Littleton. One checked his pulse, and the other shone a pencil-thin light into his eyes. At last they looked at each other, shook their heads, and then the blonde sat back on her heels and turned a quizzical gaze our way. "Are you relatives?" she asked.

"No. We're—ah—neighbors. Sort of," said Kat. I was surprised at how calm and controlled my sister's voice was, considering that not fifteen minutes ago, she'd shrieked loud enough to wake the dead. She started to edge toward the door. "I guess there's nothing more we can do here," she began, but the older woman rose to her feet and put her hands on her hips.

"I wouldn't leave just yet," she said. We all cocked our heads as the faint wail of a siren reached our ears. "The police will want to interview you."

Kat's face paled. "The police?"

I gave Kat's arm a reassuring squeeze as the younger paramedic jumped up and hurried down the hall to admit them. "Of course the police will want to interview us," I whispered to her. "We found a dead body in an armoire, for goodness' sake."

Kat nibbled furiously at her lower lip. "I hope no one from the press is tagging along. I can just see the headlines now. Shelter director and shelter's publicity director find dead body."

In spite of the old adage that any publicity is good publicity, I was forced to agree. "Yeah, I have to admit, finding a dead body wasn't exactly on my agenda for today. Or on my bucket list, for that matter. It could be worse, though."

"How?"

I gave her a thin smile. "His body wasn't very cold. I don't think he's been dead all that long. Which would mean we probably just missed the murderer."

"Yow, I didn't think of that," Kat admitted. She glanced at her watch. "I hope this interview doesn't take too long. I told Maggie I'd be in early to help with the new brood of cats."

"Why don't you give her a quick call? Don't give her any details—just say we've run into a bit of a snag, and we might be a bit late."

"A bit of a snag?" Kat snorted as she took out her phone. "That seems a gross understatement to me."

Kat moved off into the corner to make the call, and I leaned against the desk just as the paramedic returned, followed closely by two men. One was tall and muscular, the other shorter and built like a barrel. The barrel-shaped one looked to be in his early fifties and had silvery-blond hair that looked a bit thin on top, bushy eyebrows, and a walrus mustache that drooped around his mouth. I half expected him to start twirling it any second. He wore an ill-fitting jacket and pants that might have been just a tad too tight in the waist. The taller one, dressed in a neat sport coat and pants, looked to be in his midthirties—just around my own age, which would make him a good fifteen years younger than his companion. From the way he stood, I could only see his profile, but he appeared to be the better looking of the two. He glanced over in my direction, affording me an excellent view of his face. I took in the high forehead, black curly hair that begged to have fingers run through it, sparkling blue eyes, wide, generous, and very kissable mouth—and then I gave myself a mental slap. Now was so not the time to start ogling men, particularly one about to question me regarding a possible homicide. He seemed familiar somehow, and as he drew closer, recognition stabbed through me. I gave my head a swift shake. Nope, I had to be wrong. It couldn't be him—or could it?

He murmured something to his companion and then walked over to where I stood. "Good morning." He reached into his breast pocket and removed a badge. "Detective Worthington, Deer Park Homicide. I understand you found the body?"

My mind barely registered the shiny badge he dangled in front of us. "Worthington?" I squealed. "Will Worthington! I thought that was you! You probably don't remember me . . ."

His lips parted in a friendly smile. "Of course I do. You're Sydney McCall, the prettiest girl in our senior class." He inclined his head toward Kat. "And that's your sister Katherine."

For a few seconds, we just stared at each other, wide smiles on our faces.

Will Worthington had transferred to Deer Park High in his senior year, and we'd been thrown together when he'd been assigned to tutor me in chemistry. Conversely, I'd also been assigned to help him with English. We'd spent lots of time together in study hall and chem lab, and everyone had remarked what an odd coupling we made: the overweight boy who was a science whiz and the class cutup who was head of the cheer squad and president of the glee club. It had been the beginning of a beautiful friendship that might have blossomed into something more had we not gone our separate ways for college. At graduation, we'd promised to keep in touch no matter what, and of course, neither one of us had made good on that promise.

"I confess, for a few minutes there, I wasn't sure it was you. You've lost weight," I said at last.

He shot me a wry grin and patted at his stomach. "Yep. Ninety pounds. Once I decided to enter the police academy, I had to get in shape."

I was tempted to say that he'd never posted his photo on Facebook, but then that would be tantamount to admitting that I'd glanced at it over the years—more than once, in fact. I smiled. "Well, you look good."

"Thanks." His lips split in a genuine smile as his gaze raked me up and down. "So do you. Your hair is a bit lighter than I remember."

I ran my hand self-consciously through my hair. Apparently he'd never felt the urge to check out my Facebook photo. "I put in some gold highlights to brighten it up. It was such a dull, mousy brown." Or at least that's how Preston always used to describe it.

"It always looked great to me." There was an awkward pause, and then Will cleared his throat. "You've lost most of your southern accent."

"I guess I have. That's what happens when you live up north for twelve years."

"Yeah, I heard you were knocking 'em dead in New York, New York. That's why I was surprised to see you here in Deer Park."

"Yeah, well, the big city isn't all it's cracked up to be." I shifted my weight from one foot to the other. "I came back to help Kat with the shelter."

"I know what you mean about big-city life. It can wear you down. I transferred here from Raleigh just last week." He smiled again, and I was reminded of how much I'd liked him in high school. He might have been overweight, but Will had always been a total gentleman; he'd always been the guy who could make me laugh, no matter how bad my day had been—and he was also the first boy I'd ever kissed.

Now, it seemed, he'd also be the first detective to ever interrogate me in a possible murder investigation.

Kat had finished her call and now came up to us. She did a double take and then said, "Wow, Will Worthington! You look great. But what are you—" She stopped speaking as her gaze fell on the badge he still held in his hand. She paused and looked from him to me and back to him. "Wait—*you're* the homicide detective?"

He nodded. "Yep. I'll be working this case with my partner, Detective Bennington." He motioned toward the barrel-chested man who was speaking with the blond paramedic.

Kat managed a thin smile. "He looks a little on the mean side to me."

"More addled than mean," I said. "With that wrinkled jacket and blank stare, he reminds me more of Columbo."

Will chuckled. "What's that they say, appearances can be deceiving? My partner might appear a bit discombobulated on the outside, but he's one sharp cookie."

"That's right. Make no mistake, miss. I'm way sharper than Columbo."

I jumped. Bennington had come up behind us, and now he tugged at the lapel of his rumpled jacket as he regarded Will with narrowed eyes. "Everything all right here, Detective?" he asked. "Or do you need me to take over questioning?"

Will shook his head. "No, it's fine. I'll handle this."

Bennington regarded us for a minute, then turned and walked back over to the paramedics. Will looked after his partner for a second, then pulled a small notebook and a pen out of his breast pocket, flipped a few pages, then held the pen poised. He looked right into my eyes. When he spoke, his tone was all business. "You said both of you found the body. May I ask where that was, exactly?"

I pointed to the armoire. "Inside that wardrobe. He fell out when we jerked open the door."

Will paused in his scribbling, lifted a brow inquiringly. "You opened the wardrobe door? Why?"

"It's a beautiful antique," Kat answered. "When I saw it, I couldn't resist. But the door was stuck, it wouldn't open. So I asked Syd to help, and when we pulled hard on the handle, the door flew open, and Littleton just . . . he just kinda fell out."

As Will scribbled on his pad, I said, "I didn't notice any gunshot or knife wounds on the body. There is a bluish cast to the skin, though."

Will glanced up. "Pretty observant of you, Syd."

"Yeah, well, I read a lot of Nancy Drew growing

"I remember."

I glanced up sharply, tempted to ask what e remembered, but his expression had turned imp He tapped on his notebook with the edge of his pen. ME will determine the cause of death. Why don't you me through what happened. How did the two of you to be in Littleton's shop so early?"

"We had something we wanted to discuss with M tleton, and we thought the earlier the better," I said.

"I see. And just what was the nature of this discussi

I shifted my weight to my other foot. "Friendly has teamed with Dayna's Treats and Sweets for a cat event to benefit the shelter. For a nominal fee, people have their coffee and goodies in a room with shelter that are available for adoption."

Will glanced up, and I could see a light of interest in eyes. "I've heard of those cafés. They're mostly in Euro[

"There are a few in the States, big cities mostly. T will be the first event of its kind in North Caroli We're hoping to increase revenue for both the café a the shelter."

"Let me guess. That idea didn't sit well with Littleton

Kat and I both shook our heads in unison, and K exclaimed, "I should say not! He was in the shop yeste day, and he made his feelings pretty darn clear. He thoug having the cats around would be detrimental to busines Heck, he thought the shelter in general was a detriment t the town."

"A sentiment you two didn't agree with," he said slowly.

"I should say not!" Kat returned, her cheeks starting to flame. "Syd and I tried to reason with him yesterday, but he didn't want to hear it."

"And that's why you decided to come here this morning?"

I nodded. "Yes. I put together a pretty good argument of pros for the event. I was hoping to appeal to his sense of business acumen."

"Why did you feel this was necessary? Had he threatened you?"

"Not in so many words," I said carefully. "But he did say yesterday that he was determined to put a stop to the proceedings and that we hadn't heard the last from him."

"Mm-hm." Will made another notation in his book. "So when was the last time you saw Littleton?"

"Yesterday around one thirty." I cleared my throat. "If that's all the questions you have, we need to get going."

He snapped his notebook shut. "You're free to go for now," he said, "but I will probably need to talk to you some more later on."

"That's fine," I said. "We'll be here."

The corners of Will's lips twitched slightly. "Good to know."

*   *   *

Once we were back out on the street, Kat hauled off and punched me in the arm—hard.

"Yow!" I cried. "What was that for?"

"For thinking that you could come here and face Littleton without me, for one," Kat said. "I knew you had your fingers crossed last night."

I rubbed at my arm. "Can't put anything over on you, can I?"

She gave me a shrewd look. "So how did it feel, seeing Will Worthington again after all these years? I heard he was back in town, but I had no idea he'd become a detective—homicide, no less. Wasn't that always your secret ambition?" She cut me a sidelong glance. "Funny, isn't it, how you two came back to Deer Park almost at the same time. Like karma or something."

"Well, I'd rather deal with Will than his partner, Columbo Jr.," I said. "Come on, let's get my car and get to the shelter. I hope Maggie isn't too worried."

We walked through the alleyway, and when we were almost at the spot where I'd parked, I suddenly stopped short. "Hey," Kat cried as she ran full tilt into my back. "What's wrong?"

I pointed to the empty space beside my car. "There was a white Lincoln there when I came, parked pretty badly. The license plate read TLITTLE. I thought for sure it was Littleton's car, but if it's gone . . ."

"A white Lincoln? That's his wife Petra's car," Kat said. She glanced around and then pointed to the gym. "She must have parked it here instead of the gym parking lot, like she usually does. I wonder why."

Another disturbing thought occurred to me as I slid behind the wheel. It would have been impossible for

Littleton's wife not to have seen the ambulance and police cars parked in front of her husband's shop. Why hadn't she come to see what was wrong?

Unless, of course . . . she didn't have to. Because she already knew.

Chapter Five

It was a few minutes past seven thirty when we arrived at the long, one-story gray brick building that housed the shelter. We walked around to the back entrance, pausing before the nine-foot-tall chain link fence that housed the exercise pen. Viola was inside, watching as a tan-and-white puppy ran happily back and forth. She gave us a wave as we let ourselves in through the back door and were greeted almost instantly by Sissy. She was cradling a gray-and-white kitten in her arms. "Did you guys see anything on your way here?" the teen asked.

Kat avoided meeting Sissy's gaze as she answered, "Why do you ask?"

Sissy leaned against the doorjamb. "There was quite a bit of excitement downtown this morning. Did you hear that ambulance and the police siren? I thought something happened at the gym, but Viola insists she saw the ambulance stop in front of The Brush and Canvas."

I shifted my tote bag on my arm. "Score one for Viola. She was right. Trowbridge Littleton is dead."

Sissy's eyes almost popped out of her skull. "What? How?"

Everyone followed me as I walked into the small kitchen. I breathed a silent sigh of relief when I saw that the coffeepot on the stove was nearly full. I crossed over, got a mug out of the upper cabinet, and poured myself a steaming cup. It was the new blend Dayna had given us to try, and it smelled wonderful. As I opened the refrigerator, looking for milk, I answered, "Hard to say. It might have been natural causes."

Sissy frowned. "As opposed to what? Unnatural?"

Kat came over, holding a mug that had "Friendly Paws" emblazoned across it. "Speculation is pointless right now until the police complete their investigation."

"The police are investigating? Uh-oh!" Sissy shifted the kitten against her chest and waved a finger in the air. "Say, how do you guys know all this?"

"Easy," Kat said, setting the coffeepot back on the stove. "We're the ones who found him."

Sissy staggered backward with a loud gasp and placed her free hand over her heart. It was easy to see why she'd been elected president of the drama club. The girl had a dramatic streak a mile wide. "Oh gosh! You found him? What was that like? How did you feel? Was there a lot of blood?"

"It wasn't exactly a picnic," I answered. "And no, there was no blood to speak of."

"No blood? Bummer!" Her lips curved downward in a disappointed scowl. "How did he look? It had to be an improvement, 'cause he sure didn't look that great alive."

"Sissy!" Kat said reproachfully. "That's not nice—the man is dead."

"Yeah, well, he wasn't too nice to me yesterday," the girl grumbled. "And it was an accident! I didn't mean to bump into him like that, but he acted like I did it on purpose."

"We know that," Kat said evenly. "But you should still show some respect."

"What for?" the girl snorted. "He sure had no respect for anyone." She raised a defiant glance my way. "I bet he didn't look too hot dead either."

"Who's dead?"

We all turned to see Maggie standing in the kitchen doorway. She moved forward, wiping her hands on the white apron she wore. "I'd like to report that Mama Cat and babies are doing just fine," she said with a wide smile. "The kitties are feeding, and everyone seems content."

Kat let out a deep sigh. "Good news—finally."

Maggie's features arranged themselves into a worried expression. "Did something happen? On my way here, I noticed that the top of the street is blocked off, and The Brush and Canvas has yellow-and-black tape around the outside."

"You could say that," I began, but Sissy interrupted me, her eyes round.

"That man I told you about who yelled at Kat and Syd yesterday? He got iced."

"Iced?"

"As in finished, kaput, the big chill . . . he's dead."

Maggie swung her startled gaze to me. "What? Good Lord!"

"Okay, he wasn't exactly yelling at us," I said. I wagged my finger at Sissy. "And 'iced' is such a crude term." Turning back to Maggie, I added, "It's not official whether or not there was foul play involved, but . . . it's true. Trowbridge Littleton is dead."

"My word!" Maggie's hand fluttered over her chest. "I take it all that crime scene tape means he didn't die of natural causes?"

"That's yet to be determined," Kat said.

"Well, one good thing," Sissy observed. "At least you don't have to worry about him making trouble about the cat café event now."

"No," Kat sighed. "I guess not."

We were all silent for a moment, and then Maggie abruptly turned to me. "Well, onto more pleasant topics," she said briskly. "I spoke with Dayna last night. She's going to have a special menu printed up, just for the participants in the cat program."

"That's an excellent idea," Kat and I both chorused.

Maggie grinned. "I thought you'd think so." She pointed to a cake plate on the counter. "She sent some brownies that she's going to serve for us to sample, along with some other treats. Said to let her know if there was anything we didn't like."

"Good." I motioned toward the small table. "Why don't we all sit down, have a cup of coffee, and sample Dayna's treats?"

"Sounds good to me," Sissy said. "Just let me put Harley back."

I arched a brow. "Harley?"

"Sure," Sissy said, grinning. "She's purring just like my cousin Brad's motorcycle."

"We'll go with you," Maggie said abruptly. She looked at us. "I've got something to show you."

We all trooped into the cattery. As Sissy replaced Harley in her cage, Maggie went over to the table in the far corner. There was a large box on top. Maggie opened it and whipped out two manila folders. She handed one to Kat and one to me.

"I had them made up at the Staples on the highway," she said. "Doug Schooney gave me a 40 percent discount. Viola and I made them up last week."

I opened my folder. Inside were several sheets of paper with photographs of cats on them. Next to each photo was a small bio of the cat.

"The first pages are the cats we'll be showing," Maggie said, "and the rest are all the ones we've got available for adoption right now."

There was silence for a few moments as Kat and I riffled through the folders. Finally, Kat looked up at Maggie. "What a great idea," she said.

"Yes," I agreed. "If one of the cats at the event doesn't appeal, perhaps one still here at the shelter will." I walked over to one of the cages, where an entirely black tomcat lay. He perked up as I approached, then sat up. He pressed his head against the wire cage and let out a soft meow. I wiggled my fingers at him, and his pink tongue darted out to lick them. I looked at the name tag on the cage. "Take Jet here. He's not a part of the event, but he's a sweetie. Someone might want him, even though he's an older cat."

"Most people want kittens. They shy away from the older cats. It's unfortunate," Maggie shook her head emphatically. "Older cats are usually more docile. They're actually the perfect pet." She moved over to another cage that contained a pretty brown Seal-point Siamese with incredible blue eyes. "This sweetie is a sure thing. I can't imagine anyone not wanting Karma."

I walked over for a closer look at the cat, who was indeed beautiful. "Is she a pedigree?"

"Oh, yes. Karma came to us when her owner got transferred to Philadelphia and couldn't take her along. He was really heartbroken to leave her. As a matter of fact, the moment she's adopted, I have to send him a photo of Karma with her new family."

Kat shot me a mischievous glance. "Getting the itch to adopt, Syd?"

"Maybe." I glanced down at the folder I still held in my hand. The top sheet had Toby's picture on it. "Pedigrees can be a bit finicky, though."

Both Kat and Maggie burst out laughing. "Admit it, Syd. You like Toby." Kat pointed to my folder. "You've been stealing glances at his picture ever since you fished it out of the folder, and I saw you look over at his empty cage more than once."

"Guilty as charged." I gave them both a sheepish grin. "I've always been partial to what Gram used to call the 'ginger' cats," I admitted. "I have to say, though, I'm surprised to see you included him in the event grouping."

"Well, technically Toby isn't ginger. He's got a lot of white in him," said Maggie. "We included him in the group because, quite frankly, I'm afraid if we left him here at the shelter, he'd just find a way to wander off," said Maggie. "To be perfectly honest, I'm not expecting anyone to want to actually adopt him. And if by some chance, someone does . . ." She shrugged. "Unless that person fits Toby's bill of the perfect human, mark my words, no one's getting him. He'll find a way to discourage the adoption."

"I thought I saw him," I blurted. "Last night, at the window in the storage room." *And today, in Littleton's office.* But I didn't say the latter out loud.

"Really? Well, what do you know?" Maggie reached out and patted my hand. "Maybe it's a sign."

I glanced toward the cattery door. "Is Toby in there? I could have a look."

Maggie shook her head. "He was in his cage earlier, but now he's out again." Further conversation was halted by a loud banging on the shelter door. "Goodness!" Maggie jumped out of her chair. "Who could that be? The hours are clearly posted—we don't open till eleven." She pulled down the edges of her jacket and set her jaw. "I'll politely tell whoever it is to come back later." She paused and then snatched up a flyer from the table. "Never hurts to advertise," she mumbled.

I looked at Kat. "I think maybe you made a mistake. Maybe you should have made Maggie your director of publicity."

Kat laughed. "What, you think you were my first choice? Mags turned me down flat. She didn't want all that responsibility."

We laughed and then stopped abruptly as Maggie appeared in the kitchen doorway. She pushed her glasses down on her nose and said in an agitated tone, "Syd, Kat, there's someone here to see you." I turned my head slightly, and my breath caught in my throat as I saw Detective Bennington standing to Maggie's left. His expression was impassive as he regarded us, and he inclined his head slightly in greeting. Kat touched my arm. "Now what does he want?" she muttered.

"Will said they'd probably have more questions for us. I was hoping he'd be the one to ask them, though." I jumped up and hurried over to him. "Detective Bennington," I said. "What a . . . pleasant surprise. We didn't expect to see you again so soon." I glanced around. "Will's not with you?"

"*Detective Worthington* had a few other things to attend to." He glanced over at the table where Kat sat, the folders spread out in front of her. "Is this a bad time?"

Every time is bad, I thought, but I smiled and said, "Not at all. We were just going over some paperwork for the event Saturday."

"Event?" He looked puzzled for a few seconds, and then his expression cleared. "Ah, yes. The cat café." He glanced again at the myriad of folders. "Sounds . . . interesting."

"Are you an animal lover, Detective?" I asked smoothly. "If so, you're welcome to drop by."

"I just might do that," he murmured. "I had a little Pekingese pup, but she passed away last year. Fourteen years old. I figured with my job, I wouldn't take on another dog, but . . . cats are much easier for a working person." He sniffed at the air. "What smells so good?"

"We've got a pot of cinnamon-caramel coffee on, and we have some samples that Dayna Harper sent over for us to try. Double-fudge brownies and a walnut cheesecake." He sniffed at the air again, and the phrase *Keep your friends close and your enemies closer* popped into my mind. "Could I get you something?"

He hesitated, but apparently his rumbling stomach won out over his desire to question me. "I'll have a cup of that coffee and a brownie," he said.

"Surely. Why don't you have a seat, and I'll get it for you?"

Bennington pulled out a chair across from Kat, who looked to me like she'd like to crawl down into the floor and take the floor right along with her. Maggie and Sissy beat a hasty retreat into the cattery, but I had the feeling curiosity would win out and Sissy would be listening at the door before too long. I pointedly pushed the kitchen door open all the way as a deterrent before pouring coffee into another Friendly Paws mug. I set it on a small tray along with a large brownie, some sugar packets, and creamers and brought the whole thing over to Bennington. His eyes lit up when he saw it, and he immediately plucked the mug from the tray and put it to his lips without adding anything to the coffee. He took a long sip, set the mug back down.

"Heavenly. You make a mean cup of coffee, Ms. McCall." He pulled the plate with the brownie in front of him and picked up the pastry. He waved it in the air, motioning me to sit down. I slid into the chair next to him and watched as he took a bite of the brownie. He chewed, swallowed, then took the napkin off his lap and dabbed daintily at his lips.

"Delicious. My compliments to the chef."

"I'll be sure to let Dayna know you enjoyed it. So"—I let out a breath—"what can I do for you?"

He took another bite, dabbed at his lips again, and then stuck his finger out at me. "I understand that you and your sister went to Littleton's office to confront him regarding the shelter event?"

I squirmed a bit in the chair under his hawklike gaze. "I wouldn't say confront, exactly. We wanted to have a discussion. We'd learned that there was a possibility of his initiating a petition against the event, and we wanted to nip it in the bud."

"I see." He shoved some more brownie into his mouth, chewed, and washed it down with another swig of coffee. "What time did you arrive at the office?"

"Shortly before six AM."

Bennington's eyebrows rose. "Rather early for a meeting, wouldn't you say?"

I shrugged. "We heard that Littleton always got into the gallery early, and we—we wanted to get it over with."

"Uh-huh."

His head jerked up, and he jabbed a finger in the air. "What else did you touch in that office, besides the armoire?"

"Not too much, really. Kat touched the wall looking for a light switch. We both touched the armoire, and I—I touched Littleton's body." As Bennington's eyebrows rose, I stammered, "I-I felt his neck for a pulse. I wanted to see if he might still be alive."

"I see." He bit off another chunk of brownie. "Did anything strike you as out of place?"

I looked at him. "Well, it's hard to say, because it was the first time either my sister or I were in that office, but I did get that impression, yes. Some of the drawers looked to me as if they'd been pulled out—maybe hastily looked through."

He wiped a crumb from the side of his mouth. "You were never in his office before?"

"No."

"And your sister wasn't either?"

"That's right," I said evenly. "We never had a reason to ever go there to see Littleton—until this morning, that is."

"The man have any enemies you know of?"

"I didn't know him all that well. I've only been back in Deer Park a few weeks. But according to what I've heard, people weren't too fond of him."

"You and your sister weren't particularly fond of him either, were you?" Bennington bit out.

"I told you, I hardly knew the man. I can't speak for my sister."

Kat, who had been moodily silent up till now, turned to face the detective. "I can speak for myself. No, I wasn't fond of the man. He was selfish and overbearing."

Bennington leaned forward. "It's no secret that Littleton wanted not only to stop your upcoming event but to close the shelter permanently—isn't that correct?"

My lips thinned, but it was Kat who answered. "Apparently Mr. Littleton had . . . issues with the shelter, but I assure you I was quite unaware of the depth of his feelings until very recently."

"I see." He popped the last of the brownie into his mouth, washed it down with a large gulp of coffee, and pushed back his chair. He half rose from his seat and then paused. "One more thing. You and your sister are aware that removing anything from a crime scene is a punishable offense?"

I stared at him. "Yes, I'm well aware that's a big no-no, and my sister is too. Why in the world would you ask a question like that?"

He shrugged. "No particular reason. I just thought that if you weren't familiar with the law, I'd . . . remind you."

I had the distinct feeling there was more to it than just a gentle reminder, but I chose not to belabor the point. I smiled and said evenly, "Well, unless you have other, more pertinent questions, we have work to do, so . . ."

"I think we're done—for now," he murmured. He whipped out his wallet, slid out a business card, and placed it on the table. "If you should remember anything of significance in the meantime, please call either me or *Detective Worthington* immediately."

And with that, he strode out of the shelter. I picked up the card and turned it over in my hand. Something else was up—I could just feel it. There was some reason Columbo Jr. had decided to get up close and personal with us. His veiled accusation that we might have removed something from the crime scene bothered me. Why would he think that? I thought about calling Will but then changed my mind. I didn't want to put him in an awkward position. After all, Bennington was his partner.

It was only after I'd jammed the money and the card into my jacket pocket that it dawned on me that I hadn't been truthful with Bennington—I had removed something from The Brush and Canvas.

The note that Toby—or a cat that looked remarkably similar to him—had led me to.

Chapter Six

After Bennington's visit, Kat and I got down to shelter business. Since she had a meeting with some potential shelter donors that was scheduled to take up most of her afternoon, I decided to write up some more ad copy for the event. I'd just finished and was on my way to the kitchen for a much needed cup of java when I heard the strident ring of the backdoor buzzer. Since Maggie and Viola were busy at the moment with the newborns, I answered the summons. Leila stood on the stoop, her eyes bright, finger poised to ring the bell again. She pushed past me into the foyer and without any preamble said, "Have you heard the news? Littleton's dead."

"Yep," I said as I swung the door shut. "We heard, all right."

She eyed me. "That's all you've got to say? It's Littleton— you know, the king of mean, the guy who was giving you guys a hard time about Saturday's event."

"What else is there to say?" I inclined my head toward the kitchen. "Want some coffee? I think there's still some Mocha Java left from lunch."

"Sure." She eased past me into the kitchen and plunked herself down at the table. "They're calling it a suspicious death, from what I understand. Phil Cooper spent the afternoon down at the station. He tried to get more details out of the detective assigned to the case, but the guy was a real pill. Gave him the runaround."

I filled a mug with steaming coffee and then set it in front of my friend along with some creamers. "That sounds like Bennington. He was here earlier."

"He was? Why was he—oh, wait!" Leila paused, creamer in hand. "You and Kat were going to go see Littleton this morning, weren't you?" Her eyes sparkled. "Don't tell me you got to his shop at the same time as the police?"

"Actually, we beat them to it. We found Littleton's body."

"WHAT?" Leila squealed. Her arm shot out, nearly upending her mug, and her nails dug into my sleeve. "You and Kat found the body? And you weren't going to tell me?"

I grinned at her. "I was getting to it."

"Well, you know how we reporters are! Details please."

I lightly disengaged her nails from my sleeve. "Why are you so interested? Are you looking for a promotion to the crime beat?"

"You bet I am. I'd love to get out of reporting on garden parties, social teas, and dog-and-cat shows—present company excepted, of course."

"Well, don't get your promotion until after Saturday. We're counting on you to give the shelter a stellar write-up."

She pushed the half-empty mug to one side. "Of course I will, you know that, but—come on, give!" She leaned in close to me and hissed, "Was it . . . murder?"

"Not sure," I replied. "And apparently neither are the police."

Leila frowned. "So I take it he wasn't shot or stabbed— what about blood? Was there any blood spatter?"

I rolled my eyes. What was this fascination everyone seemed to have with crime scenes and blood? "None that I could see, and I bent down and looked pretty close. His skin was still slightly warm, so I don't think he died much before we got there. And there was a decidedly bluish cast to his skin."

"Bluish cast, huh?" Leila started digging in her massive brown-and-taupe Dooney and Bourke tote bag. She whipped out her iPhone, called up Google, and started to type.

"I thought cyanosis," I supplied. "It happens when the blood doesn't get enough oxygen."

"Meaning what? Someone strangled Littleton?"

"Maybe—I didn't see any marks on his neck though."

My friend shot me a searching look. "Sounds like you took a real good look at that body."

"It was hard not to. He fell out of the armoire in his office practically at my feet."

"He—fell—out of an armoire?" she asked slowly, placing one hand over her heart. "Good God, no wonder they labeled his death suspicious. Sounds like someone did him in and then hid the body." She tapped her phone against the counter. "I'll bet the list of suspects is a mile long."

I took a sip of my own coffee and leaned forward. "Yeah? Like who?"

Leila held up her hand and started to tick off on her fingers. "Well, for starters, there's Petra. Isn't the spouse always suspect number one?"

"Sure, if there's a motive," I said. "But why would she want him dead? From what I've heard, it seems she had it made in the shade."

"Maybe she got tired of him holding the purse strings," suggested my friend. "Or maybe she wanted the insurance money. I bet he had a whopper of a policy."

I wrinkled my nose. "Who else?"

"Well, there's his stepson, Trey."

"Stepson? So he's Petra's son?"

Leila nodded. "I heard there's bad blood there. Trey was pretty vocal about his dislike over the way Littleton treated his mother."

I tapped at my chin. "Unless the kid's got a Norman Bates complex, that doesn't seem like much of a motive to me. Next?"

"His gallery partner. I heard they had some pretty public arguments."

I frowned. "Littleton had a partner? That's interesting. What were they arguing over? Money?"

"No, I think it had something to do with running the gallery—what?" she cried as I let out a sigh.

"Nothing, just . . . money would be a more compelling motive. Anyone else?"

Leila brushed her hand through her curls. "Only practically the entire town, which would include the other shopkeepers in that complex. None of 'em could stand him. And God knows how many customers and artists he might have pissed off over the years." Her lips curved in a sly smile. "It will probably take your pal Bennington months to interview all of 'em."

"Hey," I waggled a finger at her, "watch who you call my pal. Anyway, Bennington's not the only detective on the case."

"No? Who's working it with him?" Leila cut me an eye roll. "Not Silas French, I hope. I wonder sometimes how he even made detective. I doubt he'd know a dead body if he fell over one." Her frown deepened. "I thought he got transferred to robbery, though?"

"He did." Kat had emerged from her office and now stood in the doorway, a sly grin spreading over her face. "There's a new guy in town, and it's someone we all know. Someone who went to Deer Park High with us, as a matter of fact."

Leila's head jerked up. "Yeah? Who?"

Kat walked over, gave me a sharp jab in the side. "Go on, tell her."

"Okay, okay. Will Worthington," I mumbled.

Leila let out a squeal. "Will? Your Will? He's back in town? When did that happen? Oh my God! What does he look like? There's no photo on his Facebook page."

I turned to give her an astonished look. "You check out his Facebook page?"

"I check out lots of people. It's the reporter in me." She tossed me an impish grin. "I bet he finally lost that baby fat, huh? If he's a detective, he would have had to."

"He said he transferred back here from Raleigh a few weeks ago," Kat supplied. "I can see why he doesn't post his photo, if he wants to maintain a low profile. He looks like a GQ model now."

"I can believe that," Leila said. She gave me a lopsided grin. "Your Will wasn't bad looking even when he was overweight."

"Please stop calling him *my* Will," I sputtered. "After all, it's been ages since we've seen each other."

"He used to be your Will, though," Leila said teasingly. "And who knows, he could be again. You two were quite the item in high school."

"Yeah, high school, exactly. Over fifteen years ago. And I'm not sure a few Friday-night pizza dates and a prom night qualify us as being an 'item.'" *Or one memorable kiss.* I cleared my throat. "Out of the two of them, though, I confess I'd much rather deal with Will. Bennington is too . . . too . . ."

"Crude? Boorish? Overbearing? All of the above?" supplied Kat.

"All good choices. However, the word that came to my mind was 'mistrustful.'" I rapped my knuckles sharply on the counter. "He has a very suspicious nature."

Leila cocked her brow. "Pardon me, but isn't that a good quality for a homicide detective?"

"Maybe so, but I didn't much care for his insinuation that Kat or I might have removed a clue from the scene of the crime," I snapped.

Kat and Leila both stared at me. "He said that?" Kat flared. "What a nerve."

"He didn't come right out and accuse us, but that was the impression I got. But to tell the truth—he's right. I did take something." I pulled out the crumpled note and laid it on the counter. "I found it on the floor."

Kat and Leila both bent their heads over the note. "Doesn't look like much to me," Leila said at last. "This writing is so cramped, you can hardly make out the words. Where did you find it?"

"In the hallway leading to Littleton's office."

Leila tapped a pink-tipped nail against the paper. "Technically, that wasn't the crime scene. Plus, you don't know if it's any sort of clue or not. Anyone could have dropped it."

"True . . . including Littleton." I fingered the note. "I should probably should show it to Will, though. Just in case."

Leila and Kat exchanged a glance. "Oh, by all means—show Will," Leila crooned. "Any excuse to call him, right?"

"Shut up." I fished out my cell phone and the card that Bennington had given me with both their cell numbers on it. I punched in Will's number and was directed to his voice mail. I left a quick message: "Hey Will, it's Syd. Sydney McCall. From high school. We met at the crime scene this morning. I mean, we didn't meet there—we already know each other. We ran into each other there. Ah—when you get a chance, give me a call. There's something I'd like to run by you. Okay? Thanks."

"Oh, smooth!" Leila chuckled as I put the phone down. I stuck my tongue out at her, and she grinned. "Feel better now?"

"Not particularly." I stared moodily at the note. "It looks like K-A-H-N L-E-E. Someone's name?"

Leila brandished her phone. "Let's find out." She called up Google, typed in Kahn Lee, and hit Go. As the screen shifted, she let out a low whistle. "Wow. 991,000 results. It'll take forever."

"Great," I sighed. "Obviously this needs to be narrowed down somehow. What about trying it as one word?"

Leila typed that in, then hit enter. "4,320, but look—most of them separate the words."

"Maybe the spelling's off. Try it as one word and leave off the last e."

Leila plugged that in. "Here's one for Tommy Kahnle, but I doubt that'll do you much good. He's a pitcher for the White Sox. Littleton hated sports, so I greatly doubt this refers to him."

I let out a deep sigh. "Maybe Will might have some ideas."

Leila snapped her fingers. "I've got one. You could ask Littleton's partner. If it has anything to do with the business, he might know."

"Oh, yes. What do I do, walk up to him and say, 'Excuse me, sir, but I found your partner's body and this strange note on the floor. Do you have any idea what this might be about?'"

"Of course you don't say it like that. You query him subtly."

"Uh . . . How can I query him when I don't even know his name?"

"I think it's Colin something. Myers, Mills—no, wait. Murphy. Colin Murphy." Leila leaned back with a self-satisfied smile. "The police have probably gotten in touch with him by now—oh, and Petra. Poor, poor Petra." She made a motion of wiping a tear from her eye. "I'd have loved to have been a fly on the wall and seen her reaction to the news."

"She was in the area," I said thoughtfully. "I parked next to her car in the lot by the back alley. It was gone when we left—there's no way she could have missed the ambulance and police cars. You'd think she would have wanted to know what happened."

"She was probably too busy dancing for joy and wondering how she was going to spend her inheritance—unless, of course, she's the killer." Leila rubbed both her hands together gleefully. "Everyone knows killers don't inherit a dime."

*　　*　　*

Leila left shortly afterward, and Kat and I returned to our respective offices. At five o'clock, she rapped on my office door and then stuck her head inside. "Hey! Want to grab some dinner? My treat."

I glanced up from the sheaf of papers that littered the top of my desk. "I really want to finish these press releases for the event tonight," I said. "Tell you what—Leila's working late, so how about you come over for dinner?"

She gave me a dubious look. "You're going to cook?"

My lips twitched. As my sister well knew, my culinary skills are pretty much nonexistent. As a matter of fact, if it weren't for TV dinners, I'd have starved in college. Preston had done the lion's share of the cooking when we'd been together, although I have been known to put together a mean omelet—that is, if you like them slightly browned. "Of course not," I assured her. "I'll pick something up. What are you in the mood for?"

"After the day we had today?" Kat rolled her eyes. "Surprise me."

"Fine. I'll see you at seven."

Kat left and I spent another half hour writing up several different ads. Finally, I put my pen down, put the ad copy into a manila folder, and grabbed my jacket. I had to pass the cattery on my way out, and I paused briefly, then stuck my head in the door. Maggie and Viola each held a kitten in their arms, and Maggie was feeding hers with a tiny bottle. She looked up, saw me, and tossed me a grin.

"Peggy Sue here is finicky. She doesn't like mama's milk. Isn't that right, Peggy Sue?"

"You gave the kittens names already?"

"Oh, sure. This one is Peggy Sue, because she's got red fur, just like Kathleen Turner. Viola's got Elvis, and little Calvin and Hobbes are happy just feeding off Mama Cass."

I chuckled as I took note of the jet-black kitten in Viola's arms. "I can see why you named him Elvis. Dare I ask where the other names came from?"

"Well, I've always been a big Calvin and Hobbes fan," admitted Maggie. "And Mama Cass just seemed to fit the mother somehow." She winked. "And no, Toby isn't back yet."

I frowned. "He's been gone quite a while, hasn't he?"

Maggie shrugged. "If he were an ordinary cat, I'd say yes. Don't worry, he'll show up soon. I just hope he stays put for Saturday."

I said good-night and left, still wondering if it had been Toby that I'd seen in Littleton's office and if so, how the heck he had gotten in there.

*   *   *

Since it was such a nice spring evening, I decided to leave my car in the shelter parking lot and walk the short distance to the square where most of the retail shops were located. It was Wednesday night, and The Fin and Claw always had a fish-and-chips special that was pretty good, so I headed in that direction. As I passed The Printed Word, the used bookstore, the door flew open, and a plump figure beckoned to me from the doorway.

"Sydney! Got a minute?"

I smiled at the woman who stood there. "For you, Natalie, I've got two."

Natalie Helms was a pleasant, round-faced woman in her mid-to-late fifties who, thanks to skillfully applied makeup and Lady Clairol Mahogany Brown, looked more like late forties. Kat had told me she'd worked as an art historian at a Boston museum for years, and when they'd downsized her job, she'd taken her savings, moved to Deer Park, and opened the used bookstore because, as she put it, "books are like an old friend you just can't get enough of." She still had a love of art in her blood too—she frequently visited the galleries and artists colonies in North Carolina and the surrounding areas, and she sold small prints and pieces of sculpture in her store.

I stepped inside the store and breathed deeply. I've never been a big reader, but there's just something about the smell of old books that I find comforting. There was another smell I detected, too, and I glanced down at the floor. "New rug?"

Natalie nodded, wrapping her coral-colored sweater tightly around her. "Yep. I came into a little bit of money, so I thought I'd spruce the place up a bit." She picked up a stack of books on a nearby table and motioned for me to follow her.

The carpeting was a thick, lush shag pile that my feet sunk into as I followed Natalie to her office situated just in back of the counter. The office radiated cozy. Floor-to-ceiling bookcases covered one entire wall, jammed to overflowing with hardcovers and paperbacks. A beautiful cherrywood desk was in the far corner, two thick padded Queen Anne chairs in front of it. I had a quick glimpse of what appeared to be an ornate glass paperweight in a lovely shade of cobalt on a shelf directly behind the desk before Natalie plunked the stack of books down in front of it. She slid into the lush leather chair behind the desk and motioned for me to sit. "Looks like you did some revamping in your office too," I said.

"That I did. Life's too short to be uncomfortable, wouldn't you say?" She leaned back, steepled her hands underneath her chin, and shot me a questioning gaze. "I heard you and your sister found Littleton," she said. "Are you okay? Want to talk about it?"

"I'm fine, although I confess finding a dead body was the last thing I ever expected to do in my life."

Her shoulders hunched in a shudder. "I hear tell the police are regarding it as a suspicious death. That means it wasn't natural causes, right?"

"They're not sure," I said carefully. Natalie was a sweet woman, but I'd heard she liked to gossip. I didn't need her repeating details that might get back to the police and entail another visit from Bennington. "I didn't see any marks on the body, but of course I'm not a trained ME."

"Oh well." She leaned back in her chair. The light from the desk lamp caught the stone in the massive ring on her pinky finger, made it twinkle. Natalie caught me staring at it, and her lips twisted into a wry smile. "Too showy? It was such a bargain, I couldn't resist."

"No, it's lovely. I've never seen a diamond that size."

"It's not a diamond, it's a white topaz. I'm a November baby, so topaz is my birthstone." She cleared her throat. "I'm sorry that you had to go through that, but honestly it doesn't surprise me that the old buzzard finally bought it. Lots of folks around here are mighty curious as to just what happened to him. And mark my words—they won't be shedding too many tears."

The vehemence in her tone surprised me, and I suddenly wondered if Natalie might be one of the shopkeepers who had issues with Littleton. As I contemplated how to ask about her relationship with Littleton, she solved the problem for me. "I'm one of 'em," she said softly. "I hate to speak ill of the dead, but all I can say is good riddance. The world's a lot better place without Trowbridge Littleton in it."

"You had issues with him?"

She barked out a short laugh. "Who didn't, love? Every shopkeeper in this complex had an unpleasant dealing with the man at some point or another. Devon, Buck, Dayna, Grace, me, Antonio . . . all of us." She picked up a pen, scissored it between her long fingers. "He was in all the shops about two months ago, letting us know that when our leases were up—and most of them are up at the end of this year—he was raising the rent. By 30 percent."

My hand fluttered in the air. "Wait a minute. I'm missing something here. How could he raise your rent?"

"Easily. He is—or rather he was—our landlord." She studied me for a moment. "You didn't know?"

"I had no idea. I mean, I knew he was rich, but I didn't realize he dabbled in real estate."

"Oh, it's a bit more than dabbling. His father owned a good bit of Deer Park. Practically all commercial properties, too."

I leaned back in my chair. Wow, talk about a shock. And about a motive. If Littleton had been about to raise everyone's rents exorbitantly, then that meant there were a whole bunch of suspects in his death, indeed. I leaned forward. "Did he ever ask you to sign a petition to evict the shelter?"

Her eyes widened. "No, but then again, he probably figured he didn't have to. Once he hit the town with the increase on the shelter, he'd more than likely achieve that goal anyway. The shelter would most likely have to move, and he could get double the rent the town was paying on that building. Kill two birds with one stone, so to speak."

"What? Wait a minute." I gave my head a brisk shake. "Littleton owned the shelter building too?"

She gave a swift nod of assent. "His father, unlike him, was an animal lover, and he gave the city a long-term lease on that building right before he died, and it's up this year. I know your sister wasn't too happy about the prospect of the shelter's rent increasing, either. Not too happy at all."

My stomach gave a little lurch. I'd been right . . . Kat had been keeping something from me, something pretty important. I leaned forward, intent on quizzing Natalie more, but just then we heard the bell above the shop door tinkle.

"Ah, customers. Tonight's my late night." She pushed her chair back, walked around to me, and patted my shoulder. "I'm sorry I had to bring up such an unpleasant subject, dear. I hate to say it, but it's such a relief as well to know that—codger—won't be making our lives miserable anymore. You don't mind seeing yourself out, do you?"

*   *   *

Back out on the street, I paused, letting Natalie's words sink in. I was particularly distressed to learn Littleton had owned the shelter building. I wondered if Bennington knew; if so, it would explain a lot. I whipped out my cell and punched in Will's number once more, and once more I got voice mail. I decided not to leave another message and slid the phone back into my tote bag. I stood for a moment, debating my next move. My appetite, which had been tenuous before my chat with Natalie, had diminished even more—fish and chips was definitely out now.

I started up the block at a fast clip. As I approached the top, I noticed the police tape stretched across the front of The Brush and Canvas swaying in the light breeze. A swift movement off to my left made me turn my head just in time to see a dark shape ducking under the crime scene tape. I stared openmouthed for a few seconds. Who would be stupid enough to do that? I whipped out my cell, intending to punch in 9-1-1—and then I hesitated. According to Natalie, practically everyone was curious about the circumstances surrounding Littleton's demise—was one of them taking their curiosity a step too far? I hated to get someone in trouble, and if truth be told, I was a bit loath to make another 9-1-1 call to the police. With my luck, Bennington would show up and be as happy to see me as I would to see him. I punched in Will's number, and when the voice mail kicked in, whispered, "Will, it's Syd. I thought I saw someone enter The Brush and Canvas. Please, if you're anywhere in the area, come over."

I rang off, slid my phone back into my pocket, and hurried up the block. I dipped under the yellow tape and up to the front entrance. I tried the door. Locked. I glanced around, then quickly made my way around the side of the building to the rear entrance. More crime scene tape covered the glass-and-wood door. I ducked underneath, turned the handle—and just as it had this morning, the door creaked open. I frowned. Had the police neglected to lock this door, or had the intruder somehow managed to open it?

I stepped cautiously across the threshold and stood for a minute, letting my eyes adjust to the abject darkness. If someone else was inside, I reasoned, they must have eyes like a cat's, because it was dark as Hades. I tiptoed over to the corridor and stood silently for a moment. I was just about to retrace my steps when I saw a bright circle of light suddenly explode at the far end of the corridor, right about where the office door was. Either the intruder had found one of the lamps, or they'd turned a flashlight on. Holding my breath, I inched down the corridor until I came to the office entrance. I peered in.

The small lamp on the desk had been turned on. A figure, clad all in black, was hunched over the desk, pulling open the drawers. Without thinking, I cried out, "What are you doing?"

The figure turned around. In the dim light from the desk lamp, I saw her face—I also caught a glint of blued steel. Without a second thought, I cried out, "Devon McIntyre, what are you doing with a gun? Did you kill Trowbridge Littleton?"

Chapter Seven

Devon McIntyre cocked her gun toward my chest and said in a shrill tone, "Me? Kill Littleton? What are you, crazy?"

"No," I said, inclining my head toward the weapon in her hand, "but what else am I to think when you're waving that thing at me?"

"Oh." She stared at the revolver as if it were the first time she were seeing it and then slowly lowered it to her side. "Sorry. I carry it for protection. A gal can't be too careful these days."

I eyed the gun. After all, what did I know about Devon McIntyre? She was a nice-looking woman in her midforties with an hourglass figure who liked to dress as if she were still twenty-one. I'd been in her shop a few times, admiring the lovely jewelry she had for sale, and she'd always been pleasant—then again, most shopkeepers were pleasant in light of a potential sale. Devon's manner had always seemed restrained, almost as if she were keeping a secret. I looked the woman straight in the eye. "Do you even know how to shoot that? It might go off accidentally."

"Wouldn't matter even if it did." She raised the gun, pointed it at the wall, and pulled the trigger. I heard a click but nothing else. "It's not loaded," Devon admitted. "I just thought if I carried one and someone went to attack me, it might scare them off."

"Not too bright," I said dryly. "What if they also had a gun and shot first?"

Devon's face paled beneath her heavy makeup. "Ooh—I never thought of that."

I shook my head. "What are you doing here, anyway? This is still a crime scene."

Devon set the gun down on the desk and dropped into the chair. She folded her arms across her chest and looked at me. "You're here," she said, her tone slightly accusing.

"I followed you."

She slapped her palm against her temple. "You followed me, but you thought I might be the killer returning to the scene of the crime? Now that wasn't very bright!"

"No, I guess it wasn't," I confessed. "I thought it was just someone curious about Littleton's death." Inclining my head toward the open desk drawers, I added, "You weren't just curious, though, were you? You came here looking for something."

Devon's lips twisted into a grimace. "Why would you think that? Maybe I was just curious to see the place where Bridge—where Littleton died. The whole town's talking about it."

"He didn't die inside one of those drawers," I said dryly.

Devon gave her head a quick toss, and a black ringlet spilled across her eyes. Brushing it away, she said, "If you must know, I lost my medical identification tag. That's a—"

"I know what it is." I was well acquainted with the item, since both my parents and two of my aunts had had them. A medical identification was a small emblem usually worn on a bracelet, on a neck chain, or pinned to an article of clothing that advised that the wearer had an important medical condition that might require immediate attention. The tags were often made out of stainless steel or sterling silver, shiny metals that a first responder would immediately notice and then become aware of the condition. I raised a brow inquiringly. "What makes you think you lost it here?"

"I had an appointment with Bridge the other day, and I know I had it on my bracelet then. When I went to put it on this morning, I realized the tag was gone, and the last place I actually remember seeing the tag was here."

My eyes narrowed. "Wouldn't Littleton have called you if he'd found it?"

She shrugged. "Maybe, maybe not. Knowing him, he just might have shoved it in one of these drawers, and since I can't ask him now . . . I had no choice but to come and look for myself." She turned a pleading gaze my way. "I'm a diabetic, so it's important I find it. Will you help me?"

I hesitated. Her story didn't ring quite true to me, but I had no way of disproving anything she'd said. "Okay, but let's make it quick."

"No problem." Devon turned and resumed pulling out drawers. "Thanks for helping me, Sydney. I can understand why you don't trust me, but believe you me, if I'd killed Bridge, I'd have made sure I didn't leave anything behind that might point to me. Besides, there's a long line of better suspects in front of me. Take that trophy-licious wife of his, for one. Don't the police always look to the spouse first?"

"Usually." I started flipping cushions on the small love seat, ran my hand beneath them. "But why would she want him dead? From what I understand, he turned a blind eye to her spending and ah, other activities."

Devon glanced up from rummaging through the middle drawer. "There was no love lost between him and his stepson, either. Trey hated him and vice versa." She let out a hollow laugh. "If you thought his mommy was a spend-thrift, then you haven't seen anything yet." She slammed the drawer shut, jerked open one on the right.

Since Devon seemed in a talkative mood, I decided to press on. "What do you know about his business partner, Colin Murphy?"

She shrugged. "Not a whole lot. Bridge brought him on to do the buying for the gallery. He came highly recommended. Lately, though, there was trouble in paradise."

"What sort of trouble?"

She shrugged again. "I'm not sure. Bridge was pretty closemouthed about it. All I heard him say once was that Colin's ideas would sully the gallery's reputation—whatever that meant."

I pushed the cushions back into place and straightened them. "So this appointment you had with Littleton—was it about the rent increase?"

She shut the last drawer on the desk and started running her hand under the cushion on the chair behind the desk. "Yes. I was trying to work out a deal with him."

"It doesn't look like your tag's here, Devon." I hesitated and then added, "You know there is the possibility that perhaps the police might have found it when they were here."

Her eyes popped, and her whole body sagged. "Oh, swell. That means they'll want to question me right?"

I walked over to her and laid a hand on her arm. "You were having an affair with Littleton, weren't you?"

Her head snapped up, and a sigh escaped her lips. "Had. Past tense. How did you know?"

"Not too many people call him Bridge. The name just seemed to roll off your tongue."

She bit down on her lower lip. "Damn. I'll try to remember that. Anyway, the affair's been over for months, but we were still friendly—or at least I thought we were."

"You came here to try to talk him out of raising your rent?"

She nodded. "I thought I could trade on our past relationship and get a more favorable lease, but—it was a no go. He was alive when I left, though," she added quickly. "I swear. Getting involved with him, well, it's not something I'm proud of. And I certainly don't want Harry finding out."

"Harry?"

"My husband. Ex-husband," she amended. "We were separated for a few years, but he's back in town now. We've been trying to work out our problems. Something like this . . ." She waved her hand helplessly. "Well, this could put a real damper on things." She shot me a beseeching look. "Bridge could be a scoundrel, but he had a soft side, too. I didn't kill him, Syd. I couldn't."

Oddly, I believed her. "I won't volunteer anything," I said at last, "but my advice to you, if the police should ask about your relationship with Littleton—don't lie."

We walked out of the office and back down the corridor. When we reached the anteroom, I pulled the note out of my pocket and held it out to her. "Have you ever seen this before?"

She peered down at the note and shook her head. "It sounds foreign. Possibly an artist Bridge might have dealt with? I know he had a lot of Asian art on display."

"Maybe. Thanks." I slid the note back into my pocket, then stiffened as I saw a police cruiser glide up and park. Devon saw it too, and her face paled. "Oh my God. What are they doing here?" She looked around like a trapped rabbit searching for a means of escape. "I can't face them now. I just can't."

I felt a sudden surge of sympathy for the woman. Against my better judgment, I heard myself say, "Maybe you can let yourself out that side door. I'll go talk to them."

Devon reached out, grabbed my hand, and squeezed it. "You're a good egg, Syd. Anything you need, anything at all—just let me know." And then she was gone.

I walked over to the back entrance and opened the door just as Will bounded up the steps. He took one look at me and said, "Syd? I got your message. Are you okay?"

I nodded. "I just feel foolish. I was certain I saw someone cross the barrier and come in here, so I followed, but . . . I was wrong. There's no one here. I must have seen a shadow or something."

Will was looking at me speculatively. "That was a fool-hardy thing to do," he chided. "What if it had been the killer? What if he or she had a gun?"

"I know, I know. My inner Nancy Drew kicked in. It won't happen again," I assured him.

"See that it doesn't." He pushed past me into the foyer. "I suppose I should have a look around, though. Just in case."

"I'll come with you."

He hesitated, then nodded. "Fine. But stay behind me."

We walked down the hall. I stayed a short distance behind Will. When we reached the office, he stood for a minute on the threshold, looking all around. I held my breath. Would he notice that the drawers on the desk were slightly ajar or that I hadn't pushed the love seat cushions all the way back? Apparently not, because he holstered his weapon and turned to me. "You're right. Looks like no one's here."

"Told you." I paused and then said, "Your partner paid a visit to the shelter earlier."

Will had moved over toward the desk, was looking around again. "So he said."

"Did he mention he asked if Kat and I were aware removing anything from a crime scene is a punishable offense?"

Will glanced at me sharply and then shook his head. "No, he didn't. I can't think why he'd do that, unless . . ."

"Unless?" I prompted as he fell silent.

Will shrugged. "I probably shouldn't say anything—Bennington will hit the roof—but it could be because of something his widow might have said."

Oho, I was right! "So she did show up at the office."

He shook his head. "Nope. We went to see her at home when we were finished here. I must say, she didn't seem very broken up about her husband's demise. She even offered us tea."

"So she's got manners," I observed. "How nice."

He chuckled. "Under the circumstances, we didn't really think it was appropriate, but—who knows. Grief affects people differently."

I glossed right over that. "So what did she say that made Bennington race right over to question us?"

Will looked me straight in the eye. "I can't say." As I opened my mouth to protest, he held up his hand. "Really—I can't say, because I don't know. I got a call from the ME, and I was out of the room for most of the time. Bennington was finished with her by the time I got done."

My brow puckered as I thought. From the questions Bennington asked, it seemed as if Petra must have inquired about some object in her husband's office, but what? I somehow doubted it was the mysterious note. Aloud, I said to Will, "What did the ME have to say? I'm assuming the cause of death wasn't natural causes."

"It doesn't look that way." I continued to stare at him, and finally he threw up both hands. "Okay, fine. I can tell you this much. It looks like you might have just missed being an eyewitness. ME set the time of death between five and six AM."

I gulped. "I suppose you want to know where Kat and I were between those hours, right? At home, asleep—at least I was until five thirty. But I have no witness to prove it. Leila was dead asleep."

Will glanced at his watch. "Well, since there's no intruder here, I have to be getting back to the station. Can I drop you off at your house?"

"Thanks, but my car's back at the shelter. You could give me a lift over there, if you don't mind."

"If I minded, I wouldn't have asked. Let's go." As we walked out of the store and over to the police car, my hand dipped inside my jacket pocket and closed around the note. I stopped dead in my tracks. "There is something else," I said.

He turned toward me. "What?"

I pulled the note out of my pocket and held it out to him. "I found this in the hallway of Littleton's store. So I guess your partner was right. I did take something from the premises."

Will picked up the note gingerly and turned it over. "Are these teeth marks? What were you doing? Chewing on it?"

"Ah, no. Not me. A cat."

He cocked a brow at me. "A cat? Littleton kept a cat in the shop?"

"No, I don't think so. I think it might have been a stray that got in somehow."

Will squinted at the note. "The writing's cramped, and the note's kinda soggy. Hard to read what's here."

"Do you think you can get prints off of it? Or DNA?"

"Doubtful." He folded it carefully and slid it into his pocket. "It's probably nothing, but I'll check it out."

He started to move forward, but my hand shot out, pressed against his chest. "You won't tell your partner, will you?"

He stared deeply into my eyes for a few seconds, then gave his head a quick shake. "Somehow, Syd, I don't think a soggy note was the sort of thing Bennington had in mind. No, this is just between us." His lips parted in a smile. "Your secret's safe with me."

*　*　*

Kat rang my bell promptly at seven. She stepped inside, and her eyebrows rose as she saw the pizza box on the living room coffee table. "That's the best you could do?" she said.

"It's a long story." I waited until Kat had seated herself on the sofa, then I plunked myself down next to her and cut right to the chase. Fixing her with a stern look, I said, "I knew you were holding something back. Why didn't you tell me that Littleton owned the shelter building?"

103

My sister paused, a slice of pepperoni and onion half-way to her lips. Her face paled slightly. "You found out, huh? How?"

"Natalie told me earlier. She also told me he wanted to raise everyone's rent 30 percent—and that included the shelter."

Kat slid the slice onto a paper plate and set it on the table. "I didn't mention it because it wasn't a done deal yet. He'd approached the mayor a while ago, said that he was considering doing that and wanted to give everyone fair warning." Her gaze was troubled. "I won't lie—if he'd decided to increase the rent 30 percent, there's no way we could have kept the shelter going without a large injection of funding. That's why I've been trying so hard to get more donors." She worried her lower lip. "Frankly, I was hoping the whole thing might blow over." She sighed. "If you found out all this, then I suppose Will and that horrible Bennington can too. And it won't make me look good, will it?"

"Probably not." I picked up one of the throw pillows and started to toy with the tassel on its end. "Did Littleton say *why* he wanted to raise everyone's rent?"

"The usual—expenses, taxes, we've had that dirt-cheap rent forever, yada yada. We figure the real reason was that his lovely wife was bleeding him dry, and he was using any means he could to recoup some of his losses."

"Hmm. That tallies with what Devon said," I murmured.

"Devon McIntyre? You talked to her?"

"Oh, yeah." I tossed the pillow off to one side. "Did you know that Devon and Littleton were—ah—a little more than just landlord and tenant?"

Both Kat's eyebrows went straight up. "She admitted it? Wow! I mean, we all suspected for some time, but . . ." Her face arranged itself into a frown, and she perched herself on the edge of the coffee table across from me. "Just what happened tonight? You said it was a long story."

I sighed. "Yes. First, let me apologize for the pizza. I'd planned on fish and chips originally, but by the time Will drove me back to the shelter to get my car—"

"Whoa!" Kat held up one hand. "Will, huh? And just what were you doing with Will? Reinvestigating the scene of the crime?"

"Something like that. I'll tell you everything, but let's eat first. Suddenly I'm famished."

In between bites of pizza and sips of sweet tea, I recounted the evening's adventures. When I finished, Kat gave a sigh and regarded me with narrowed eyes. "My, you have had a busy night. You're not planning to keep on doing this, are you?"

I set down my glass of sweet tea and reached for my third slice of pizza. "I'm sorry. I'm not sure what you mean."

"Oh, yes you do. You're planning to investigate Littleton's death on your own, aren't you?"

"Who, me?" I turned my finger inward and pointed at myself. "Would I do anything like that?"

"Yes, you would. I know how much you love a good puzzle and how much you always wanted to be a PI . . ."

"Actually, I wanted to be a homicide detective, but that's neither here nor there. You know me well, sister dear."

"Darn straight I do. And I always promised Mom I'd try to keep you out of trouble. That's why I want you to promise me that you'll stay out of it and leave it to the police."

"Oh, really," I sat back and rolled my eyes. "It's not like I'm going to go out and deliberately confront a murderer. What I want to do is try to get us out of the spotlight Bennington's got us in—especially you."

"And I appreciate the gesture, but your safety comes first. Please, Syd."

"Okay, fine. I promise." At her black look, I thrust out both my hands and waved them under her nose. "Satisfied?"

Kat set the spoon down and shook her fist at me. "I'm serious, Syd."

"So am I. I promise—no investigating."

And thank God I was sitting down, so she couldn't see I had my ankles crossed.

Chapter Eight

The rest of the week passed rather uneventfully—thank God! Saturday morning found us at Dayna's Sweets and Treats bright and early, cats in tow. Kat and I helped Maggie, Viola, and Sissy set up the cages in the pop-up café. There were eight cats in all—besides Toby and Karma the Siamese, there was Jinx, a black female with the greenest eyes I'd ever seen; Elmo, a black-and-white male who had a meow like a locomotive; Pumpkin, a ginger female; Magnolia Blossom, a beautiful calico; and Ralphie and Norton, brothers who'd been named after the characters in *The Honeymooners*. It was easy to see why: Ralphie was a gray cat definitely on the tubby side—a decided contrast from his brother, Norton, a gray-and-white who had a much more slender physique.

"We'd really like to see Ralphie and Norton adopted together, if possible," Maggie said as I helped her arrange the brothers' cage near the jungle gym. "Of course, it's not a requirement, but they've been together since birth,

and they absolutely love each other. I'd hate to see them separated."

I peered inside the cage. Ralphie had Norton in a head-lock and was sinking his teeth into the other cat's neck. Norton had his eyes closed and actually looked as if he were enjoying this. "Is Ralphie part vampire?" I joked.

Maggie gave a soft chuckle. "It looks a lot worse than it actually is. That's how they play." She gave my elbow a soft nudge. "Your favorite has deigned to make an appearance today, by the way."

My gaze strayed over to Toby's cage, all the way at the other end of the room. Toby sat in the corner, his paws folded beneath him. He appeared to be studying the other cats. I walked over to his cage and stood looking at him.

"I wonder if he gets lonely," I murmured. I hadn't real-ized I'd spoken aloud until Viola laid a hand on my arm.

"Cats are basically solitary creatures," she said, her hands running down the sides of the printed maxi dress she wore. "I doubt they're ever really lonely."

"Oh, I know that," I answered. "But Maggie said that Toby sometimes wanders away. I thought maybe it was because he might be . . . searching for companionship? A nice female cat, maybe?"

"Either that or he's just a tom with wanderlust in his DNA. Maggie likes to say he's searching for that perfect human, but to be honest, I think she's romanticizing. It's just hormones kicking in."

"Oh," I said. I couldn't keep the disappointment out of my tone. "To be honest, I kinda like Maggie's version better."

Viola ran a hand through her short crop of light-brown hair. "Who knows? Maybe she's right. One day he'll get paired with just the right human, and then his vagabond days will be over."

Toby rolled over on his side and stretched out his long forepaws. "So he's pretty social, then?" I asked.

"He hasn't bitten anybody yet," Viola laughed. "Cat, dog, or human."

"Maggie did say he was good at discouraging potential adoptees."

"That he is. One woman was nuts over him, but every time she went to touch him, he'd hiss, and all the fur on his tail would stand on end. Another young couple with a baby took a liking to him, but he went and jumped on top of one of the newborn kittens, and the woman was afraid he might do that to the baby." Viola shook her head. "It's like he knows just what buttons to push. Spooky. And as far as interacting with the other cats . . ." She inclined her head toward Toby. "Don't worry, he gets in plenty of playtime with them. Not so much the other males as the females. He's quite the ladies' man. He loves to chase the girls around the playroom at the shelter."

Viola moved off, and I walked over to the cage, knelt down, and wiggled my fingers through the slats of the cage. "Hey there, little man. I hear you like the ladies."

Toby lifted his head and fixed his green stare directly on me. A loud purr rumbled deep in his throat.

I leaned in closer. "Do you like me, Toby? Because I definitely like you."

Toby cocked his head.

"I think you do like me," I whispered. "I saw you outside the shelter window one night, and I'm pretty sure it was you in Littleton's office the other day. How did you get in there, and where did you find that note? I wish you could talk and tell me."

The cat rose, stretched, and ambled over to where my face was pressed up against the cage. He sat down right in front of me and cocked his head to one side. And blinked those wide green eyes twice.

I felt a tap on my shoulder, and I looked up to meet Maggie's gaze. Her eyes twinkled behind her glasses. "They say receiving a blink from a cat is like getting a kiss," she said.

"Mer-owww!" said Toby.

Maggie shook her head. "Darned if that cat doesn't understand English." She brandished a stack of flyers. "I'm going to put these out on the entrance table. It's almost time to start. Isn't it exciting?"

As Maggie and her crew hurried out to the front of the shop, I lagged behind. I looked around to be sure no one else was within earshot and then whispered to Toby, "You be good today—but not too good, okay? I think I might want to take you home with me."

Toby blinked twice, and the corners of his lips tipped up a tad. I wondered if he had indeed understood what I'd said.

*   *   *

The line outside Dayna's shop for the cat café adoption event stretched around the block. Some were just curious, but others were genuinely interested in the cats and hopeful that their personalities would click. There was a separate line for the people interested in participating. They bought a separate ticket and paid the fee, which entitled them to a maximum of two hours inside the playroom. Kat and I had set up a small treat station in the far corner, where folks could purchase coffee, tea, and the human snacks that Dayna had put on the special menu. Maggie and Sissy were currently manning the station, which also included a section of edible cat treats and small toys that the patrons could use to entice the animals. Viola and Sophie, another volunteer, let the cats out of the cages and walked around the perimeter of the room to ensure that everything went smoothly. Within the first two hours, three of the cats had firm applications for adoption. Karma was the first to go, no surprise there. Edith Maxwell, the high school principal, fell in love with her at first sight. I was pleased to learn that Doug and Ida Charles had put in an application to adopt both Ralphie and Norton. Doug was a lawyer who'd just started a new practice, and Ida worked as a telemarketer out of their home. I had no doubt that they would all pass with flying colors. The other cats received their fair share of oohs and aahs, and the people loved playing with them while they noshed on pastries and fresh-brewed coffee and tea. Around noon, Leila stopped by and interviewed several of the volunteers and prospective "parents." She glanced up and gave me a thumbs-up sign.

I grinned at her as she passed me. "So I take it you approve of Toby as a roommate?" I asked.

"Well, he certainly seems more docile than some of the humans I've dated recently," she chuckled. "Handsomer, too. But seriously, Syd, I told you, if you want to adopt him, I'm cool with it. Just let me know so I can order that pet-hair attachment for the vacuum."

I made a face at her. "Very funny." I glanced over toward the far wall. Toby was huddled against it, and two young girls were leaning over him, giggling and wiggling their fingers at him. Toby looked as if he could care less. He flopped over on his side, facing the wall. A few seconds later, the sound of loud snoring reached our ears.

"That's one way to discourage a potential adoption," chucked Leila as the two girls turned toward some of the other cats roaming around. She shot me a mischievous grin. "Maybe he's waiting for you, Syd. Go on over and see if he perks up."

I resisted the urge to stick my tongue out at my friend, but once she breezed out the door, I did amble over toward where Toby lay. I leaned down and wiggled my fingers at the supposedly sleeping cat.

"Hey Toby," I said. "Is Leila right? Are you waiting for me?"

Toby's tail suddenly flicked to and fro, and he twisted his head slightly so that he was facing me. Then he opened his eyes and blinked twice.

"Two kisses," I laughed. "Maybe you were playing possum after all."

"Looks like our rogue cat has his eye on you."

I jumped and whirled around to see my sister standing behind me. She grinned. "Isn't it great, though? Everyone seems to love this event, and the cats are going like wildfire. I think we should have brought more."

"We'll know for next time," I said. "There will be a next time, right?"

"I think so. The seating area outside in the café is full, and Dayna's got a long line. She had to pull Sissy back outside to help out." She glanced over at Toby, who was now sitting up. "He'd certainly make a good mouser," she said. "But how do you feel about his habit of wandering?"

I shrugged. "Maybe if he were in his very own home, with his very own humans, cat bed, and toys, he might be persuaded to stick around."

"You could be right. Maybe you are that special human Maggie's always talking about," Kat laughed.

I grinned at her. "From your lips to God's ears."

*   *   *

The afternoon passed swiftly. Dayna got really busy in the café, and her other part-timer called in sick, so I went over to lend a hand. By the time it slowed down enough for me to return to the playroom, a welcome sight greeted my eyes. All the tables we'd set up in there were still filled with people. I noticed that Magnolia Blossom was at one table with a gray-haired woman who was petting her soft fur and whispering to her and that Pumpkin was twining around the ankles of Mr. Petrie, the grammar school custodian who'd lost his wife two months ago. I walked up to Mr. Petrie's table and smiled down at the man. "Looks as if you've found a friend."

He reached down to stroke Pumpkin's head. "She's a sweet little thing. I've been sorta lonely since Marjorie passed on. I thought—now don't think I'm foolish or anything, but—I kinda thought maybe Marjorie led me here today. Maybe led me to this sweet girl."

"I'm sure she did. I think the two of you make a splendid pair."

He nodded in agreement, lifted his coffee cup to his lips. "That settles it. I'm going to fill out the application— just as soon as I finish this coffee and apple tart."

"Don't wait too long," I cautioned. "There's still another hour left on the event. You don't want someone else to put in an application for Pumpkin."

Mr. Petrie gulped down the last of his coffee, scraped back his chair, and swooped Pumpkin into his arms. "Absolutely not," he said, then started striding toward the volunteer table. I looked around for Toby and finally saw him curled up in the far corner of the room. Viola was waving a catnip chili pepper at him. Toby appeared less than interested. I hurried over. "Everything okay?" I asked.

Viola looked up with a smile. "Oh, yes. Just more of the usual."

"The usual?"

Viola pointed to a young couple with a little girl at a table in the far corner. Jinx sat complacently in the little girl's arms. "They took a shine to Toby—especially the little girl. But when she tried to pick him up, he hissed at her and smacked her with his tail! Then he took off for this corner and hasn't budged since."

I looked over at Toby. Once again, he gave me a slow blink. Then he rose, stretched, and padded right over to me. He twined himself around my ankles, looked up with an almost beseeching look, and said, "Merow."

Viola shook her head. "Well, imagine that! He's never done that before—not to any prospective owners, and certainly not to any of us volunteers." She grinned at me. "You know, Syd, you must have something special."

"Maybe you're right." I exhaled a deep breath. "I'm going to do it, Viola. I'm going to fill out an application to adopt Toby."

I looked down at the cat. He met my gaze, then reared up on his hind legs and held out one paw.

"Mer-oooow."

"Well, what do you know?" Viola called over to Maggie. "I think we finally have a winner in the Toby adoption sweepstakes."

*   *   *

I filled out the required papers and wrote out a check for the deposit. Maggie tucked them into her portfolio. "I hope I qualify," I said as Maggie snapped the portfolio shut.

"Well, I can't see why you won't." She inclined her head over toward Kat, who was talking with some people over by the door. "It's not like you won't have good references."

I wrinkled my nose. "I don't have a permanent job though, at least not yet. If this director of publicity gig doesn't pan out . . ."

"Let's not think that way," Maggie said. "You have a job now, and that's what counts. Anyway, push come to shove, your roomie has a job, right? Or I'm sure your sister will vouch for you." She reached out and squeezed my hand. "I'm glad you turned out to be Toby's special human. And now"—she glanced at her watch—"it's almost time for us to wrap things up here."

I stole a glance at my own watch and saw she was right. The time had passed so quickly! It was four o'clock, and the last cat adoption customer had just departed. Now that I'd filled out the application, all of the eight cats they'd brought today had found forever homes. Kat hurried over to me. "This was a huge success, Syd. So much so that I want to talk to Dayna about doing this again, maybe once a month?"

I bobbed my head in agreement. "Sounds good. And if that works out, maybe we could expand it to every other week. And we don't have to limit it to Dayna's either. Any interested venue can set up a pop-up. You know, we don't just have to limit it to cats. A dog café could be a possible expansion."

"True. Maybe Natalie could have a book-signing-slash-shelter-event at her store," Kat said enthusiastically. "There are several writers from this area who've written both fiction and nonfiction books featuring dogs and cats. I'll put it on my agenda to discuss." She glanced over at the cages and saw the white sticker on Toby's cage. "Oh—Toby got adopted?"

I couldn't help the grin that spread across my face. "Yep. By yours truly—as long as I pass the screening, that is."

Kat let out a whoop and grabbed me around the waist. "What do you mean? Of course you pass!" She turned and waved at Maggie with her free arm. "Maggie, leave Syd's papers on my desk. I'll process them first thing Monday." She gave me a wide smile. "So . . . you can pick him up any time after noon on Monday. That work for you? Or is it too soon?"

Now it was my turn to whoop. "Too soon! Heck no. It's just too bad that it's a weekend and that I can't take him home tonight."

"Now now, calm down," Kat grinned. "You need time to go shopping for supplies."

"Oh, darn." I slapped my forehead with the palm of my hand. "You're right. I forgot about that little detail."

"We can help with some of it," Maggie said from behind me. "We can provide you with some toys, but you'll need a food bowl, food, a cat bed . . ." She rummaged in her portfolio and whipped out a sheet of paper. "Here's a checklist."

I stared at all the items and knew just where this week's pay would be going. But it was all worth it.

*　*　*

Viola, Sissy, and Maggie took the cats back to the shelter while Kat and I sat down at the counter with Dayna to iron out details about another possible event. We'd only been talking for a few minutes when the bell above the café door tinkled, and in walked Will and Detective Bennington.

"Oh, great," Kat muttered under her breath. "What do they want?"

"I don't know, but I bet it's not to adopt a cat."

Will offered me a fleeting smile as he and Bennington strode up to the counter. Bennington tapped one chubby finger on the counter. "I guess we're too late to have a look at the kitties, eh?"

I pointed to the clock on the wall. "It ended at four," I said. "But don't worry, we'll have another event."

"I gather it was a success, then?" Bennington observed.

"Oh, yes," Kat piped up. "Very much so."

"Ah." Bennington shot us a piercing glance. "Any of 'em get adopted?"

"All of them, actually," I said. "It really went off like clockwork."

"How . . . nice."

The silence hung heavy in the air, and I felt as if I could read Bennington's thoughts: *So Littleton's death proved rather fortuitous, eh?*

Dayna eyed the newcomers rather suspiciously. "Can I get you gentlemen something to eat or drink?"

Bennington sniffed at the air as he patted at his bulging stomach. "Something to eat would be nice. Smells really good in here."

"That would be my apple tart," Dayna responded. "Would you gentlemen like one? And some coffee to go with?"

"I think we can make time for that." Bennington glanced meaningfully at Kat and me. "I really need to talk to the McCall sisters."

"I was rather hoping to impose on them to give me a hand getting your treats," Dayna said quickly. I glanced at her set jaw, and I could read between the lines. The faster they were served, the faster they might leave.

"Sure. I'll make the coffee," Kat said quickly. She gave me a little push. "You can start with the detectives." She tossed Bennington a tight smile. "I trust that's okay?"

He nodded. "Perfectly fine." He turned and pushed his way toward a table near the middle of the café. Will started to follow, but I reached out and touched his arm.

"Any more word on Littleton's cause of death?" I whispered.

Will stole a quick glance over at the table where Bennington had already made himself comfortable. "Not yet," he said shortly.

I leaned forward. "What about the note? Did you check that out yet?"

"Not yet."

My eyes narrowed. I had the distinct feeling he was being deliberately dismissive. "Are those the only two words you know?"

His lips twitched. "Nope."

I made an exasperated sound. "What about the other suspects? Did any of them have alibis for the TOD?"

Will's brows drew together. "Other suspects?"

I widened my eyes. "You've got other suspects, don't you? Or are Kat and I the only lucky ones?"

Will's hand shot out and gripped my elbow. He inclined his head in Bennington's direction. "Can we talk about all this some other time?"

I thrust my jaw aggressively forward. "I'm not afraid of your partner."

"No? Maybe you should be." He turned on his heel and stalked over to where Bennington sat.

"What got him hot under the collar?"

I turned. Kat stood behind me, holding a tray on which rested two steaming cups of coffee.

"How on earth did you make that so fast?" I cried.

She shrugged. "I used Dayna's French press," she said. "Brewing a fresh pot would take too long. I'd like to get this over with as quickly as possible too. Will I don't mind so much, but his partner gives me the creeps."

"No argument here," I muttered. "Will turns into a different person when he's around Columbo Jr." I saw Dayna pulling tarts out of the microwave. "Go serve them the coffee, and I'll get the pastry." As Kat walked over to their table, I decided I'd be very circumspect in what I told them. I meant what I said. It seemed to me that Will walked on eggshells around Bennington. I'd have to manage to get him alone somehow.

Dayna emerged from the kitchen and pressed the tray containing the tarts into my hand. "Here. Try to make it fast, will ya—what the heck?"

A loud cry made us both whirl around. Bennington had half-risen from his chair, and I noticed that he had coffee spilled on his shirt. Will looked like he wanted to drop through the floor and disappear as Bennington reared back and pointed an accusing finger under Kat's nose.

"Young lady," he bellowed, "are you trying to kill *me* now?"

Chapter Nine

I shot out from behind the counter like a flash and raced over to my sister's side. Bennington had grabbed a handful of napkins and was attempting to wipe off his shirt. He glanced up briefly, his eyes blazing. "That coffee!" He gestured toward Will's still full cup. "Take a taste. It's horrible!"

Will hesitated, then raised his mug to his lips and took a tentative sip. His eyes bulged, and he made a face as he lowered the cup back to the table. "It—it isn't too good," he said.

"Isn't too good! That's an understatement!" Bennington rasped.

"Oh, for goodness' sake." I snatched up Will's cup and raised it to my own lips. A moment later, I spat out the liquid. "Uck. Tastes like dirt." I turned my gaze to Kat. "What kind of coffee is this?"

"Oh my stars." Kat turned on her heel and hurried back behind the counter. Fortunately, there weren't too many other customers in the café at the moment, but the few that were craned their necks, trying to ascertain what had made Bennington make such a fuss. I picked up Will's cup and carried it back with me, over to the rear counter where Kat was standing by the French press she'd used to make the coffee. She had a purple container in her hand and was just standing there, staring at it.

I waved the cup in front of her. "What in heck did you do to that coffee?"

She looked up at me, her lips white. "I was in such a hurry—I wanted to get rid of Bennington. Not in the strictest sense of the word, but . . ."

Dayna bustled up to us. "What on earth happened?" She cried, then stopped as she caught sight of the purple container in Kat's hand. "Oh, Lord! Don't tell me you grabbed the chicory by mistake?"

Kat nodded, her expression miserable. "I'm afraid so. You said the purple container, and I grabbed the dark one. I should have grabbed the light one, I guess."

Dayna sighed. "I'm so sorry, Kat. I should have been clearer. After all, you were doing me a favor, and now . . ."

Suddenly, I started to laugh. I just couldn't help it.

Kat stared at me, and I saw tears start to form in the corners of her eyes. "It's not funny, Syd. That man—I think he's got it in for us already, and now . . ."

"Oh, I'm sorry." I gasped for breath. "I didn't mean to laugh. It's just nerves I guess. But this just shows you why we don't run a coffee shop." I reached up, snatched the other container from the shelf, and headed back toward the table. Bennington had finished wiping off his shirt and had started to dig into the apple tart. He wiped some crumbs from his upper lip as I approached and laid the two canisters side by side on the table. "It was an honest mistake," I said. "Kat just pulled down the wrong canister."

Will leaned over, took a sniff. "Chicory. Oh, gee."

Bennington arched one shaggy brow. "A mistake. Of course. Seeing as Ms. McCall doesn't normally brew coffee here, I can understand it."

I stared at him in surprise. "You can?"

"Of course." He dabbed at his lips with his napkin. "Of course, I must also question just why your sister decided to turn café worker now."

"Because she was helping me out," Dayna said evenly. She placed fresh mugs of coffee in front of both men. "I trust this will be more to your liking?"

Bennington eyed the mug, then picked it up and took a tentative sip, then another. "Ah. Now *this* is coffee."

I crossed my arms over my chest and said in an even tone, "I have a question. You said quite plainly to my sister, 'Are you trying to kill me now?' Are you inferring that she might have killed someone else?"

Will paused, the mug of coffee halfway to his lips. "Syd!" he said, a warning note to his tone.

"It was merely an expression. I didn't mean anything by it, I assure you." Bennington's gaze raked me up and down. "Unless, of course, you or your sister have a guilty conscience about something?"

"Absolutely not. Not one thing," I answered with a curl of my lip. I could feel Will's gaze on me, and I studiously avoided looking his way.

"Well, that's good to hear." Bennington picked up his fork, broke off a large hunk of tart. He shoved the tart into his mouth, chewed, swallowed, and then picked up the mug of coffee. He took a sip and then started to cough.

"My Lord," I cried. "What now?"

He looked up, raised two fingers in the air. "I'm fine. It just went down the wrong pipe." He patted at the stain on the front of his shirt. "We're all good—well, all except my shirt. I'll have to send this to the cleaners. But other than that . . ." He turned an accusing stare at me. "Do you or your sister have any first-aid training?"

I turned back slowly. "First-aid training? We know the basics, I suppose. Why?"

"Would you know how to administer CPR, or . . . oh, an injection, if one were needed?"

"I know how to bandage a wound and maybe perform a Heimlich, and that's it," I said evenly.

"Hmm. And you, Miss McCall?" He fixed Kat with his hawkish stare. "How about your skills?"

Kat's lips thinned. "Pretty much the same as Syd's."

"Ah."

Further conversation was precluded as both Will and Bennington suddenly dipped into their jacket pockets for their cell phones at almost the same instant. Kat plucked at my sleeve, and the two of us started to move back toward the counter. Will and Bennington scraped back their chairs and started to head for the door, still on their phones. As Will passed me, I caught the tail end of his conversation.

"Put those toxicology reports on my desk. We'll want to go over them ASAP." He clicked off his phone, glanced up and saw me looking at him. "Sorry we have to rush off," he said, slipping his phone back into his pocket.

"Oh, think nothing of it," Dayna said from her position behind the counter.

Bennington appeared behind Will. "Yes, sorry we have to leave so soon. It's been swell. Don't bother with the change." He whipped out his wallet, slapped a twenty-dollar bill on the counter, and then turned and hurried out the front door.

I grabbed Will's sleeve. "Your partner is a real charmer."

Will's tone as he answered was gruff. "Don't push it, Syd."

I gripped his arm more tightly. "I heard you got a toxicology report in?"

He raised a brow. "Eavesdropping now?"

I returned his stare. "You weren't whispering."

"Yes," he said shortly. "And don't ask me for the results."

"But does that mean—you think Littleton might have been poisoned?"

Bennington stuck his head back in the front door. "Are you coming, *Detective Worthington?* Or do you have something else to do?"

I let go of Will's arm and made a shooing motion with my hand. "Go on, before he arrests me for fraternizing with the police. We can talk later."

Will opened his mouth to say something but then apparently thought better of it. He shrugged and followed Bennington outside. The two of them stood on the sidewalk outside the store, talking in low tones. Once, Bennington looked back into the shop, and our gazes locked for a brief instant. He raised a brow at me, then took Will's arm, and the two of them walked off.

"Well, that was a crappy ending to what started out as a reasonably good day," sighed Kat. "Nothing against Will, but since he and that horrid man seem to be joined at the hip, I hope they don't feel the need to interrogate us again anytime soon."

I silently agreed. Kat didn't show much emotion outwardly, but I could tell that Bennington's innuendo had really gotten to her. And despite my brave front, the offensive detective was getting to me too. Something—or someone—had put a bee in his bonnet about us, and it was becoming increasingly apparent to me that the only way to get Bennington off our backs was to figure out who'd killed Littleton. That certainly wouldn't be easy, especially since it was pretty evident I'd get precious little information out of Will. I needed another source—but who?

And then the shop doorbell jangled again, and Lady Luck stepped in.

Chapter Ten

The girl who stood on the threshold looked to be around my age, maybe a little younger. She had on a neat navy-blue skirt and jacket, and her makeup was artfully applied, not a curly blonde hair on her head out of place. She hurried toward us, a wide smile on her face, and looked straight at Kat. "How'd the event go?" she asked. "Did all the kitties get adopted?"

"They did," Kat responded. "Even Toby."

The girl clapped her hands. "Toby finally got a home! That's great. Who adopted him?"

"I did," I piped up. As the girl turned a curious stare my way, I added, "I'm Kat's sister."

The curious stare melted into a warm smile. "Oh, you're Sydney!" The girl thrust a beautifully manicured hand at me. "It's so nice to finally meet you. Kat always talks about you. We were all thrilled to hear that you were joining the shelter staff."

"Well, it's not permanent—at least not yet," I said as I shook her hand. "I take it you're one of the volunteers here?"

"Yes," Kat said, throwing me a meaningful glance. "This is Diane Ryan."

Diane Ryan. The name seemed vaguely familiar to me, but I couldn't quite place it.

"I told you about Diane," Kat went on. She gave my shoulder a little nudge. "She took Betty's job at the police station."

Ah. Light dawned. Diane Ryan was the one who'd told Kat about Petra's being involved with her gym instructor. Kat's words came back to me in a rush: *And just like Betty before her, she loves a good gossip session.*

Well, well. Talk about Lady Luck! I'd been wondering who I could cultivate as a source other than Will, and here she was, standing right in front of me. I turned to Diane and flashed her a smile. "Yes, my sister's mentioned you. You're the admin down at the station, right?"

Diane's smile got wider. "That's me." She leaned in toward me and added, "Your sister is a perfect dear. Everyone at the shelter loves her."

Dayna emerged from the back room and caught sight of Diane standing with us. "There you are," she said. "I was just gonna call you. I'm closing a little early tonight. Today was a busy day." She reached under the counter and pulled out two large boxes. "I hope the guys at the station like these. I'm trying out two new recipes: Butternut brownies and caramel cream puffs."

"They both sound delicious. Those guys would eat sawdust as long as you prepared it, Dayna. Everyone loves your baking." She started to open the tote on her shoulder, but Dayna gave a wave of her hand.

"On the house today, Diane. Tell 'em it's all part of being a test case."

"Really? Wow, thanks."

She shoved the tote back on her shoulder and started to reach for the boxes, but I stepped in front of her and grabbed one. "Why don't I help you with these? They're a little heavy, and I'd hate for you to drop one."

She flashed me a grateful smile. "Thanks, I'd appreciate that. I had to park two blocks away."

Kat glanced at her watch. "I've got to get back to the shelter." She smiled at the two of us. "You two should really get together. You've got a lot in common."

Diane and I each grabbed a box, and Dayna held the door open for us. Sure enough, Diane's maroon-colored sedan was parked not two but three blocks away, just across from the park. She balanced her box in one hand and started to fumble in her purse for her keys with the other. I set my box on her car roof and reached out to rescue the box of brownies before they ended up on the concrete.

"Thanks," Diane said. "I'm so clumsy sometimes."

"Not a problem." As she pressed the button on her key fob to unlock the doors, I added, "Are you in a hurry to get back? Dale's Soda Shop has a special on green tea smoothies, and I'd love to try one. Besides, I agree with Kat. I'd like to get to know you better. I don't know many people here anymore, other than Kat, my pal Leila, and the shelter volunteers."

"That's so sweet," Diane said. "Sure, I'd like to try one of those smoothies. After I delivered these, I was just going to go on home anyway and wash my hair. So if you don't mind going on ahead and ordering, I'll be back in about fifteen minutes?"

I smiled. "Perfect."

*   *   *

By the time Diane returned to the soda shop, I was seated at a table in the back of the small store with two delicious green concoctions sitting in front of me, prepared with grapes, spinach, avocado, honey, and, of course, green tea.

"Oh, it's heavenly," Diane said after taking a sip. "I've tried to make these at home, but somehow they just don't come out the same."

"That's so true, isn't it? Some things just taste better when someone else makes them." I set down my glass and leaned forward. "So, working at the police station. That's got to be exciting."

"It has its moments. It's a very demanding job, though."

"I can imagine. Especially with all the excitement lately, what with the murder and all."

Diane's head bobbed up and down. "Oh, yes. Murder isn't exactly a commonplace occurrence here. We're lucky to have homicide detectives with experience who transferred here, like our newest recruit."

"Will Worthington. I went to high school with him. Of course Kat was two years ahead of us, but she knew him quite well too."

"He mentioned he grew up here," Diane nodded. She leaned forward and said in a conspiratorial whisper, "Just between you and me—I don't think he's too crazy about working with Bennington. Then again, neither is anyone else."

Gee, I wonder why. Aloud, I said, "I'd agree with that assessment. He's rather . . . brash."

She barked out a laugh and twirled a stray curl around one finger. "That's putting it mildly." She cocked her head. "I guess you've had your own up-close-and-personal with him, since you discovered Littleton's body. I'm sure that must have been very upsetting."

"Yeah, not an experience I'd care to repeat. He's got a swell bedside manner."

We sipped our smoothies in silence for a few minutes, and then I said casually, "I was wondering if Littleton might have died of natural causes, you know, like a heart attack."

Diane made a loud sucking noise with her straw. "Why'd you think that?"

"Because of the blue tinge on his skin. It's a condition called cyanosis. It happens when the blood doesn't get enough oxygen, like if the victim had a heart attack or a stroke."

"Umm. I never heard of that, but I can tell you what else would produce the same symptoms. Poison!" She pushed her empty glass over to one side and leaned both elbows on the counter, her eyes sparkling. "I probably shouldn't say anything, but . . . I overheard the detectives talking. Apparently Littleton had enough of some sort of toxic chemical in his system to choke a horse."

I widened my eyes. "No!"

"Oh, yes. They found some sort of small mark on the back of his neck, like someone might have given him an injection." She shuddered. "Someone really had it in for him."

"Sounds that way." An injection of poison? Hmm, that explained Bennington's interest in whether Kat or I had first-aid training—although how much training did you need to plunge a needle into someone? I tried to make my tone casual as I said, "I'd sure like to see that suspect list. I bet it's pretty long."

"Long enough." She reached for her glass and took another sip of her smoothie.

I tapped a nail against my glass. "I understand the widow wasn't all that grief-stricken."

Diane frowned into her glass. "From what I heard, she took the news well. Then again, she and her husband hadn't been all that close lately." She leaned forward and said in a low tone, "Littleton had a roving eye, if you catch my drift."

"I heard," I said carefully. "I also heard Mrs. Littleton had one as well."

"I guess you can't really blame her if that's true, can you? You know that old saying: what's good for the goose is good for the gander." She scooted to the edge of her seat and said, "I heard his most recent affair was with one of the single shopkeepers in this complex." She tapped one nail after every word for emphasis.

Poor Devon, I thought. I should have known. Secrets have a way of coming out. I only hoped that when the police interviewed her, she'd own up to it. Aloud, I said, "I heard a rumor about that. Truthfully, I would never have thought that. He certainly didn't seem the type."

Diane giggled. "No, he certainly didn't. He was more like a crotchety old bear. Guess some women find that appealing. Grace sure did."

I frowned. "Grace?"

"Yeah." Diane sipped the last of her smoothie. "Grace Topping, the mousy little thing who owns the hat store. She's the woman Littleton had the affair with."

Chapter Eleven

"Grace Topping? And Littleton? Are you sure?" I'd finished my conversation with Diane, and after telling her that I'd see her soon at the shelter, I had made tracks for Kat's apartment. Now we were sitting at the table in her cozy kitchen, sipping tea and looking out the window at her small garden. I set my cup down and laced my hands behind my neck. "That's what your pal Diane Ryan seems to think. How accurate is her gossip, anyway?"

Kat leaned back in her chair and closed her eyes. After a few seconds, they fluttered open, and she looked at me. "Pretty accurate," she admitted. "Everything that she's ever told me has been spot on. It is kind of hard to imagine those two together, though. I wonder if the affair was still going on when he died?"

"Diane didn't know. She didn't think so. And she didn't . . ." I stopped. I'd started to say, "She didn't seem to know about Devon's affair," but I'd caught myself. After all, I had promised Devon I wouldn't say a word to anyone. And anyone included my sister. "She didn't know names, but she was fairly certain he'd had a number of affairs." A mental picture of Littleton flashed through my mind, and I couldn't help it. I giggled. "Sorry. It's just really, really hard to imagine."

Kat was also finding it hard to stifle her grin. "I know, but looks aren't everything. Maybe he treated his women really well." She paused. "I can't picture Grace in the role of murderer, though. She's got such a sweet face."

"True," I admitted. "Still, Leila did say she saw them in the mall last week, arguing . . . Maybe I should have a little talk with Grace. If nothing else, maybe she has an idea who might have wanted to kill Littleton."

"Well, if you do, try to be tactful," Kat said. "Grace is so sensitive—I can just imagine how she'd react to that Bennington plying her with questions. I hope, if the police do interrogate her, that Will's the one to do it."

"Hmm," I said.

Kat looked up. "What's that 'hmm' mean? You don't think Will would be more tactful?"

"Hard to say. He would if he were alone. He seems to turn into a different person when he's around Bennington— like one of those hard-boiled homicide detectives from a 1940s noir movie."

"True. Still, maybe we should cut him some slack. Will's new to the force, and Bennington is his superior. He's probably just trying to impress."

"Maybe." I drummed my fingers on the edge of my chair. "According to Diane, there was a good deal of some sort of toxic substance in Littleton's system. Sounds to me as if whoever killed Littleton must have planned well—it wasn't a spur-of-the-moment murder." I jumped up from my chair. "Do you still have that old whiteboard?"

"In the hall closet. Why?"

"I'll show you." I vanished down the short hallway, returning a few minutes later with a medium-sized whiteboard. I propped it up on Kat's kitchen counter. "Got markers?"

Kat opened a drawer in the kitchen island, whipped out a black marker, and handed it to me. "What are you going to do?"

I drew a large box in the center of the board. "What every good homicide detective does when they start a case. I'm making a murder board."

"A what?"

"Actually, it's more commonly known as a crime board. Police use them to track the status of their investigations. Most these days are magnetic, but this will do." I printed Trowbridge Littleton's name in the large square and then drew six other boxes: two to the right, three to the left, and one directly above Littleton's box. "In the top box here, we'll put his wife." I printed Petra's name. Next to the box, I printed: "Possible motive: Wanted to control entire fortune; beneficiary of large insurance policy? Able to have affairs unencumbered." In the top box to the right of Littleton's, I wrote: "Trey, Stepson. Was heard arguing with Littleton. Didn't like the way he treated his mom."

In the other box on the right, I put Colin Murphy's name, and next to that: "Disagreements over running of gallery." In the other three boxes, I put: "Shopkeepers," "Artists," and "Scorned Mistresses." Then I stepped back to view my handiwork.

"Well?" I asked my sister. "What do you think?"

Kat studied the board for a few minutes, then walked over, picked up the marker, and drew another box in between the mistresses and shopkeepers. Inside it, she printed her name and next to it wrote: "afraid Littleton would find a way to close shelter." She set the marker down and eyed me. "If we're being perfectly honest about this, my name belongs on the suspect list. Even though we both know I didn't kill him."

"True," I agreed. What I didn't add, as I studied the board, was that out of everyone listed, right now it appeared Kat had the best motive. I tapped my nail against the board. "I need to find out more about these suspects."

Kat's eyebrow rose. "So much for you not investigating, huh?"

I looked at her. "Come on, Kat. As long as Bennington's on your tail, do you really think I'll just sit back and do nothing?"

She sighed. "No, I suppose not."

"Good." I chewed at my lower lip. "Where to start. Maybe with Colin Murphy?"

Kat snorted. "What makes you think he'd tell you anything? You're not a homicide detective or even a PI."

Toby rolled over on his side, muttering.

"Not too fond of that, huh? Well, maybe I can find something in the fridge to tide you over, okay? Let's take a look."

Toby sprang to his feet, pranced over to me, rubbed against my ankles, and purred.

Leila's door was still shut—she'd been out late on an assignment—so we padded quickly downstairs. I put on a kettle for a quick cup of tea and then checked the refrigerator. No chicken breast left, but there was a small amount of smoked turkey we'd had for lunch on Wednesday, along with a few slices of American cheese. I crumbled a slice of turkey and some cheese into a small plastic bowl and then rummaged around in the cupboard and found a can of tuna. I spooned some of that out on top of the cold cuts and set it down on the floor. Toby padded over to it, sniffed, then squatted and started to chow down.

"You're not too fussy—that's a good thing," I chuckled as I poured the hot water into my cup. "Kat did say you were like a garbage pail when it came to food."

Toby glanced at me over his shoulder, made a small sound deep in his throat, and went back to slurping.

I plopped my peppermint tea bag into my mug, walked into the living room, and settled myself on the chintz-covered window seat. I opened the shutters and peered outside. There wasn't a hint of a breeze, and even at this early hour, I could tell the day was going to be a scorcher. I sipped my tea slowly, making a mental to-do list in my head. First, obviously, was getting over to the Pet Palace to pick up a few things for Toby. If that didn't take too long, I'd hoped to make a quick stop at Hats Off. I knew Grace Topping generally opened her shop on Sundays at eleven thirty, which would be perfect.

A soft *thunk* against the front porch alerted me that the Sunday paper had arrived. I opened the door and scooped it up. Tucking it under my arm, I headed back into the kitchen, where Toby was just finishing up his breakfast. He looked up as I entered and put one paw on the now empty bowl. "Ar-owl?"

I laid the paper and my mug down. "Seconds? Well, okay, just this once." I got another slice of turkey and more cheese out of the fridge and crumbled them into his bowl. He attacked it happily, and I turned my attention to the paper.

Leila had written a lively account of the cat adoption that was featured prominently on page six along with some photos. There was one of Jinx, her nose pressed up against her cage, looking into the eyes of a little girl; another of Norton and Ralphie playing; a nice shot of the beautiful calico Edith Maxwell had adopted; even one of Toby, lying against the wall, paws crossed, his ears flicked forward. I made a mental note to ask Leila for a print of that one. The caption read, "Cat Café: A Success in Deer Park." I read the article, which praised the shelter and was definitely slanted in favor of our partnership. I was smiling when I finished the article; my friend had outdone herself.

Leila stumbled into the kitchen, her pink, fuzzy bathrobe tightly drawn around her slender body. "Good

pieces that found their way to the floor. After dinner, I took Toby upstairs and led him into my bedroom. I got an extra blanket out of the closet and laid it down on the floor next to my bed.

"I'll get you a regular cat bed tomorrow," I told him. "But this should do nicely in the meantime."

Toby went over and sniffed at the blanket; then, with one graceful leap, he hopped up on my bed, turned around twice, and made himself comfortable at the foot of the bed.

I laughed. "Or you could sleep on the bed. But I'm gonna have to get a hand vacuum. Leila said that picking up your gold hairs would be my job."

Toby stretched himself out full length, an action that enabled him to take up three quarters more space. "Merow."

"Okay, I know you must be tired after walking all the way here from the shelter," I said. "Even though I know you've done it before. You take a little cat nap, now."

Toby curled himself into a ball and closed his eyes. I went back to the kitchen and returned in a few minutes with the whiteboard. I propped it up against the far wall and stood back to survey it.

"Merow?"

I glanced down. Toby had left the comfort of my bed and now wound himself around my ankles, his gaze fastened on the whiteboard.

"This isn't a toy," I told him. "This is my suspect list."

Toby raised his head slightly. "Er-ow?"

141

"A suspect list. People who had a reason to do in Little-ton." *Oh my God*, I thought. *Am I really talking to this cat like he's a person?*

Toby blinked at me twice, then jumped back on the bed and closed his eyes. A few seconds later, I heard soft snoring.

"Bedtime," I said. "Not a bad idea, actually. Get a good night's sleep, and my perspective will be better in the morn-ing. Tomorrow, I'm going to start tracking down some of these leads."

I undressed quickly and slid into my favorite sleepwear—a thin pair of baby doll pj's peppered with butterflies. Pres-ton had always hated them.

While I'd been changing, Toby had arranged himself on the right side of the bed, stretched full length, so I turned down the covers on the left side, which was the one I usu-ally slept on anyway. Before I turned in, I decided to check my e-mail. I booted up my laptop and scrolled through my inbox, deleting the junk. Toward the end, I saw an e-mail from Pres982gmail.com. I clicked on it. Short and to the point.

Sydney:

Do you want that mission-style coffee table you bought in Salem? Need to know. I imagine it would go more with your decor than my new one. If you don't want it, Cindi plans on donating it to Goodwill, so let me know. If I don't hear from you within 48 hours, I'll assume you don't want it.

Hope all is well.
Preston

I sighed. I remembered when we'd bought that coffee table. I'd been so full of hope for our future. Apparently Cindi was redecorating the apartment I'd so carefully arranged. Oh well.

I hit the delete button, then powered down my laptop and set it on the nightstand.

I shut off the light, slid under the covers. Toby shifted and snuggled against me. I smiled in the dark, confident I'd made the right decision.

That part of my life was definitely over. I had other things I wanted to accomplish now—and I had to admit, right now solving Littleton's murder before Kat officially became suspect number one topped that list.

Chapter Twelve

I awoke the next morning to find Toby sprawled across my chest, purring loudly. "Ow-owrr," he said, lightly touching my cheek with one paw.

I turned my head slightly so that I could see the clock. Six AM. "Really? On a Sunday?" I said, reaching up to stroke his soft fur. On Sundays, the shelter was open by appointment only, and I knew there were none scheduled for today. I swung my feet out of bed, grabbed my robe, and headed for the bathroom, Toby following close behind. He stretched out under the sink and waited patiently while I showered and dressed in jeans and a long-sleeved T-shirt. As I ran a brush through my tousle of curls, I said to him, "The Pet Palace doesn't open till eleven, but I bet Hugo's Market has some cat food. I'll take a quick run up there and get you something, okay?"

He lay down, rested his head on his paws, and looked at me with soulful eyes. "Ow-owl."

"Too hungry to wait? Okay, well . . . more oatmeal?"

"You know that, and I know that. But Colin Murphy doesn't have to know that. I'll think of some way to interrogate him." I tapped at my gut. "I just know that the sooner either the real killer or a very viable suspect is found, the sooner we can get Bennington off our backs." I rubbed my hands together. "Looks like I have a full schedule ahead of me." I gestured toward the whiteboard. "Mind if I borrow this?"

Kat made a sweeping gesture with her arm. "Be my guest. Say, did you ever give Will that note you found?"

I pulled a face. "Yes. He apparently doesn't think too much of my clue, because he hasn't looked into it yet."

"Maybe you should add that name to your list," Kat suggested. "Maybe this Kahn Lee, whoever he is, plays a part in Littleton's murder."

"Good idea." I snatched up the marker, drew another box next to Petra, and wrote "Kahn Lee" inside it. "I'm going to have to try to find a way to talk to Will alone . . ." I stopped, my head cocked. "Did you hear that?" I asked Kat.

Kat glanced up. "Hear what?"

"That scratching sound." I stood still, listening. Yep, there it was again.

Scritch, scritch. It sounded like nails on a chalkboard. I walked over to the door that led out to Kat's garden. The sound was louder here. I flung open the door.

"Merow."

I took a step backward and rubbed at my eyes. "Toby?"

Sure enough, the large gold-and-white cat squatted on the small step. As I said his name, he rose, stretched, and then, with his tail held high, walked right into the kitchen and planted himself in front of me.

"Merow."

Kat tried to suppress a smile but failed miserably. "Well, look who followed you," she grinned. "I guess he didn't want to wait either."

"Well, I was planning to go to the Pet Palace on my lunch break tomorrow and pick up food and cat supplies." I leaned over, my hands on my knees, and smiled at Toby. "I wasn't expecting to pick you up until Monday night, boy. What happened? You didn't want to spend any more time in that cage at the shelter, huh?"

Toby cocked his head and looked at me. "Merow," he said again. Then he closed his eyes in a slow blink.

I glanced at the clock on the wall. "I think the Pet Palace is closed now," I said. "I don't have any supplies yet. Maybe I should take him back to the shelter till Monday."

"He'll only follow you again," Kat said. "I have some canned food I can spare till you get to the store, but it would also be okay to give him a taste of your dinner—not too much," she cautioned. "He also likes oatmeal."

"In other words, he's a feline garbage pail."

"That pretty much sums it up," Kat said cheerfully.

*   *   *

I took Toby home and fed him the oatmeal concoction. Just as Kat predicted, he gobbled it down and half a bowl of water too. I made myself a salad with some leftover cooked chicken I found in the fridge, and he scarfed down some morning," she mumbled. Her gaze fell on the table. "Oh good, the paper came," she said. She moved toward it, and her eyes rested on Toby curled up underneath the far chair. "Ah—I see we have a new roomie?"

"Yep. You said it was okay," I responded, almost defensively.

"Of course it's okay." Leila leaned down and gave Toby a scritch behind one ear. He opened one eye and let out a soft meow. "Like I said, he's probably better behaved than most of the males I know." She pulled out a chair and eased herself into it. Her nail tapped at the paper. "You saw the article? And you liked it?"

"It was perfect."

Leila riffled some of the pages. "Did you see this?" She held up the "Crime Blotter" section and pointed to the headline: "Investigation into Local Businessman's Death Continues."

I made a face at the photo beneath the caption. "Couldn't they have found a better photo of Littleton?"

Leila laughed. "Is there a better photo? I doubt it."

I walked over to look over her shoulder and then pointed to another photo directly beneath. Littleton, looking decidedly uncomfortable in a tux, stood next to a stunning brunette in a tight-fitting sheath. The brunette was smiling, revealing perfect teeth I was willing to bet were caps. They both held glasses of champagne. "This must be the missus. Wow! I can see why Littleton was attracted to her. She's gorgeous!"

Leila nodded. "That's our Petra. Doesn't she look like the perfect first runner-up for Miss North Carolina?"

"Oh, definitely. I'm surprised she didn't win. She could easily be a Miss America." I tapped at the photo. "Who's the hunk standing behind her?"

Leila rubbed at her eyes, then bent for a closer look at the photo. "Ah, that's Kevin Devine the Third, the son of Petra Devine Littleton and stepson of Trowbridge Littleton. I understand he likes to be called by his nickname, Trey."

"Not bad looking. He doesn't look too fond of Littleton, though, does he?" Trey Devine's head was turned slightly, facing Littleton, and the expression on his face seemed strained.

She nodded. "Rumor is they've had their share of issues. Whether they're big enough to kill over is anyone's guess."

I scanned the article quickly. "It says here that the police are still investigating various angles of the case. Oh! They've released the body to the family. A viewing will be held at St. John's tomorrow night, with a memorial service and interment on Tuesday morning. Now isn't that interesting."

Leila arched a brow. "You're thinking of going?"

I pushed the paper off to one side. "The thought did cross my mind. It would be a golden opportunity. I mean, think of it. All the suspects will most likely be there."

"What, to make sure he's dead?"

I made a face at her. "I wonder if Will is going," I murmured.

"Probably. And his charming partner too. I don't think you should go, Syd. You probably wouldn't learn anything, and you might piss Bennington off."

"That alone is reason to go," I said.

"I'm serious. No one's going to admit to anything untoward at a funeral viewing, for goodness' sake."

"Maybe not, but I still think it's a great opportunity. I'll think about it." I reached for my purse and slung it over my shoulder. "Right now I've got more important things to do—like getting Toby settled in."

"Priorities," Leila said with a grin as she headed for the coffeepot on the stove. "That's what life is all about."

*　*　*

The Pet Palace was located on the opposite end of town, a large, white modern building with large plate glass windows in which pet supplies of every size and shape were prominently displayed. The parking lot, macadam and newly painted, was the size of a city block and three-quarters full. Apparently, Pet Palace was the new "in" spot for people and pets on a lazy Sunday morning. The store was packed. People meandered up and down the aisles, some with large dogs on leashes, others with small ones tucked into shopping carts. I didn't see anyone with a cat, but one woman had a small carrying case tucked into her cart—as I passed, I saw two beady brown eyes staring out from behind the mesh.

"It's a ferret," she told me. "They make really nice pets."

"I'm sure they do," I murmured. "I'm actually looking for the cat section, though."

"Last aisle on the left."

I thanked the woman, said good-bye to the ferret, and pushed my cart in that direction. Sure enough, in the last aisle on the left, I found a wide selection of cat supplies. I grabbed a box of dry kibble, then mulled over several choices of cat beds before choosing a large sherpa one with a soft red-and-green plaid cushion. Maggie had said Toby had some toys she'd be glad to drop off, but I wanted him to have some special ones, so several more minutes went by as I picked through the immense rack of cat toys. I finally decided on some soft round balls and a large toy filled with catnip in the shape of a banana. Wet food was next on the list—I headed for that rack and once again stood staring. Who knew there were so many choices?

"Got a new kitty?"

I jumped at the voice almost at my elbow and whirled around to find a dark-haired, pleasant-faced woman smiling at me—the very same woman I'd planned on visiting today. I smiled back and responded, "Hello, Grace. As a matter of fact, yes. One of the cats from the event we held yesterday."

"Good for you," Grace Topping said. She shifted the plastic shopping bag she held into her other hand. "I meant to stop by, but the day just got away from me, and by the time I was able to get away, it was too late."

"Were you thinking of adopting another cat?" Kat had told me Grace had a lovely tortoiseshell cat named Ol' Moody that she absolutely adored.

Grace laughed. "Are you kidding? Ol' Moody would have a snit for sure. It's tough to bring a new cat into a home where one has reigned supreme for nine years. But I confess I love to look at them, and I thought your concept was a fun one—eat some treats and play with some cats."

I hesitated, wondering how I might broach the subject of Littleton. Turns out I didn't have to worry. "I understand you and your sister are the ones who found Bridge," she said. "That must have been . . . a shock."

"Oh, definitely. Not something I'd care to repeat," I replied. The fact she'd called him by the short version of his name wasn't lost on me. I picked up a few cans of Fancy Feast and tossed them into my cart. "It's hard to believe he's gone."

"Yes, it is. I know that everyone in town perceived him as a tyrant, and make no mistake about it—he could be. But he had a softer side, too." Her lips twisted into a wry expression. "He just didn't show it to many people."

Ah, now here was my opening. "You sound as if you've seen that side of him."

"Yes, I have." She let out a breath. "He was very supportive when I first opened my shop and was even one of my best customers. I guess you could say we struck up a friendship of sorts. Recently, though, we, ah, sort of drifted apart." She raised a hand, started to play with the buttons on her sweater. "The last time I saw him, we had a disagreement over his raising everyone's rent."

"Was that at the food court in the mall?"

Grace's brow wrinkled. "Direct, aren't you? I haven't been to the mall in months. Home Shopping takes care of most of my needs. No, it was at my store when he dropped off the letter. I'll always regret my last words to him were harsh ones."

"It sounds to me like the two of you were close. Really close."

"You don't have to fish for information, Sydney," Grace said with a low chuckle. "You can come out and ask. You've heard the rumors about Bridge and I being more than friends."

I plunked some Nine Lives into my cart. Since she'd invited me to be blunt, I had no problem with that. "I've heard that the two of you had an affair."

To my surprise, Grace threw back her head and laughed. "That's flattering, especially to a spinster like myself," she said at last.

I thought that in her stylish peplum top and crop pants, her dark hair cut in a becoming pageboy, she looked like anything but a spinster. "So you didn't have an affair with him?"

She shook her head so that her curls bobbed up and down. "Lord, no. Bridge liked his women a lot younger than me. No, we were just friends. I think he looked on me as the sister he never had."

"Right," I murmured. "He was an only child."

"Yes. Bridge would confide things in me, about his family, about his marriage. He trusted me to keep everything confidential and never repeat it, and I never will. Except now . . . I'm wondering if maybe I shouldn't break my silence on some things. It might matter."

I moved closer to her. "Do you know something that might help the police find out who killed him? If so, you definitely should speak up."

"Well—mind you, I don't know anything for certain. But from what Bridge told me, it seems to me there were a few people who might have had a reason to kill him."

Some more people pushed down the aisle and stopped in front of the pet food display. I took Grace's arm and steered her and my cart over into a corner. "Like who?"

She put a finger against her chin and regarded me curiously. "You certainly are interested in all this, aren't you? Don't tell me you're helping the police investigate?"

"Not exactly," I responded, "but the lead detective seems to like Kat as suspect number one for some reason, so I guess you could say I'm trying to help steer them in another direction."

"Of course." Grace nodded. "I can understand your concern. Who could possibly think Kat would murder anyone?" She gave her head a quick shake and then said, "Okay then. I'd have to say Bridge's partner, Colin Murphy, for one. Lately he and Bridge weren't seeing eye to eye on the management of the gallery. They had a couple of pretty good arguments, one just a few weeks ago. Bridge called me afterward, upset."

"What was the argument about?"

Grace clucked her tongue. "Bridge didn't go into specifics. He just told me that Colin was getting out of control, and his recklessness might endanger the future of the gallery."

"Reckless? In what way?"

Grace shrugged. "I have no idea. I do know that in recent weeks, he'd become terribly disenchanted with Colin. At one point, he said he'd only agreed to the partnership because an old friend had highly recommended him." Grace's lips curved into a lopsided smile. "Bridge loved that gallery. Art was his passion. He didn't need the revenue from it, but he enjoyed seeking out new talent and showcasing it. He'd rather display pieces crafted from local artists that showed promise than established ones that they could get a large sum for. I believe that was one area he and Colin butted heads over." Her hand fluttered in the air. "It hardly seems like a motive for murder, though, does it?"

"It's hard to tell what sends some people over the edge," I replied carefully. "What about his wife?"

"Petra?" Grace wrinkled her nose. "Theirs was one of those love-hate relationships. In spite of his wandering eye, Bridge loved Petra, and in her own way, I think she loved him too."

Or his money, I thought. Aloud, I asked, "What about Petra's love life? I heard she was getting it on with her gym coach."

"Oh, that!" Grace waved her hand dismissively.

"She wasn't having an affair with her gym coach?"

"I have no idea. Natalie said that she saw them in a clinch at the gym, but . . ." Her shoulders lifted in a shrug. "Petra's come into my shop a few times, and she doesn't impress me as being stupid. If she were going to fool around, she'd be damn sure no one saw her." Grace let out a breath.

"Frankly, it wouldn't surprise me if Natalie made the whole thing up."

"Why would she do that?"

"Possibly to get back at Bridge for arguing with Colin. She and Colin are quite close, you know."

"They are?"

"Oh, yes. She knew him in Boston, I think. If I'm not mistaken, Bridge took Colin on per Natalie's recommendation."

Now that was interesting. Devon had said Bridge took on a partner on the recommendation of an old friend. Natalie was the friend? She hadn't sounded like one the other day. It had sounded more like she hated Bridge. Had something happened to taint the friendship? I made a mental note to investigate that angle. Aloud, I said, "Anyone else you can think of?"

Her hand reached up and she fiddled with one of the buttons on her sweater. "There's the stepson—Trey. They hated each other. Bridge thought he was a slothful sponge who couldn't hold down a job. Trey thought Bridge was a hateful martinet who treated his mother badly."

"It didn't sound as if he treated Petra badly. He turned a blind eye to her spending and, from what I've heard, her extracurricular activities as well. As a motive for murder, it's pretty thin."

"There were other . . . circumstances." Grace hesitated and then said, "Trey got in a bit of trouble a while back and had to borrow money from Bridge to get out of it. Bridge was insistent Trey pay back the sum—that's why he's working at the gallery."

"How much money, do you know?"

"Bridge didn't volunteer the information, and I didn't ask." Her lips twisted into a wry grin. "And then there's Devon."

I swallowed. "Devon?"

"Oh, yes. She was having an affair with Bridge, and they were pretty hot and heavy, let me tell you—until Bridge broke it off. In spite of what she says, Devon was devastated. And honey, believe me—there's nothing worse than a woman scorned."

* * *

I said good-bye to Grace and wheeled my purchases over to the checkout line. Fortunately, there was only one other person in front of me. I trundled everything out to my car, and as I drove back home, I sorted out everything I'd learned from Grace.

She'd said she and Littleton were close, that she was the sister he'd never had. I believed her when she maintained they hadn't had an affair. She'd also denied arguing with him in the food court. Was she telling the truth? I rather thought she was on that point, too. That brought me to Devon. Apparently, she hadn't been as forthcoming with me as I'd originally thought. Was Devon sincere about wanting to get back together with her ex? Or was that the defense mechanism of a woman who'd been dumped by her lover? And would said dumping drive Devon to murder? She'd seemed awfully comfortable brandishing that gun; then again, Littleton hadn't died of a gunshot wound.

I thought about Petra Littleton and her son, Trey. If Trey owed Littleton a substantial sum, that could be a possible motive. Petra's wanting to protect her son from her husband's wrath could also be deemed a good motive. Mother lions killed to protect their cubs, right? Suddenly, my suspect list was looking up.

I still wasn't too sure about what Colin Murphy's motive might be. Maybe it depended on the sort of "improvements" he'd wanted to make to the gallery. Was Littleton's blocking of them enough to kill over? I resolved to try to grill Natalie about it. If she and Colin were as close as Grace had hinted, she might know.

*   *   *

Toby greeted me at the door and sniffed at the bags in my arms. I put away the food I'd purchased and then spooned out some Fancy Feast tuna. Toby quickly gobbled it up, then turned his green gaze hopefully at me. I shook my finger at him. "Uh-uh. Sorry, pal. I don't want to over-feed you." I bent down and ran my hand along his slender frame. "You don't want to get fat. Best to wait till dinner."

Toby let out a soft bleat, then walked over to the cat bed, which I'd set down in one corner of the kitchen. He sniffed at it, then hopped inside, turned around twice, and lay down. I went over and laid the balls and catnip banana next to him. Toby immediately wrapped his paws around the toy and rolled over on his back. He chewed contentedly on the banana, his eyes round, his back feet moving rapidly back and forth. I watched him with amusement and then glanced up as Leila came into the kitchen. She was dressed impeccably in teal-colored slacks and a matching sweater set that complemented her red hair. She surveyed Toby in his cat bed with a smile on her face. "Your buddy seems happy," she remarked. She eased one hip against the doorjamb. "You remember my friend Krystle?"

"The one with the purple punk-rock hairdo and the tattoos? How could one forget her?" I chuckled.

"Yeah, well, she works at the lab, and guess what she happened to see?"

"Don't tell me—Littleton's toxicology report?"

"Yep. According to her, he was loaded up with strychnine. To quote her exactly, 'It was enough to sink a battleship.'"

"Strychnine, huh?" I struggled to remember what I'd heard about poisons, and that one in particular. Strychnine is a colorless alkaloid commonly used as a pesticide. When inhaled, swallowed, or absorbed through the eyes or the mouth, it results in muscular convulsions and death through asphyxia—which would definitely account for Littleton's blue cast to the skin, bulging eyes, and lolling tongue. It is usually introduced into the body orally, by inhalation, or by injection. Judging from Bennington's sly inquiry into my and Kat's first-aid prowess, I had an idea how the poison had been administered to Littleton.

"Strychnine is a big component of rat poison," Leila said. "You or Kat haven't bought any lately, have you?" she added jokingly.

"Heck no," I replied. "We surely don't need any at the shelter. We've got at least three dozen personal exterminators on hand right now."

"True that," Leila chuckled. "And what have you decided about the wake?"

"I'm going to go," I said slowly. "I feel I can't pass up that opportunity."

"Okay then." My friend let out a long sigh. "Then I shall accompany you. I have a new black suit I'm dying to wear—ouch, that was a bad pun."

"Yes, it was," I chuckled. "Maybe after the viewing, I'll treat you to a drink at DuBarry's."

"It's a date," Leila said. "Oh, and by the way, Kat called while you were out. They ran out of disinfectant at the shelter, and she wanted to know if you could stop by her apartment. She said that she bought a big jug at Costco last week, and it's under the kitchen cabinet."

I reached for my purse. "On my way. Want to go out for Chinese later?"

"I'd love to, but I can't. I'm meeting a few of the other reporters at the new pub in Clark. Two new reporters are starting, and we're having a sort of 'welcome to the madhouse' party." She walked over and rested her head on my shoulder. "I'd much prefer eating egg foo yong with you, but if I back out, heck, I'll never hear the end of it—and I might blow any chance I've got of getting promoted to the crime beat some-day." She gave her head a brisk shake. "Office politics. Blah!"

I grinned at her. I knew how she despised get-togethers like that. I used to hate them too, back in New York. Something else I didn't miss. "Have fun," I told her. "Have a glass of Chardonnay for me."

She slung her purse over her shoulder and cut me an eye roll. "Girlfriend, I might have two. Or maybe a whole bottle."

*   *   *

I mulled over what I'd learned on the short drive to my sister's apartment. Poison was generally considered a woman's weapon of choice, and there were surely plenty of female suspects. Not that a man couldn't use it either, of course. I sincerely hoped that I might learn something useful at Littleton's wake so attending wouldn't be a total loss.

It was a short drive to the tidy colonial where Kat lived. The people who owned the house had retired and now lived in Florida. They'd had the two-family renovated so that the bottom floor was actually two separate three-room apartments, with a larger six-room apartment on the top floor. Kat rented the one on the left side that opened out onto a small garden. I parked my convertible in the driveway, then whipped out the spare key she'd given me and let myself in. I went directly to the kitchen and the cabinet she'd mentioned. Sure enough, there was a large bottle of disinfectant right in front. As I picked it up, I noticed another bottle directly behind it. I pulled it out for a closer look. It was black and white, with a large red circle on the front label that depicted a skull and crossbones. The label read in big gold letters:

Gopher Revenge

With a sinking heart, I glanced at the contents. Sure enough, it was loaded with strychnine.

And it was about three-quarters empty.

Chapter Thirteen

I scurried through the back door of the shelter about fifteen minutes later. Kat was in the room designated for new puppies, and she was on her hands and knees, scrubbing out a large cage. She glanced up as I poked my head in the doorway, and her eyes rested on the bottle of disinfectant in my hand. "Thank goodness," she said. "Maxwell and Byron were playing, and they had a little . . . accident, shall we say. No, scratch that. They had a *big* accident."

I stepped forward and handed her the bottle. She took it from me, then frowned. "Is something wrong, Syd? You look funny."

I laughed. "Do I? I guess I'm just not used to seeing the shelter director on her hands and knees, cleaning out a puppy cage."

"Everyone pitches in to help with the animals—you know that." She set the disinfectant on the floor and sat back on her haunches, cocking an eyebrow at me. "Something's up. Spill it."

"Well . . ." I glanced around to assure myself no one else was around and then said, "The bottle of disinfectant was just where you said it would be in the bottom cupboard." I bit down hard on my lower lip and then added, "Guess what else was in there?"

Kat let out a low chuckle. "Well, since that's where I put most of the cleaning supplies, I'm going to say . . . cleaning stuff?"

"Maybe. I didn't notice after I found that bottle of Gopher Revenge."

"Oh." Kat's cheeks flushed a bright scarlet. "I know I always said I hated to poison animals, but I'm not sure I can consider that gopher a friendly animal anymore."

"Gopher?"

"Yep. There's a big fat one that's been terrorizing my neighborhood. He's eating up all the produce in my small garden, and last week, Mrs. Dinwiddie said he ransacked her garden too. I put that poison out as sort of a . . . a community service." She offered me a thin smile. "It seems to be working. None of us have been bothered all week with the varmint. He left my carrots alone—finally."

"So you used that poison on the gopher," I said slowly. "Did anyone know you bought it?"

She frowned. "I don't know. There were a couple people on line at the hardware store—and, of course, Minnie Franz rang my purchase up. But I told her I was going to use it on the gopher. What's wrong, Syd? Why all these questions?"

I leaned one hip against the sink. "Leila's friend Krystle works at the lab, and she saw Littleton's toxicology report. He died from strychnine poisoning."

"So? OH!" Kat's hand went to her throat. "Gopher Revenge is loaded with that, but you can't seriously think—"

"Of course I don't," I said quickly. "And neither would anyone else who knows you. But think how that might look to our friend Bennington. And when you add in the letter and the rent increase . . ."

"*Possible* rent increase," Kat corrected. "But I see what you mean. If he should find out I was in possession of the very poison that killed Littleton, it'll certainly add fuel to the fire."

I started to drum my fingers against the edge of the sink. "We need to find out what put the bee in his bonnet about us. It started with those sly comments about us removing something from the crime scene. I'd sure like to know what it is he thinks we might have taken."

"Me too. But how can we find out? We can't ask him, surely."

"No," I sighed, "we sure can't. I tried asking Will, but he said that he didn't know. He *thought* it might have been because of something the widow said."

"Petra? What on earth could she have possibly said? She doesn't even know us." Kat's eyes flashed, and her back bristled, just like a cat getting ready to pounce.

"I'm sure she didn't accuse us directly," I said. "But maybe she gave them a list of Littleton's office contents, and something from that list was missing. And since we were the last ones in there . . ."

I turned the faucet back on again and started loading the dishes into the sink. "I guess the only recourse left is to ask Petra Littleton point-blank. Maybe I'll get a chance tomorrow night."

"Tomorrow night?"

"At Littleton's wake."

"Syd! Tell me you're not serious about asking her something like that at her husband's wake, for God's sake!"

Kat ran a hand through her blonde curls. "Do I have to go to that viewing too, just to make sure you don't do anything that will embarrass us?"

"Don't fret, sister. I'll be well chaperoned. Leila is going with me."

"Great." Kat picked up her sponge and started to swipe furiously at a spot in the far corner of the cage. "That doesn't exactly fill me with confidence."

"Hey, Leila's a professional reporter. She knows how to get information out of people."

"Maybe so, when it comes to fashion and flower shows. A murder is another animal entirely. I repeat, you're not a professional detective. Please promise me the two of you won't do anything foolish."

I was spared from making said promise as the backdoor buzzer sounded. "I'll get it," I murmured, glad for an excuse to end the conversation. I hurried to the rear entrance and opened the door to find Will hunched against the railing.

"Hey," he said. "I saw both your cars in the parking lot as I was passing. I'm glad to catch you both here. Think I might have a word?" He reached into his breast pocket and pulled out a small notebook. "It should only take a few minutes."

I sighed, then stepped aside to let him enter. Manners long ingrained in me by my mother rose to the surface. "Would you care for a cup of coffee? I think there might be some muffins in the pantry, too."

Will smacked his lips. "A muffin sounds great. I only had a slice of toast for breakfast, and I skipped lunch."

I pointed toward the kitchen. "Go on and help yourself. I'll get Kat."

* * *

Once Will had downed two cups of strong coffee and polished off two corn muffins, Kat leaned back in her chair. "Okay, Will. Or would you rather I call you Detective Worthington?" she asked.

Will took another sip of coffee and set down his mug. "Will's fine. Unless Hank's around, then you'd better call me Detective."

I looked at him. "Hank?"

"Bennington's first name is Henry. He told me I could call him Hank."

I crossed my arms over my chest. "Lucky you."

His lips quirked slightly, and he pulled a small notebook out of his breast pocket, flipped a few pages. "He's already made a few protests about me being too biased to work this case, but that's only because . . ."

"Because?" I prompted as he hesitated. "Because why? Kat and I are suspects number one and two?"

Will tapped at his notebook. "Because of my history with the two of you. And yes, because at the moment you two are considered persons of interest."

"Persons of interest," Kat repeated. "I've always been curious. What does that term mean exactly?"

"Just what it sounds like. It usually refers to someone the police are interested in, either because they're cooperating with the investigation, have information that helps the investigation, or that the police feel warrant further . . . attention."

"In other words," I said, turning to my sister, "it could refer to someone who can help them, or it could also refer to someone they think might have committed the crime." I glanced over at Will. "Right?"

He looked away before answering. "Right."

"So—which definition applies to us? Do you think one of us did the deed? Injected Littleton with poison?"

Both Will's eyebrows shot up. "How did you know that?" he demanded. "I never said what the actual cause of death was."

"No, you didn't," I responded with a curl of my lip. "Fortunately, I have my own sources of information."

Will tapped his pen against the cover of his notebook. "You do know that if you'd said that around Hank, you'd shoot yourself up to the top of his list."

I leaned forward to look him straight in the eye. "What, I'm not there already?" I quipped.

His lips thinned. "You, not yet. Kat, however . . ."

"What!" Kat and I both cried at the same time. Kat's face had gone pale. "You can't be serious," I cried. "There are tons of people with actual motives. Just because Kat bought gopher poison—"

Will's eyes narrowed, and he swung his gaze to Kat. "You bought gopher poison?"

She let out a sigh. "Yes, last week. To try to get rid of that gopher that's been plaguing my neighborhood and tearing up everyone's gardens. It seems to have worked, too."

I saw the expression on Will's face, and I bit down hard on my lower lip. "That's not the reason Kat's on Bennington's list. You wouldn't have known about the gopher poison. Unless, of course, you got a list of people who recently purchased anything that contained strychnine and then got a warrant and went in and searched her apartment."

"We are in the process of getting such a list," Will admitted. "So Kat's name would have come up on it."

"It doesn't matter," I said quickly to Kat, "because you're innocent. You didn't kill Littleton." I turned my gaze to Will. "So why are you here, exactly?"

Will turned back to Kat. "Littleton sent you a letter about a possible rent increase to the shelter."

I avoided looking at my sister as she fiddled with the edge of her napkin. "Well, actually he sent it to the mayor and the town council. I was copied."

Will looked Kat straight in the eye. "We found a copy of that letter tucked inside a folder in his desk. Along with a letter you wrote to him."

Kat shifted uncomfortably in her chair. "Oh."

I ignored the sinking feeling in the pit of my stomach and slid my hand over Kat's. "You wrote Littleton a letter?" I said.

She sighed. "Yes. Not the brightest idea, in hindsight. I was mad when I wrote it. I'd just read the letter he sent to the mayor about the shelter building. I put down exactly how I felt. He was attacking the shelter when we were at our lowest point. I said he was a hateful man who delighted in the misfortunes of others, and the world would be a better place without him in it. Thoroughly unprofessional of me, I know, but . . ."—she spread her hands—"Where my animals are concerned, I get passionate. I let my emotions take over."

"Oh, Kat!" I cried. I turned to Will. "Kat can't have been the only person who wrote Littleton a letter. According to Natalie, all the shopkeepers got one. And they were all plenty mad at him."

Will shifted a bit uncomfortably in his chair. "That might be true, but Kat's letter was the only one we found." He paused. "And there's more. Someone called the police with an anonymous tip. They said they heard Kat threaten Littleton shortly before he was killed. Is that true?"

Kat exhaled a sharp breath. "I don't know if I'd call what I said a threat. He came into the café when we were talking about the event with Dayna. He made remarks

about stopping the cat showing and ended with we'd have the event over his dead body."

Will riffled a few pages in his notebook. "According to this eyewitness, you said 'Mess with my shelter, and it'll be the last thing you ever do.'"

Kat gulped. "I—yes, I might have said words to that effect. But I was angry. I didn't mean it."

I frowned. I recalled the incident too. Besides Kat and me, the only other people in the café at the time had been Dayna and Sissy.

Had one of them called the police on Kat? I couldn't imagine either one of them doing such a thing.

But if not one of them, then who?

Chapter Fourteen

The scent of overly sweet flowers—lilies, no doubt, accompanied by gardenias—assaulted me the moment I stepped inside the vestibule of the St. John Funeral Home. Organ music played softly in the background, and I paused to get my bearings. A dead body could drop at my feet, and I wouldn't blink an eyelash, but wakes and funerals never failed to creep me out. "Must be the organ music," I muttered; then I jumped as I felt a sharp jab in my ribs.

"Looks like the weeping widow went all out," Leila whispered, adjusting the jacket of the tailored black suit she had on. "It smells like the botanical gardens in here."

I noticed a wooden podium with a white guest book resting on top and moved toward it. "I guess not too many people are here yet," I murmured. There were only a few names entered, and none that I recognized.

"I doubt there will be a very large crowd at all," Leila said dryly. She'd moved over to stand in front of a jungle of

potted plants to my left. "Ten bucks says none of the other shopkeepers show up."

"Oh, I don't know. I think Grace will make an appearance. Possibly Devon. Right now, though, I'm more interested in the widow, the stepson, and the partner. I'd love to shift Bennington's focus off Kat and onto one of them."

"How's Kat doing?"

"Okay, considering. I have the feeling Bennington would love to arrest her, but so far, he doesn't have enough to make a murder charge stick." I picked up the pen, scrawled my name in the book, and then set the pen back down. "Buying that gopher poison isn't going to help her case."

"No, but maybe one of the other suspects made a similar purchase," Leila suggested.

"Maybe. It would help if Will would share some information, but every time I see him, either he says something that pisses me off or he's with Bennington and summarily ignores me."

"Well, that certainly doesn't sound like your Will," Leila said teasingly. "The Will Worthington I know would never deliberately ignore you."

"The new and improved Will Worthington doesn't have a problem in that area. What I need to do is come up with something to show him that I'm an asset in this investigation, not a liability."

"Good luck with that. I take it you have a plan?"

"I'm working on it." I angled a glance at Parlor A, which bore a sign that read "Trowbridge Littleton." "Shall we venture in?"

We stepped through the arched doorway into a room that felt more like the freezer aisle at Wegmans. It was done in soft shades of muted burgundy and pink.

"Oh, Petra definitely had a hand in this," Leila whispered. "These are two colors I'd never associate with Littleton."

I nodded in agreement and let my gaze wander to the front of the room. I moaned softly, and Leila's head swiveled swiftly in my direction. "What's wrong?"

"Open casket," I muttered. I glanced up sharply as Leila started to snicker. "What's so funny?"

"I was just thinking . . . The gal who can sit through six *Saw* movies in a row gets cold feet over seeing a body in a coffin. One that you saw up close and personal in the throes of death, too."

"Yeah, well, that's why. I'm really not looking forward to seeing his corpse again."

"Too late now. We might as well get it over with." Leila took my elbow and steered me along. I rubbed my palms, slick with sweat, against the sides of my black pants. Flickering white candles stood atop gleaming tapers at either end of the ornate brass coffin. There were dozens of sweet-smelling flowers banked behind it, lilies and geraniums and carnations. A purple satin cloth covered the bier. Leila gave me a little push, and I was propelled forward to the casket's edge. I steeled myself and looked down.

Littleton looked a lot better now than he had the other morning when he'd practically fallen at my feet. The bluish tinge was gone—now his skin just appeared fragile and waxy-looking. As I turned away, my gaze fell on the front

row of chairs not three feet away and the woman seated right in the middle. I recognized Petra Littleton instantly from the picture I'd seen. She looked much more sedate than glamorous right now, her head bowed, makeup perfect. She wore a simple black suit that probably cost more than I'd made at Reid and Renshaw in a year. The man seated next to her had a well-tailored suit on as well. Dark, close-cropped hair framed a tanned face with a sharp nose and chiseled jaw that just missed being handsome. He bent over, whispered something to Petra. She looked at him and nodded.

"Dior," I heard in my ear.

My head jerked up. "Huh?"

Leila gave me a swift nudge and nodded toward Petra. "Dior. That's a two-thousand-dollar suit she's wearing. I saw a similar one in *Vogue* last month." Her lips parted, and she emitted a strangled sigh. "Must be nice, being the wealthy widow."

"Hmm. Who's the guy next to her? They seem pretty chummy."

"I've only seen his photo once, and not a very good one at that, but if I'm not mistaken, that is Mr. Colin Murphy—Littleton's business partner in the gallery."

"So that's Colin Murphy." I leaned in for a closer look. "He's a lot better looking than his former partner, I'll say that."

"You got that right. Looks like he and the widow are pretty well acquainted, if you ask me."

I looked at the two of them, their heads bent close together. Murphy whispered something to Petra and patted her shoulder. She laid her hand on top of his and looked up at him with what my mother would have described as a "Scarlett O'Hara simple"—an almost worshipful gaze. Murphy gave her hand another squeeze and rose. As he stood there, his back to her, I saw Petra's expression change into one of thinly veiled contempt. He turned back toward her, and the expression once again morphed into one of dewy-eyed appreciation.

Hmm, I thought. *Perhaps Petra was a better actress than people gave her credit for.*

A tall, beak-nosed man wearing a Roman collar and carrying a Bible approached them—the minister, no doubt. He sat down on the other side of Petra and started to speak to her in low tones. Murphy stood there awkwardly for a few seconds, then turned and walked off toward the rear of the viewing room. When he reached the podium where the guest book lay, he paused. I saw his head swivel to and fro, almost as if he were searching for someone, before he turned and walked into the hall.

"Now's our chance," I hissed, and I started up the center aisle. When I reached the door, I suddenly realized that I was alone—where was Leila? I scanned the room and then saw that she'd been waylaid by Jim Wantrobski. I recalled her mentioning him as one of the new junior reporters she and her colleagues had taken to dinner the other night. Jim had no doubt been assigned to cover the tragic event. I hesitated, then decided Leila could catch up with me later.

I hurried out into the hallway. It was deserted. I walked back to the main door, pushed it open, and went out onto the porch. Colin Murphy was at the far end. I caught sight of a glowing ember in one hand and realized he'd come outside for a smoke. As I drew closer, I realized something else: he wasn't alone. A figure stood in the shadows just off to his left. The two of them were conversing in low tones, and then the shorter figure squeezed Murphy's arm and moved off toward the side door of the funeral parlor. As the door opened, light splashed across an object on the person's left hand. The large stone twinkled and glittered in the pale light, and I bit back a sharp cry as I recognized Natalie's ring.

I hesitated. Should I approach Colin Murphy or go inside and try to grill Natalie? As I stood pondering, Murphy's head suddenly swung in my direction, and his eyes widened slightly as he caught sight of me standing half in, half out of the shadows. "Yes?" he barked. "Can I help you?"

Gathering all my courage, I squared my shoulders and walked over to stand in front of him. "Colin Murphy, I presume?" At his nod, I continued. "I—ah—I just wanted to say I'm sorry for your loss. I know Mr. Littleton and you were partners in the gallery."

One side of his mouth twitched with—what? Curiosity? Amusement? "Do you now? Well, thanks." He looked me up and down again. "Did you know Bridge?"

"I only met him once. He was more or less acquainted with my sister."

"Your sister?"

I held out my hand. "I'm Sydney McCall. My sister is Katherine McCall."

His brow puckered slightly, and then his expression cleared. He took my hand. "Ah, yes. The shelter director. You work there too?"

I nodded.

"Yes. I work there as well." He released my hand, and I let it drop to my side.

"That's a fine undertaking, saving defenseless animals," he said. "You two should be commended." He regarded me with hooded eyes. "I understand you and your sister found the body. That must have been . . . shocking."

"To say the least. We'd gone over there hoping to have a discussion with him about the cat café event. He'd been in Dayna Harper's shop the day before, and things . . . well, things got a bit heated."

"A bit?" Colin Murphy leaned back against the porch railing, folded his arms across his chest. "I heard that your sister threatened him. Well, I can't say as I blame her. Bridge had a way of pushing people's buttons."

I held my head up high. "I'm afraid you're misinformed, Mr. Murphy. My sister didn't threaten Littleton."

He waved his hand in a careless gesture. "Whether she did or didn't is immaterial in the grand scheme of things, I suppose. My partner wasn't famous for his ability to win friends."

"Did Littleton have any enemies you're aware of?"

He eyed me, then jabbed his finger in the air. "Oho, I see what's happening here. Your sister is high on the suspect list, so you're—what? Fishing around for someone to take her place?" He leaned in a bit closer to me. "Is this the part where you ask me, 'Mr. Murphy, just where were you on the morning of the seventh?' And I answer, 'I was on a plane coming in from San Francisco—red-eye flight. I'd just returned from a buying trip to the Summerfield gallery out there.' The police have already vetted my alibi, Miss McCall. The airline records show that I was on that plane, circling to make a landing at Raleigh-Durham at the time they estimate my partner was killed." He looked me up and down. "I'm sorry to disappoint you."

"What makes you think you've disappointed me?"

"Isn't it obvious?" He threw back his head and let out with a rich baritone of a laugh. "I suppose I should be flattered you'd think I'm the killer type, but . . . though there were many times when I might have wished him dead, I did not kill Bridge." He paused. "And then there's the question of motive. I may have disagreed with my partner on the running of the gallery, but that's as far as it went."

"I heard it was a bit more involved than that. That Littleton was against some improvements you wanted to make to the gallery."

He brushed a hand through his hair. "Yes, well, Bridge always was resistant to change—even when the change would have netted him more money. We disagreed on a few key points, but I assure you, it was nothing serious. The gallery was thriving with or without my improvements. I had no reason to want him dead. If anything, his death is a giant pain in the you-know-where for me. Bridge took care of most of the day-to-day management issues. Now I'm stuck with everything."

"I understand his stepson works at the gallery," I offered. "Surely he will be a help to you."

Colin Murphy threw back his head and laughed. "Hardly, Miss McCall. One thing Bridge and I did agree on—Trey's a lazy so-and-so. He takes after his mother. He'd rather spend money than make it." He glanced at his watch. "As lovely as this chat has been, I've got to go, sorry."

"One last thing." My arm shot out, and my fingers dug into his forearm. "Does the name Kahn Lee mean anything to you?"

"Kahn Lee? Never heard of him," Murphy said in an irked tone. "Should I have?"

"I don't know. I thought perhaps he might be an artist that Mr. Littleton dealt with, or perhaps a customer?"

"Well, Bridge had his own listing of select clientele so . . . maybe. Who knows? Name's not familiar to me." He started to brush past me, then stopped and looked me directly in the eyes. "Want some advice? If you're dead set on finding a good suspect, I suggest you go back in there and give dear Petra a grilling. Our grieving widow is putting on quite a show, but that's all it is, trust me—a show. She's ecstatic the old boy is dead—now she's got her hands on his fortune and no longer has to account for every penny. Plus, Bridge had a nice insurance policy that she was named as beneficiary on. So it's a win-win for her. As for that son of hers, well, he and Bridge absolutely hated each other. Bridge hated his spendthrift ways, and Trey hated his stepfather for—ah, for oh so many reasons." He paused. "Two hundred fifty thousand reasons, to be precise. And mommy was in no position to help. I'll let you in on a little secret, Ms. McCall. Bridge was getting ready to divorce Petra. He had an appointment with a lawyer set up, and he told her she should watch her step. She didn't take that threat very kindly."

I swallowed. "Have you mentioned any of this to the police?"

He shrugged. "I told those two detectives all this when they questioned me. I'm not sure they'll do much about it, though. The one who looks like a sorry bulldog didn't seem too interested in what I had to say. Perhaps you can convince them to take a closer look."

He turned on his heel and started to go back inside, then paused and fixed me with a piercing gaze. "You know, Petra and Trey both had their reasons for hating Bridge, and she and her son, well—they're thick as thieves. They'd do anything to help the other. It wouldn't surprise me if they planned his murder together."

And with that, Colin Murphy touched two fingers to his forehead in a salute and strode off around the side of the building. As I turned to go back inside, I caught a flash of movement out of the corner of my eye. I turned my head just in time to see a curtain in one of the windows slide back into place. Someone had been watching me with Colin Murphy.

Chapter Fifteen

I stood on the porch for a few minutes after Colin Murphy departed, mulling over what he'd said. I'd never even considered the possibility of two people working in tandem with each other, but . . . heck, it was possible. It even sounded plausible. My thoughts wandered briefly to who might have been watching us. One possibility came to mind: Natalie. I had to speak with her too, as soon as possible.

I retraced my steps back to the viewing room and saw a harried Leila still engaged in conversation with Jim Wantrobski. She caught my gaze over his shoulder and bounced both eyebrows, her usual signal for *Help me*. I moved swiftly over to where they stood and tapped Leila on the shoulder. "Hey, there you are," I said cheerfully. "I've been looking for you."

Jim Wantrobski smiled as he reached up to brush an errant blond lock of hair out of his eyes. "Sorry, my fault. The paper sent me to do a story on Littleton's service, and since I'm a relatively new resident of Deer Park, I was just picking Leila's brain about the local color." He made a sweeping gesture with his arm. "She's all yours now," he said, and there was no missing the reluctance in his tone. He tossed Leila an almost worshipful gaze. "Thanks for all your help."

Leila flashed Jim a wide smile. "No problem," she murmured. Her fingers dug into my arm as she propelled me toward the back of the room. We reached the large potted plant next to the podium, and she pulled me behind it. "About time you showed up! God, can that man talk."

"I noticed. I also noticed he seems pretty interested in you."

Leila's expression turned horrified, and she waggled her finger to and fro. "In me? Oh, no, no, no. He's just new, and he wants to make a good impression on Seth Warner— that's his editor. He wanted to know stuff about Littleton, his business, what he did for the community, that sort of thing."

"I'm surprised he didn't ask the widow."

"I think he tried to, but she blew him off—and then he got me in his sights."

I shot her a sly grin. "It looked to me like he might have had you in his sights for quite a while. I got the feeling his questions weren't entirely fueled by business. Take it from me—I think he's got a crush on you."

She rolled her eyes. "Great, just what I need. Another clingy male, like Jackson."

I remembered Jackson Hornsby, Leila's ex-boyfriend, and had to agree. He'd been extremely needy, the total opposite of my friend. I'd always wondered what she saw in him other than his movie-star good looks. Aloud, I said, "Your ex? No way. Jim Wantrobski didn't seem clingy to me. He seemed kind of . . . sweet."

Leila grimaced. "Yeah, well, he's not my type. Anyway, what took you so long to rescue me? I kept looking around for you, but I couldn't find you."

"I followed Colin Murphy outside."

"Ah, so you got your chance to talk with him. Learn anything?"

"Actually, I think I might have." I hit the highlights of my conversation with Murphy, ending with his insinuation that Petra and her son might have jointly plotted Bridge's demise. "What do you think?"

Leila tapped at her chin with her forefinger. "Not sure. I know Petra and her son are close, but plotting a murder together seems a bit over the top. Are you sure Murphy wasn't just trying to blow smoke, maybe divert suspicion away from himself?"

"Well, he said the police checked out his alibi. It's kind of hard to kill someone when you're in a plane forty thousand feet above the ground. Besides, he's right. Littleton's death is more of an inconvenience for him than anything else. He doesn't benefit at all that I can see."

"But the widow definitely does," Leila said. "His estate and an insurance policy! She's rolling in it now." She placed her hand on her hip. "So now what? Or are we done here?"

I glanced toward the front of the room. A slender man with dark hair dressed in a three-piece suit had taken the seat on Petra's right. Their heads were bent close together, and I saw him slip a protective arm around her shoulders. "I see Trey has come to console his mother," I whispered. "I'd sure like to have a little chat with one or both of them, if I could only think of a good reason."

"How did you start things off with Colin Murphy?"

"I said I was sorry for his loss, then I introduced myself. He seemed to know who I was." I stopped, frowning. "He even knew Kat had threatened Littleton."

"Well, you said someone reported it to the police, right? Gossip spreads through this town like wildfire." She reached out and grabbed my arm. "Oh, oh! Look who just came in."

I turned. Grace Topping and Devon McIntyre were both framed in the doorway. Grace made a beeline for the podium and the guest book while Devon hung back on the fringe of the room, her eyes darting to and fro. Devon's gaze fell on me, and her eyes widened slightly. She spun on her heel and hurried back into the hallway. Before I could make a move to follow her, I heard a sharp gasp and then Grace's voice: "Sydney? For goodness' sake, what are you doing hiding behind that plant?"

Out of the corner of my eye, I saw Leila glide off in the direction Devon had gone. I turned to Grace with a smile. "I'm not hiding. I just—ah—wanted a quiet moment."

Grace looked toward the front of the viewing room, and a small sigh escaped her lips. "It will be strange, looking at him lying there. Bridge was always so full of vitality and life." Her gaze fell on the front row and the two people seated there, and her brow furrowed. "I see Petra is playing the grieving widow to the hilt. Sitting there, dabbing at her eyes as if Bridge meant something to her. I doubt they ever really loved each other in the truest sense of the word."

I was surprised at the vehemence with which Grace spoke. Perhaps their "friendship" hadn't been as platonic as Grace wanted me to believe.

I smiled at her. "You didn't see Natalie anywhere around, did you?"

Grace nodded. "She was just leaving as I came in." She cleared her throat. "Well, I suppose I'd best say my final good-bye and offer my condolences to the family." She reached out and gave me a pat on the shoulder. "Take care, dear."

"Grace!" I caught her arm. "I spoke with Colin Murphy earlier. He said something to the effect that Trey had two hundred fifty thousand reasons to hate Littleton."

"Did he?" she said thoughtfully. "Well, I could easily see Trey owing his stepfather such a large sum. It would explain why he was so bitter about having to pay it back." She glanced around and then leaned closer to me. "Trey has—had, rather—a bit of a gambling problem. But he's getting help."

With that little bombshell, Grace turned and walked away.

I watched her glide down the aisle toward the casket and then made a beeline for the hallway. As I stepped over

the threshold, I ran smack into Leila. "Hey, where's the fire?" she asked.

"Did you see where Devon went?"

"Oh, yeah. She went outside on the veranda. Stood there for a couple minutes, and then she got a call and whipped her cell out of her bag."

"Did you hear who she was talking to?"

"I heard her say, 'Why are you calling me now?' and then she was quiet for a minute, and then she said, 'You know why I had to come here. I had to make sure' . . . and then that was it."

"That was all she said?"

"No, all I heard. I was trying to get a bit closer when I saw Wantrobski coming out the door. Thank God I ducked back into the shadows before he saw me. He went into the parking lot, but when I looked around for Devon, she was gone."

"Curious. I'd love to know who she was talking to."

"Me too. I'm sorry I couldn't hear more. Did you learn anything from Grace?"

"Actually, I did," I began, but I stopped cold as I felt a hand drop on my shoulder. I saw the myriad expressions that ran across my friend's face, and I knew who was behind me even before he spoke.

"Well, Syd and Leila. Fancy meeting you here, of all places."

I turned. Will Worthington stood there, looking very handsome in a dark-gray jacket and pants, crisp white shirt, and gray-and-black-striped tie. Leila turned her

triple-wattage smile on him and leaned forward to envelop him in a hug. "Hey, Will. I heard you'd come home." She stepped back and surveyed him, her head cocked. "You look fantastic!"

"Thanks. I understand you're a reporter now. You're not covering this, are you?"

"Oh, God, no!" Leila waved her hand in the air. "That would be Jim Wantrobski's misfortune. My beat is fashion shows and garden parties, with the occasional dog show—and cat shelter event—thrown in."

His gaze wandered back to me, and I made a point of looking first right, then left. "Where's your charming partner? Don't tell me he decided not to attend and harass these people in their hour of grief."

"Bennington couldn't make it." Will arched a brow at me. "I do sincerely hope that *you* just came here to offer condolences, Syd. That you didn't have anything else in mind."

I widened my eyes. "Why else would I be here?"

"Oh, I don't know. Maybe you thought it'd be a good opportunity to ask a few discreet questions?"

"Isn't that your job?" I asked sweetly. "Nine times out of ten, the murderer shows up at his victim's viewing or funeral, right? And it seems to me most of the prime suspects are here, although if Colin Murphy is to be believed, he's been eliminated from the pool."

"Aha, I knew it! You've been asking questions." Will jabbed a finger in the air. "You just can't help yourself, can you?"

"Not when I know Bennington's eyeing my sister for murder I can't."

"Excuse us for a moment, Leila." Will grabbed my elbow and steered me toward the exit. We went out into the hall, down the archway, and back out onto the porch. No one else was out there, but Will marched me over to the far corner before he let go of my arm. "Look, Syd, I know you have a natural curiosity, and I know you're trying to help, but . . . we are dealing with a murderer here. You could get hurt . . . or worse."

I shook his arm free and took a step back. "I'm glad you called it my natural curiosity," I said. "Some others might call it a penchant for snooping. Either way, I hope you realize that I can't just sit by and do nothing, not when I know Bennington's eyeing my sister as suspect number one."

"We're not eyeing anyone as the prime suspect yet," Will said. "We're still investigating."

"I hope you're investigating the widow," I said. "I just found out that she's the beneficiary on Littleton's very large insurance policy."

Will started. "How did you find that out?"

"I told you, I've got my sources. Money, as you well know, is an excellent motive for murder. Did you find out where Petra was the morning of Littleton's death?"

"She gave us a statement. Said she was at the gym."

Something in his tone made me raise both eyebrows. "She said she was at the gym—but you don't believe her?"

He shifted his weight from one foot to the other. "Look, Syd, I really shouldn't be discussing details of an ongoing case with you, and especially not here."

I grabbed at his arm. "So let's go somewhere else and share information—off the record."

"Even off the record, if Hank found out . . ."

"Then we'll make sure he doesn't."

Will stared at me, and then his lips twitched upward in a half smile. "You're incorrigible, you know that?" He took my arm and led me into a secluded alcove just outside the viewing room. "What I'm going to say stays between us," he said. "You say nothing to Kat, or to Leila, or to anyone . . . not even your cat. Promise."

I wasn't particularly sure I could keep the part about not sharing with Toby, but Will didn't have to know that. I made a crossing motion over my heart. "I promise. And anything I tell you is off the record. You don't share with Bennington. Right?"

He hesitated, then nodded. "Okay. Mrs. Littleton told us she was at the gym the morning of her husband's death."

I nodded. "That's true. I parked next to her car."

"She was scheduled for a Zumba class, but it was canceled at the last minute. She opted for a massage instead but felt ill and went outside for some fresh air."

I lifted an eyebrow. "Did anyone see her?"

"That's what we're still checking on. So far, we can't find anyone to substantiate that part of her alibi. The masseuse said she looked flushed when she returned."

I gripped Will's arm. "Oh my God! It's only about a five-minute walk from the gym to the gallery. She could have slipped away, injected her husband, and gone back. The brisk walk, as well as committing murder, could account for her flushed appearance."

"First of all, ouch!" He gently disengaged my fingers from his arm. "Second, we're aware of that. We're not ruling Mrs. Littleton out as a suspect."

I scowled at him. "But she's not number one, is she? That honor belongs to Kat."

"I can't comment on that, but I can tell you this." Will's tone became a bit gentler as he added, "You're forgetting one important thing, Syd."

"Yeah? What might that be?"

"I know both you and Kat, and I know that neither one of you is capable of murder. Trust me. We'll find the person who really did it, I promise. Have a little faith in me."

"I do have faith in you. But if I were helping you, we might get to the bottom of this a lot sooner." I smiled up at him and batted my eyelashes. Heck, Leila was right. It had always worked in high school.

Will sighed. "What else do you want to know?"

"I spoke to Colin Murphy. He said you'd checked out his alibi."

"Yeah, kinda tough to commit murder when you're thirty thousand feet above the ground."

"What about Petra's son? I heard he owed his stepfather a lot of money and resented having to pay it back."

"We checked him out right away. Turns out he'd gone to stay with some friends in South Carolina, and they were about to tee off on the golf course at around that same time."

"Convenient. Maybe too much so," I muttered.

He shoved his hands deep into his pants pockets. "We're looking into every angle, trust me. I won't let Kat get railroaded for something she didn't do."

"That's a very nice sentiment, Will, but you and I both know that happens to innocent people more than you'd think."

His expression was grim. "True, but it won't happen here. I won't let it. Oh, and before I forget." He reached into his jacket pocket and pulled out a little baggie and pressed it into my hand. "Your note. It was just as I thought. There was too much cat saliva to retrieve any useful fingerprints or DNA from it."

"Great," I said. I took the baggie and turned it over in my hand. "What about the name? Did you find any connection to Littleton?"

"Not yet. We're still working on it." He reached out, chucked his thumb under my chin, and raised my face to his. "Now do me a favor. Go inside, get Leila, and go home before Hank gets here." As I hesitated, he said in a stern tone, "Or do I have to arrest you?"

The twinkle in his eye told me the last remark wasn't serious, so I managed to bark out a laugh. "No, I guess we're done here for tonight."

"And mum's the word?"

I made a gesture of locking my lips and throwing away a key. I started to walk away, but he reached out again and caught my arm. "Say, once this is all over . . . maybe you and I . . . maybe we . . ."

I smiled at bit at his discomfiture. "Maybe we can get reacquainted?"

He grinned. "Something like that."

"Well, how about this. Get Kat off the hook, and I'll make you a nice home-cooked meal. How does that sound?"

He shook his head, eyes twinkling. "I'd rather take you out for a nice dinner. I remember your cooking, Syd, and I've got an idea it hasn't improved over the years."

"Smart decision," I flung over my shoulder as I headed back inside to find Leila. "It hasn't."

* * *

Leila and I got back home a little after ten. Toby greeted me at the door with a soft *merow* and wound his furry body around my legs, then pranced off in the direction of the kitchen, his tail held high.

"Your bud must be hungry." Leila put her fingers to her lips to stifle a yawn. "Go on, feed him. I'm going to bed. Got a big day tomorrow. Fashion show in Derry—woo-hoo."

Leila went upstairs to her bedroom, and I followed Toby into the kitchen. The cat twined himself around my ankles, purring and glancing over at his food bowl. I spooned out some of the wet food I'd purchased, then sat down on one of the kitchen chairs and propped my chin in my hands, watching as the cat attacked the food hungrily.

"This is a real puzzle, Toby. In all the mysteries I've read, the detective's rule of thumb is 'follow the money.' Nine times out of ten, the killer is usually the person who stands to gain the most from the victim's death. In this case, that answer's pretty obvious. It would be Petra, right? She got it all, but she wouldn't if Littleton had managed to divorce her, would she? I wonder who else would have benefitted from his death. Maybe Colin Murphy, somehow? Darn, I'd love to be a fly on the wall when that will is read."

Toby glanced up from his bowl. "Ow-owr?"

"Yes, speaking of Colin Murphy—just what were these improvements he wanted to make to the gallery that Littleton was so against? According to Grace, Littleton thought they'd be very detrimental—or should I even worry about it, considering the guy was up in an airplane at the time of the murder?

"Maybe I should concentrate on another strong motivator: jealousy. That might put Devon back into play—and maybe Grace, too. Devon got a suspicious phone call tonight, and Grace . . . well, let's just say Grace's feelings for Littleton might run deeper than she let on. Maybe that 'woman scorned' aspect Grace mentioned applies to her and not Devon after all. Or who knows? Maybe this mysterious Kahn Lee is a suspect too. If only we knew who he—or she—is."

Toby padded over, rubbed against my ankles. I got up and started for my bedroom, Toby following right behind me.

It would seem, as far as suspects were concerned, that I was back to square one. There wasn't one, so far, with a clear-cut motive. Still lots of work to do in that area, but . . . something had to give. And I was hoping for sooner rather than later.

Chapter Sixteen

Around one thirty the next day, Kat poked her head into my office. "Say, feel like going over to the diner? I haven't had lunch yet. The meeting with the mayor took longer than I expected."

I could tell from the expression on her face that her meeting hadn't gone well. I opened the bottom drawer of my desk and reached for my purse. "Sure. I could go for a nice club sandwich." I looked her straight in the eye. "Meeting not go well?"

"Not really. Since no one knows yet just what's going to happen with Littleton's estate, we figured we should look into a plan B." She gave me a tired smile. "Let's just say there aren't very many buildings that could accommodate the number of animals we house at the same rent we pay now."

"There must be something," I cried. "Surely, once people learned it was for the animals, they'd be more willing to cut a deal . . . right?"

"One would hope." Kat's lips twisted into a wry expression. "Bottom line? We need a lot of prayers, we need to scrounge up some major donors, and we need some kick-ass fundraisers over the next few months."

I gave her hand a reassuring squeeze. "Don't worry, sis. Things usually have a way of working out. This will too—you'll see."

She smiled at me. "You sound so confident."

"You betcha. Now let's go get some lunch." I smiled back, wishing I felt half as confident as I sounded.

*　　*　　*

I drove my convertible over to the center of town and parked in the back lot of Rosie's Diner. I glanced at my watch. "It's a little after two, and there are still a lot of cars here. Lots of people must be having late lunches today."

Kat shrugged. "I think her special today is meatloaf. And Rosie makes a mean one."

We entered the diner, and much to my surprise, most of the tables and the counter were empty. Kat touched my arm and nodded toward a large circular booth near the kitchen. "Looks like we've interrupted a conference."

I followed her gaze. Sure enough, the booth was occupied by most of the square's shop owners: Natalie, Grace, Buck, Antonio, and Ioan. Kat gave me a nudge, and I followed her as she made her way over to them. "Hey guys," she greeted them. "Fancy seeing you all here. Is something up?"

"You could say that." Buck Noble's head bobbed up and down. He was a short, squat man with a rather prominent nose. "We heard that Littleton's will was to be read immediately after his interment. Those were his instructions."

I let out a low whistle. "That's interesting. How did you find out?"

Ioan, a tall, solidly built man with iron-gray hair and shaggy eyebrows to match, spoke up. "From Randy, one of my part-timers. His older brother is a part-time law clerk in Littleton's lawyer's office." He let out a chuckle. "Apparently, law clerks love to gossip—and snoop. The lawyer left some notes from the meeting on his desk, and, well, to make a long story short . . . Petra gets everything."

"So we want to be prepared," Antonio Muriello put in. He wiped his hands nervously on the sides of the stained apron he wore knotted about his ample waist. "We thought maybe we should have an impromptu meeting of all the shop owners, you know, just in case it is true, and she decides to go along with what her husband had in mind."

Rosie came out of the kitchen just then, carrying a large tray of coffees. She set the tray down and started to hand out the mugs. "And they're here because . . . guess what? Littleton owned this property too! I mean, I make good money, but a 30 percent increase would definitely cut into my profit margin." She eyed me and Kat. "So, you two want to join the group? Littleton owned the shelter building too, right?"

"Right." Kat slid into the space next to Natalie, and I plunked down across from Grace. "Do you think she would pick up where her husband left off?" I asked no one in particular.

"Maybe," Natalie said with a scowl. "She likes money, that one. And everyone knows she's the main reason Littleton wanted the rent increase. To keep her in designer clothes, cars, and jewels."

"I'm not so sure about that," said Ioan, crossing his arms over his chest. "Littleton was just plain mean, and he liked having people under his thumb. I wonder if Petra had anything to do with that decision at all. It would be just like Littleton to raise our rents just because he could."

There were murmurs of assent from the others. I stole a quick glance at Natalie. From the expression on her face, it was evident she didn't agree with the majority consensus. I remembered what Grace had told me—about her starting the rumor about Petra and her gym coach and also about her recommending Colin to Littleton—and I touched her arm. "Might I have a word with you in private?" I asked.

She looked surprised but nodded, and we slid out of the booth and moved off a bit to a nearby corner. I decided to get right to the point. "I heard that you were the person who recommended Littleton take on Colin Murphy as a partner in the gallery," I said.

Her eyes widened, but her expression remained neutral. "I did," she said. "I knew Colin from back in Boston, and he's a very talented art appraiser. He'd been downsized and was looking for work. Why do you ask?"

I shrugged. "I was just surprised. When we last spoke, it certainly seemed as if you had no love for Littleton. I didn't realize you were that close."

"We're not—at least not anymore. At one time, though, he wasn't such a bad egg. He used to visit Boston quite a bit, and we struck up a sort of friendship there. When I decided to move here, I contacted him, and he gave me a good deal, initially, on my store." Her lips thinned as she added, "Ever since he married her, though, he changed. He became more money-hungry than ever. I blame her for the change in his attitude."

"Surely you can't also blame her for the disagreements Littleton and Murphy were having over the gallery?"

Her eyes narrowed. "I'm not sure what you mean. They were having more tiffs than usual lately, but they're both strong-willed men with definite opinions. I'd have been surprised if they didn't argue."

I nodded. Natalie started to turn away when I remembered the note. "One last thing," I said quickly. "Did you ever hear Littleton talk about someone named Kahn Lee?"

Her eyes darkened for a split second, then cleared. "Kahn Lee, you say?"

"Yes. I thought perhaps it might be an artist?"

She gave her head a brisk shake. "Never heard that name. If he's an artist, I've never heard of him. We'd best get back," she added, turning on her heel. I started to follow her but paused as a collective gasp of astonishment went up from the booth. I looked over my shoulder to see what had attracted their attention, and my jaw nearly dropped as I saw the source of their consternation—Petra Littleton. "Well, what do you know," Natalie muttered. "Here's the grieving widow now."

Petra certainly didn't look the part of a grieving widow—far from it. My first thought was that the photo in the paper hadn't done her justice. Her dark hair was pulled back into an elegant French twist, and her makeup was flawlessly applied. Her dress, a brilliant cobalt-blue knit, shaped and molded every curve of her well-toned body. As she approached the counter, I noticed how extraordinarily tall she was, due no doubt in part to the killer stilettos she had on—pale blue, with a slim strap around the ankle, a peep-toe style that showed off her pedicure—toenails painted a pale shade of blue and dotted with little stars. I was positive I'd seen those same shoes in *Vogue* last month. They retailed for nine hundred dollars. Not too shabby.

She walked right up to our booth and stood—maybe posed would be a better word—for a few seconds before her crimson lips parted to reveal gleaming white teeth. "How fortuitous, catching the group of you together," she said. "I was going to call a personal meeting with each of you, but since everyone's conveniently here . . ." Her gaze swept over us, and I noted it rested for a moment longer than necessary on Grace. She cleared her throat and announced, "I'm sure rumors have been swirling. Let me say right now that my husband left the bulk of his fortune to me, including his rental properties. So, for the time being, I'm going to continue on as general manager of this complex, as well as his other holdings."

Anxious glances were exchanged. No one spoke. We had no idea what to say.

"I know most of you, of course," she went on. "I've eaten at Buck, Antonio, and Ioan's establishments many times. I've ordered books from Natalie, and I am familiar with Ms. Topping's hat shop." I noted she made no mention of Devon. Then she turned her sharp gaze on Kat and me. "I'm sorry, I don't know you two."

Kat thrust out her hand. "I'm Katherine McCall. I'm the director of Friendly Paws Animal Shelter. This is my sister, Sydney." She indicated me with a flick of her wrist. "She's been helping the shelter with publicity."

Petra pinned Kat with a sharp gaze. "Ah, so you are Katherine McCall. I understand you had a little run-in with my husband before his unfortunate demise."

"It really wasn't that bad," Kat began, but Petra held up a bejeweled hand and waved it carelessly in the air.

"Oh, sweetie. Don't fret. Half the town made idle threats at Bridge at one time or another. Hell, I did it all the time." She shrugged as if it were no big deal and then turned to face everyone. "As I said, I'm going to be the general manager of this complex, but it's only a temporary thing. I have no desire to do this permanently, and I have no desire to dabble in real estate as my late husband did."

Ioan's head shot up. "If you've no desire to dabble in real estate, does that mean you're going to sell off the properties?"

Petra threw her head back and laughed, a low, throaty sound that would have been grating coming from anyone else—but from Petra, it sounded sexy. Her hand reached up to toy with the magnificent diamond solitaire pendant that dangled from the gold chain around her neck. "Goodness me, no. They provide quite a nice income. I have no plans to sell at all. I just can't be bothered with the mundane day-to-day management of my late husband's empire. I've already set the wheels in motion to locate a suitable business manager. Until then, though, I shall do my best."

"Does your best include rent increases?" piped up Grace.

Petra eased one slender hip against the table. "Let me put your fears to rest right now. I'm aware my husband stirred up a hornet's nest when he mentioned a possible rental increase to all of you. I'd just like to go on record as saying that as far as I'm concerned, there is no need for any increase on the shops, at least not at this time."

Antonio leaned forward and said excitedly, "You mean that? You're not going to raise our rents?"

"I repeat—there will be no increases at this time. Let me go one step further. If the issue should be revisited in the future, I can assure you any increase will be nowhere near 30 percent. That's exceedingly steep. I don't know what my husband was thinking. Then again, he was a greedy bas—person." She turned on the full-wattage smile again. "I hope that sets all your minds at ease."

Antonio leaned across Natalie and held out his hand to Petra. "It certainly puts mine at ease. Thank you so much, Mrs. Littleton."

She clasped Antonio's hand and bestowed a dazzling smile on him. "You are very welcome."

Everyone started to slide out of their seats, and everyone save Natalie crowded around Petra, murmuring their thanks. Natalie made a beeline for the door while Kat and I stood awkwardly by and exchanged a glance that said more plainly than words: *What about the shelter?*

Apparently satisfied, the shopkeepers all started to file out of the diner. Kat looked at me, then squared her shoulders and marched right over to Petra. She touched her arm and said, "That's wonderful that you aren't planning to increase the shops' rent but . . . does the same hold true for the shelter?"

Petra's eyes widened, and then she slid into the booth, motioning as she did so for Kat and me to do the same. Once we were seated, Petra folded her hands on the table in front of her. "The shelter's situation is a bit different from the others, I'm afraid," she said slowly.

I felt my stomach plummet. I stole a glance at Kat out of the corner of my eye and saw her jaw was set, her lips compressed in a thin line. "How so?" she asked in a tight voice. "If you ask me, not raising the rent on the shelter should be number one on your list of priorities. We are one of the few no-kill shelters in this area, and we provide top-notch care for the animals in our charge. We work tirelessly to find them good homes, and . . ."

Petra held up her hand. "I'm aware of all that, Ms. McCall. Unlike my husband, I've always been a staunch supporter of animals. As a matter of fact, I've given anonymously to your shelter, as well as other animal rescue groups, on various occasions. This is purely a business matter. There is another prospective tenant who wants that location and who is willing to pay top dollar—heck, more than top dollar—to acquire it."

Kat's lips drooped. "Oh."

She reached out and gave Kat's hand a pat. "My financial advisor and I plan to meet with the mayor early next week, though, to discuss the situation. I know it's not exactly what you want to hear, but . . . I'll try my best to work with you, believe me. I'm not against the shelter. I'm hoping a deal satisfactory to all parties can be worked out. As a matter of fact, I always wanted to adopt a dog from there, but Bridge wouldn't hear of it."

"We specialize in cat rescues, but we also have some lovely dogs," Kat responded. "A few are pedigree rescues. You should stop in. I guarantee you'll find a puppy you'll fall in love with. My staff and I will do our best to accommodate you."

Petra looked slightly amused. "You guarantee it, eh? Well, Ms. McCall, I just may take you up on that. I certainly would love to have a dog, especially now that Bridge is gone. I've always been a sucker for unconditional love." She brushed at her eyes and then turned her gaze on me. One long nail tapped at her chin before she pointed it right at me. "I'm sorry, it's just that . . . you look so familiar. Are you certain we've never met before today?"

"Actually, we have. At your husband's wake Monday night."

She snapped her fingers in the air. "That's where I saw you," she murmured. "I remember now. You had a black pantsuit on. Tailored, very nice." Her lips quirked. "I never forget an outfit—especially one as well made as that one."

I paused, part of me flattered that such a fashion plate as herself would notice my simple outfit. Then again, it was one of my more pricey articles of clothing—I'd splurged on a really great suit when I'd worked at Reid and Renshaw. The set also boasted a matching skirt and vest. "Thanks. I realize I should have come over and offered my condolences, but to tell the truth, I felt a bit . . . awkward."

Her finely penciled brows drew together. "Awkward? Goodness, why?"

"Well, for one thing, my sister and I are the ones who found your husband's body."

Her eyes widened a bit. "You two are the ones who found him?"

"Yes. Didn't the police tell you?"

"They said it had been found by some people who'd had an early morning appointment. No names were mentioned. I'd assumed . . ." She gave her head a little shake, leaned back in her chair. Rosie appeared, set a mug of steaming coffee in front of her, and quickly withdrew. "Never mind. It doesn't matter."

I leaned forward. "Could you think of anyone who would have wanted your husband dead?"

She plucked the creamer from the table and poured some into her cup. Then she picked up a spoon and gave it a quick stir. "Honey, that list would take ages to recite. You either loved Bridge or you hated him. Unfortunately, most people were in the latter camp."

"Including you?"

She paused, coffee cup halfway to her lips. "Bridge and I had a very . . . open marriage. Things were very rosy at first, as they usually are, but little by little, I could feel him drifting away from me. He found fault with my spending, with the company I kept, with my son—in short, with practically every aspect of my life."

The words tumbled out before I gave them a second thought. "Is that why the two of you had affairs?"

Kat gasped, but Petra didn't seem at all bothered. She leaned back in the booth and took another sip of coffee before she answered. "Most folks around here have me pegged as a real shrew," she said, "but nothing could be further from the truth. I was a loyal and faithful wife to Bridge. As for his infidelities, well . . . they didn't please me, but sometimes that's just the way a man is made up. One thing I'll say—he always came home to me. Then again, the way our premarital agreement was worded, he pretty much had to." A small sigh escaped her lips. "I wasn't happy with my husband's affairs, which he took care to flaunt in my face, and he suspected me of sleeping with practically every man who looked at me sideways. I knew Bridge had a roving eye before we married, so I had the agreement worded so each of us was allowed our little dalliances, if we chose to have them. But if either one of us wanted to end the marriage, there would be consequences. In my case, I could walk away with everything I'd accumulated during the marriage. In Bridge's case—well, let's just say I got well compensated for my time."

"I'm surprised a businessman as savvy as Trowbridge Littleton would have agreed to that."

She made a little clucking sound in her throat. "Oh, honey. Back then he was so besotted with me, he'd have signed anything. Come to think of it, we both had stars in our eyes back then . . . but I've always had this annoying practical streak. A gal's gotta look out for herself. I found that out the hard way. In spite of it all, though, I think we did love each other in our own ways—at least I did. I loved him enough to know that no matter what I thought, he would do what he wanted to do."

"But he'd decided recently that he did want a divorce?"

She waved her hand. "He threatened that at least once a month. Then he'd take a look at his bankbook and forget all about it."

"How did your husband get along with your son?"

Her eyes darkened, and she let out a sigh. "That's a whole other story, I'm afraid. Trey and Bridge were constantly at odds."

"I heard he owed your husband a large sum of money."

Her eyes widened, and two spots of color appeared on her cheekbones. "Gossip sure travels fast in a small town," she muttered. "Yes, unfortunately my son got into a few . . . scrapes, shall we say, and Bridge bailed him out. He wasn't about to let Trey get off scot-free, though, and I supported his decision."

I raised an eyebrow. "Tough love?"

"You might call it that. As a matter of fact, I'm continuing where my husband left off, only now Trey will be making his payments to me. I'll be the first to admit that my son is a lot of things, but a murderer? Hardly. He faints at the sight of blood." She picked up a napkin, toyed with its edge. "All this speculation is so unnecessary. I told those detectives what they needed to find in order to close this case—Bridge's diary."

I stared at her. "Your husband kept a diary?"

She nodded. "Yes. Oh, I know what you're thinking. Yes, it was unusual, but Bridge was an unusual man. He wrote everything down in that diary—absolutely everything. Shortly before his death, he bragged he had enough information on people in that book to ruin lives." She drained her cup and set the mug down. "He knew plenty of secrets, and he wasn't afraid to write them down or let the people know he knew, either. He kept it somewhere in his private office at the gallery—that I know. I told the police to find that book, and they'd probably find out the name of Bridge's killer. But . . . somehow I don't think that detective took me too seriously."

Aha, I thought. Now I had a pretty good idea what it was that Bennington suspected either Kat or I had taken. Aloud, I said, "Oh, I don't know about that. You might be surprised," I murmured. "Sometimes detectives like to play everything close to the vest."

She glanced at her watch, then started to ease out of the booth. "I'm sorry to cut this short, but I've got a meeting in twenty minutes. I know you're concerned about the shelter, and I promise you, I'll keep you apprised on how the talks

207

turn out." With a wave and a smile, she walked out the door, hips swaying.

Kat turned to me with a rueful expression. "She's not at all what I expected. She's a square shooter, all right, and she doesn't pull any punches."

I had to agree. "I think Littleton met his match with her, all right. I can see why he would have been attracted to her."

"Please don't think I'm nuts, but . . . I kind of liked her."

"I don't think that at all, because I kind of like her too."

"I wish she had something more positive to offer about the shelter. Now I'm not certain what's going to happen," Kat said. "In spite of her protestations, I get the feeling she's pretty savvy when it comes to business. She might empathize with the shelter's plight, but the bottom line is dollars, and if this other place is offering more than top dollar for rent, there's no way we can possibly compete."

"She said she wanted to adopt a dog," I said. "Hopefully she'll visit the shelter before any negotiations, and you can dazzle her with how well the shelter is run and what good care the animals receive. Stress the fact that if the shelter has to move or close, many of the animals might not survive."

"Appeal to the sense of humanity in her? Maybe. It's a quality her dearly departed hubby never had, that's for sure." Kat looked at her watch and rose. "Come on. It's time we got back to work."

I nodded and rose. Our little conversation with Petra had given me a lot to think about. I had to admit, her remark about the diary had thrown me a curve. Did such a book exist, or had she made it up to divert suspicion away from herself?

In any event, the identity of Littleton's murderer was as much a mystery as ever.

*   *   *

I was just finishing up a proposal for an event at Natalie's bookshop when I heard the back door of the shelter open and close. A few minutes later, there was a tentative knock on my office door. "Come in," I called.

The door creaked open, and Diane Ryan popped her head in. "Hey," she said.

"Hey, yourself," I answered. "I thought you weren't volunteering tonight."

"I thought I might have to work overtime, but it ended up not being necessary. They caught the two guys who were breaking into those homes over on the west side. One less thing we all have to worry about."

"Um, that's true." I propped both elbows on my desk. "The real news of the day, though, is the reading of Littleton's will. Kat and I ran into Petra at Rosie's. Apparently, she inherited everything."

"She sure didn't waste any time spreading the news," Diane murmured. "I'll say one thing for her—she's sure got timing on her side."

"What do you mean?"

Diane leaned forward. "I heard Bennington on the phone this morning. Apparently Littleton had a meeting set up with Pete Faversham for the morning he died. He called it rather suddenly."

I drew in my breath sharply. Pete Faversham was one of the highest-priced lawyers around. "He did? About what?"

Diane's eyes gleamed. "Faversham said Littleton didn't say why, but . . . my friend Sasha works in the law office right next door. She's pretty tight with Faversham's law clerk. Faversham had her doing last-minute research that afternoon on clauses for wills and also dissolutions of partnerships and prenups."

Now that was interesting. "Was all that for Littleton?"

Diane shrugged. "She didn't know what client it was for, but it's certainly a coincidence, if you ask me. Petra made out like a bandit." She tugged on her jacket. "So did Colin Murphy, from what I understand."

I glanced at her sharply. "Colin Murphy? He was in the will?"

Diane leaned forward. Even though she and I were the only two around, she lowered her voice to a half whisper. "Littleton willed his share of the gallery to him. So Murphy now has complete ownership."

I let out a low whistle. "You're kidding."

"Nope. He lucked out too, just like Petra did. Think about it. Littleton was fed up with both of 'em and made an appointment with his lawyer—and now he's dead, and they're sitting pretty. Some people really step in it." She moved a bit further into the hall. "Well, Maggie said they're backed up in the cattery, so I'd better start my shift. How's Toby doing?"

"Fine," I answered absently. Diane gave a wave and closed my door, and I leaned back in my chair. I wasn't a big believer in coincidence. Had Littleton made that appointment with Faversham because he was going to change his will to cut out both his wife and Colin Murphy? Why else would Faversham be researching those particular topics? Both of them stood to lose a great deal if that was Littleton's intent.

It suddenly occurred to me that perhaps Murphy's assessment about Petra coplotting her husband's murder might not have been that far off after all. And what if Petra's partner in crime wasn't her son but Colin Murphy?

And, as they say, the plot thickens.

Chapter Seventeen

Shortly before two o'clock, Sissy popped her head inside my office. "Hey! How would you like an iced cappuccino? I picked one up for Maggie at Dayna's, but she decided she didn't want it."

I grinned. "Are you kidding? Iced cappuccinos are my favorite thing in this whole wide world, next to animals, that is."

Sissy reappeared a few seconds later and laid a large Styrofoam cup on my desk. I took off the lid and saw the mound of whipped cream drizzled with caramel, then took a sip. "Caramel. My favorite."

"It's my new favorite drink," the teen laughed. We sipped our iced cappuccinos in silence for a few minutes, and then she asked, "How's Toby enjoying his new home?"

I laughed. "He definitely rules the roost. He's even mastered a way to finagle extra treats out of Leila."

"No more wandering, eh?"

"Not that I can tell."

She nodded wisely. "Maggie always said once Toby found his perfect human, he'd settle down. By the way, some people were asking if we're having another cat café event."

"We're hoping to, maybe the end of next month. Kat said the new kitties should be ready to show by then."

"Great." Sissy drained the last of her drink. "At least now we won't have to worry about that horrible man making trouble. I don't blame Kat at all for the way she answered him. He deserved it." She paused. "I don't mean . . ."

"I know what you meant." I hesitated, unsure of how to broach what was on my mind. Finally, I decided to just have out with it. "Sissy, you didn't call the police station and tell them Kat threatened Littleton, did you?"

The teen stared at me, wide-eyed. "Of course not! I would never do something like that! Where did you get such an idea?"

I sighed. "Sorry. I didn't think so, but I had to ask. I found out that someone told the police, and since you and Dayna were the only other two people in the café at the time . . ."

"Wait a sec." Sissy held up a finger. "There was someone else around. She was standing right outside the door when I came in, and she might still have been there when Littleton pushed through. He and Kat were shouting pretty loud. Maybe she overheard and reported it."

I pounced on her words. "You said 'she.' Did you recognize the person?"

"Yeah. The woman who owns that lovely vintage jewelry shop. Starts with a 'D' . . . Dara, Denise, no—Devon. That's it. Devon McIntyre."

*   *   *

City Jewel was the type of shop I'd love to own if I were into vintage jewelry—or anything vintage for that matter. Devon had given the place a homey feel with its white-washed walls and ceilings and the thick shag carpets scattered across the hardwood floors. Even though the shop was jammed to the rafters with a spectacular array of inventory, it didn't seem cluttered. Busy was more the word I'd have chosen to describe it. Glass showcases displayed rows and rows of bracelets, necklaces, earrings, and rings, most of them estate pieces that Devon picked up for a melody and sold for a song. She carried other articles too: silk handbags, flowing scarves, jeweled opera glasses and gloves—there were even a few tiny lamps with beautiful stained-glass shades. The shop was empty when I entered—no big surprise, seeing as it was nearly six o'clock. As I approached the main counter, a pair of curtains parted, and Devon emerged, lugging a large cardboard box. She glanced at me, then slammed the box down on the counter. I heard a rattle as she did so and hoped that whatever was inside hadn't broken.

"Sydney. Hello. What can I do for you?" Devon brushed a curl out of her eyes with the back of her hand and eased one hip against the counter.

"I got off a little early tonight, and I just thought I'd come by and check out your shop," I lied. "I'm afraid I haven't really been able to do too much exploring in all these lovely shops. The shelter keeps Kat and me hopping."

"That's not a bad thing." Devon pushed the box off to one side. "Are you looking for something in particular?"

"Um, I just thought I'd see if anything catches my eye." I gazed into the jam-packed counter and pointed to a pin of a cat sitting up tall and straight, wearing a bow tie. The cat's body was made up of white-and-orange crystals. "Oh, that's cute," I exclaimed. "He reminds me of Toby—my new cat."

"That's a nice piece. Costume jewelry. Those crystals aren't Swarovski, but they're very nice." Devon reached inside the case and plucked the pin from its velvet cushion. She turned it on its side, and I could see a tiny white sticker fastened to the cat's back. "$39.99. A bargain, actually. The craftsmanship is very good."

"Yes it is." Impulsively, I reached into my tote bag and pulled out my wallet. "I'll take it."

I passed Devon my American Express card, and as she rang up the purchase, I glanced again at the case and pointed to a large brooch in the shape of some sort of bug. It had a massive dark-blue stone for its belly. "That's beautiful. I love the shade of blue."

Devon reached down and pulled out the pin. "You have good taste. That stone is lapis lazuli. In ancient times, it was known as the stone of royalty."

"It's striking. It reminds me of the color of the dress Petra wore to Rosie's Diner earlier." I reached up to slap my forehead with my palm. "Oh, duh. That's right. You weren't there."

"I had to pick up a shipment," Devon said shortly. She placed the cat pin in a small velvet-lined box and slid it inside a burgundy-colored paper bag before passing me the credit card receipt to sign. "Grace filled me in on what I missed. So Petra got everything, eh? That figures." Her expression turned stormy. "It's so unfair. She didn't love him, and I know he didn't love her."

"How do you know?" I signed my name to the slip and passed it across the counter. "Did he tell you that, Devon?"

Her eyes flashed. "Not in so many words, but I could tell he'd reached his limit. I don't know how to explain it—it was as if he'd had an epiphany of sorts. He was tired of living a lie with Petra. He realized she'd never be the wife or companion he wanted or needed." She tossed my credit receipt copy into the bag and held it out to me. "I confess I saw red when we broke things off, but it wasn't long before I realized he'd done me a huge favor."

I took the bag, tucked it into my tote, and looked her right in the eye. "You called the police and told them that my sister threatened Bridge, didn't you?"

Devon's eyes bugged. Her lower lip started to quiver. "How—how did you know?"

"That's not important," I said, making a dismissive motion with my hand. "What I'd like to know is why on earth you would do that. My sister never did anything to you."

Devon let out a sigh. "You're right. Okay, I admit it. I did it, and I'm sorry, but . . . I had a good reason."

I arched a brow. "And that would be?"

"I had to direct their suspicions to someone, so they wouldn't look too closely at me." She started to wring her hands. "I know, I know, it was horribly selfish, but I honestly couldn't think of any other way. I knew his witch of a wife probably couldn't wait to name me and Grace as women her husband had an affair with, and I—I just didn't want to get in the middle of a murder investigation." She looked at me defiantly. "I know Kat wouldn't hurt a fly, and I knew they wouldn't turn up anything on her. I just didn't want them looking at me, stirring things up, and making things uncomfortable. Not now . . . not when Harry's back and things are going so well."

I sighed. "Your convoluted logic certainly has made both my sister and me very uncomfortable around that detective, not to mention the spotlight that's being thrown on Kat."

"Yeah, well, think how you'd feel if you really had something to hide."

I eyed her. "Do you have something to hide, Devon?"

She goggled at me and pointed a finger at herself. "Me? Not if you don't count the fact I was foolish enough to take up with Bridge in the first place. He caught me at a vulnerable time in my life. He caught all his women at vulnerable times. If only . . . never mind."

I decided to take a chance. I leaned forward and said in a gruff tone, "You weren't looking for a medical ID tag when I caught you in his office that day, were you? You were looking for his diary."

Her head snapped up. "You know about that?" At my nod, a sigh escaped her lips. "I guess there's no sense denying it, then. I did lose my ID tag, but not in his office. Yes, I was looking for his stupid book. I wanted to see if he'd written anything in there about me, and if so, what it was."

"And if you'd found it?"

Her eyes widened. "Why, I'd have turned it over to the police, of course."

"Before or after you ripped out the parts that mentioned you?"

She gave me a shrewd look. "You're pretty good, aren't you, Syd? Of course, after. But I didn't find any book, so it's a moot point."

"But one does exist?"

"Oh yeah. I saw it. It's a dull saddle-brown leather, about yea big"—she outlined a small rectangle with her hands. "His initials—TL—are in the left corner, and the lower-right corner is pretty worn. I think it's got a small tear. Mark my words, Petra probably found it after she iced him. She's probably got it tucked away somewhere, just waiting to blackmail people to do her bidding, just like Bridge did." She waggled her finger. "But he was wise to her."

"What do you mean?"

"I spoke with him a week before his death. He said he was going to have a chat with his lawyer. 'Devon,' he said, 'I've had it. I'm sick of all these leeches in my life feeding off me and making a shambles of everything I hold dear.' He could be pretty cryptic, but I knew what he meant. He was going to see his lawyer about a divorce."

"Are you certain? It couldn't have been he was thinking of drawing up a new will?"

Devon rested a finger against her cheek. "Say, I never thought of that. Maybe. That would certainly have been a blow to Petra, too."

"Have you told the police this?"

Devon's eyes popped. "Heck no. I'm no squealer." At my pointed look, she threw up both hands. "Heck, I'm not doing a single thing that might piss Petra off. That woman hates me as it is, and now she's my frigging landlord. I don't need to add any more fuel to that fire."

*　　*　　*

After a quick snack, I went upstairs and sat at the desk in my room—pad in front of me, pen poised above it. Toby squatted on the floor at my feet, nibbling on a sardine-flavored kitty treat. I tapped the edge of my pen against the pad and closed my eyes, marshaling my thoughts. The fact that no one seemed to be able to account for Petra's exact whereabouts at the time of her husband's death spoke volumes to me. I needed to know if she could be guilty, one way or the other, and since the police didn't seem to be following that lead . . . maybe it was time they had some outside help.

I scraped back my chair, startling Toby, who dive-bombed under the desk. I picked up my purse from where I'd tossed it on the bed and reached for my car keys. "The gym's open till ten tonight," I told him. "I think it's time I checked out the possibility of signing up for Zumba lessons—what do you think?"

Toby gave me a slow blink. "Ow-orrr."

*   *   *

Twenty minutes later, attired in sweats and an old T-shirt, my hair pulled back into a ponytail, I parked my car in the parking lot of Gold's Gym. I glanced around as I walked up to the entrance. One wall was made up entirely of plate glass, and I could see the people on the different machines, exercising their little hearts out. Exercise has never been my strong suit; I've always had a thin frame, an inheritance from my mother's side of the family. Running on a tread-mill or doing reps wasn't how I liked to spend my free time, but hey, whatever floats your boat. I imagined this was how Petra kept that movie-star figure of hers. I walked inside and took a quick look around. There was a wide desk off to one side. A girl with blonde hair done up in two pigtails and wearing a tank top was behind it, slurping down what looked like some sort of pink frothy drink, probably loaded with vitamins. She glanced up as I approached and set the drink down after taking one long, loud slurp on her straw. "Good evening." Her smile was wide, revealing nice, even white teeth. "Can I help you?"

"I hope so"—I glanced at the name tag pinned to one of her tank straps—"Judy." I leaned both my elbows on the counter. "I've been a bit remiss with my exercise program, and I heard this was just the place to get back in the swing of things."

"It sure is." Judy reached beneath the counter and came up with a fistful of brochures. "We offer a wide range of group exercise classes." She held up her hand and started to tick them off on her fingers. "Pilates, Step Aerobics, Mixed Martial Arts, Yoga, Tai Chi, Core, Aqua, and Zumba—we've got it all."

I stared at the brochure. "Yes, I can see that. I have to admit, though . . . I've never been much for group exercise. I'm the type who needs to be pushed, and well, I just don't feel I get enough impetus when I'm in a group."

Her head bobbed up and down, making her pigtails shake to and fro. "I can totally understand that. You'd be surprised how many women—men too—thrive much better when it's a one-on-one experience. If you prefer, we can assign you a personal instructor." Her finger tapped against the brochure. "If you're unsure, you can sign up for a free seven-day VIP membership. Try before you buy."

"Hmm." I took the brochure, turned it over in my hand. "It's tempting, but I don't know . . ."

"Can I be of some help?"

I glanced up and into the eyes of the freckle-faced dishwater blonde who stood in front of me. She looked very trim in her black-and-pink exercise leotard and tights. Her hand shot out, gripped mine. "I'm Dorrie Cavanaugh. I work here. If you have questions, maybe I can answer them."

Ah, Dorrie Cavanaugh. I remembered Leila mentioning the judo instructor more than once. "That might be very helpful," I said.

"Great. Okay, shoot. What do you want to know?"

"Actually . . ." I took Dorrie's arm and steered her away from the reception desk. "I'm more interested in getting some information than I am in a gym membership. I'm a friend of Leila Addams."

"I know Leila. She works with my boyfriend." Dorrie crossed her arms over her chest and leaned against the wall. "What sort of information do you need? Are you working with Leila on a story?"

"In a manner of speaking," I said. "I'm helping out with the investigation into Trowbridge Littleton's death."

"Oh, that was a real shock," said Dorrie. "To his wife, too, I think."

"I understand she was here the morning he died?"

Dorrie's eyes squinched up as she thought. "She sure was. She gets here every morning at a quarter to five. Likes to ride the exercise bike before the early risers pile in. That particular day, she was scheduled for the five thirty AM Zumba class, but it was canceled, so she had to take the seven thirty one instead. I know, because I teach it."

"You do?" Wow, judo and Zumba. No wonder she was in such great shape. "Do you remember anything unusual about Mrs. Littleton that day?"

Dorrie reached up to fiddle with the end of her ponytail. "As a matter of fact, I do. My friend Rolina is the masseuse here. She told me that when the class was canceled, Mrs. Littleton came in for a massage, but she hadn't been on the table two minutes when she begged off, claiming that she had a bad stomachache. She said she was going to the bathroom. Rolina said that she'd looked pretty pale, so she went to check on her about ten minutes later—and Mrs. Littleton wasn't in the bathroom."

My heart skipped a beat. "She faked it?"

"Apparently." Dorrie shook her head. "As it happened, I went for a walk out back. There's a little garden right beside the running path, and I saw Mrs. Littleton on one of the benches. She was curled up, one leg tucked under her, yammering away on her cell phone. And—she looked pretty healthy to me. Looked pretty good when she got to class too." She cut me an eye roll. "Rich people, huh?"

"Yeah, go figure. Do you recall what time it was you saw Mrs. Littleton on her phone?"

Dorrie's lips scrunched up as she thought. "Around five thirty, I think. It could have been a few minutes later or earlier." Someone called out to her and she slapped her forehead with her palm. "Oh, I forgot I've got a consult with a new customer. Nice meeting you. If you need anything else, just give me a holler." She took off down the hall at a brisk canter.

I retraced my steps outside, my mind whirling with what I'd just learned. I was so focused that I didn't see the man cross in front of me until it was too late. I bumped into him full tilt. "Oh, I'm so sor—" I began, and then the words died in my throat as recognition kicked in. "You!" I cried. "What are you doing here?"

Chapter Eighteen

Will Worthington towered over me, looking mighty fit in a gray short-sleeved sweat shirt that emphasized his muscled arms and black running shorts that showed off his toned legs. He carried a gym bag in one hand. "Hello yourself, Syd. I was just going for my workout." His eyes narrowed and he gave me a quick once-over. "What are you doing here? Do you belong to the gym?"

I tore my gaze away from his physique and stammered, "Oh, heck no—but I guess you do?"

"I joined when I moved back." He patted his stomach. "I find sticking to a workout regimen helps keep me in shape." He set the bag down on the sidewalk and crossed his arms over his chest. "So, if you're not a member, what are you doing here?"

"I—ah—was thinking of becoming a member," I blurted. "I just came to check out some of their programs."

"Bzzt. Wrong answer. Try again."

I lowered my lashes and screwed my face into an exaggerated expression of innocence—or at least I hoped it looked that way. "What? You don't believe me?"

"Frankly, no. You always hated working out." His lips twitched upward. "Remember Scotto's gym class? All the excuses you used to make up to get out of it?"

"They worked quite well in the beginning, until someone tipped him off." I waggled my finger at him. "I still suspect you, you know."

"Me? Nah. Would I do that?"

"Absolutely."

His lips twitched slightly. "And I can always tell when you're not telling the truth. You do a funny thing with your nose."

My hand flew to my nose, and I rubbed at it. "What funny thing? I do not!"

"Yes, you do. Your eyes squinch up at the corners, and your nose wrinkles up."

Will reached out, tucked two fingers underneath my chin, and raised it so that he could look into my eyes. "You forget I remember you telling me about all those Nancy Drew books you read as a kid. How Nancy was your idol. So . . . were you investigating?"

I dug the toe of my sneaker into the concrete walk. "Will you be mad if I say yes?"

"That depends. Did you find out anything?"

"As a matter of fact, I did," I could barely contain my excitement. "I thought I'd check into Petra's alibi . . ."

"Wait." He held up a finger. "Not out here in the open. Let's go somewhere quiet where we can talk. Have you had dinner yet? We could go to DuBarry's."

My stomach gave a loud rumble as he said the word dinner. I didn't think cheese wedges and graham crackers counted. "It sounds good, but what about your workout?"

His eyes crinkled at the corners as he smiled. "I don't think skipping one session will hurt."

"In that case, okay, sure. I could go for a DuBarry burger and some sweet potato fries."

Will patted at his stomach and smacked his lips. "I can taste it now. Okay, so—my car's over there."

"So's mine," I said, starting off for it at a fast jog. "Last one there buys the beers."

*   *   *

Five minutes later, I screeched to a stop in front of DuBarry's. Will was about four seconds behind me. We both clambered out of our cars and made a beeline for the front door, reaching it at about the same time. I turned to him, laughing. "Tie!"

He grinned back. "I'll say this for you, Syd—you can still run."

I grabbed at my sides and pantomimed panting. "Not like I used to, though. It's tough, this getting old."

He snorted. "Yeah, we're the same age. Thirty-five isn't exactly over the hill."

"What's that they say? Thirty is the new twenty?"

His gaze roved over me, rather appreciatively I thought. "You look just as good today as you did in high school."

"You are such a liar."

"Everyone's entitled to their opinion. In mine, you look good."

"You—you look good too," I stammered.

He reached past me, his fingers lightly grazing my shoulder. A little shock of electricity coursed through me as he pushed the door open. "Shall we?" he asked. "I don't mind saying I could probably eat two DuBarry burgers and maybe a whole platter of fries."

"Not afraid of gaining that weight back?"

He looked at me searchingly. "There are ways to burn calories," he murmured.

I ducked my head, hoping he wouldn't see how my cheeks had started to flame, and entered the tavern foyer. DuBarry's had definitely "classed up" since the last time I'd visited. What had once been a down-home type of bar and meeting place had now become more of a bar and upscale eatery. The main room was wide open, with tables scattered all around. The bar was a shining block of mahogany wood, accentuated by droplights and a long mirror. Padded stools in gold and purple flanked it. The lighting was dimmer than I remembered but cozy. A blackboard to the left of the bar had a large variety of specials listed on it. We hadn't been standing there for more than two minutes when a young girl with long black hair, wearing a bright-red maxi dress that matched her lip gloss, sidled up to us, menus tucked under her arm. "Welcome to DuBarry's." She gave us both an appraising glance, but I noticed it lingered a fraction longer on Will. "First time?"

"First time since they've redone the place," Will said with a smile. "We've been away for a while."

Her eyes narrowed slightly, and I saw her glance down at my left hand. "Ah, so you're a couple who's come back to your roots?"

"We've come home, but we're not a couple," I blurted.

Will squeezed my arm lightly and turned his smile on the girl, whose nametag read "Doris." "We're friends," he said.

"That's nice," Doris purred, her gaze never leaving Will's face. "One can never have too many friends."

"Quite true. Tell me, do they still serve the DuBarry burger?"

"Oh yes. It's our biggest seller."

"And sweet potato fries?"

"Best in the county." Her laugh tinkled out. "I can tell you're hungry. Let me show you to a table."

Hips swinging, Doris moved off. We followed her to a corner table close to the bar. She set the menus on the table and said, "I'll send your server right over." Her eyes fastened again on Will. "If you need anything, don't hesitate to call me."

Will glanced up from the menu. "We could use two Michelobs. On tap, if it's not too much trouble."

"I'll have your server bring them right over." With another triple-wattage smile directed at Will, she moved off toward the bar.

"Wow, she wasn't too obvious, was she?" I quipped. "It was as if I didn't exist. I'm surprised she didn't pass you a card with her phone number on it."

Will picked up the menu. "Geez, Syd, like no guy's ever flirted with you before."

I tugged self-consciously on a strand of hair. "Well, yeah. But not for a long time."

We were quiet for a few minutes, studying the menu. A tall girl with red hair and freckles whose name tag read "Polly" came over, carrying a tray on which rested two frosty mugs of Michelob. "Good evening," she said. She set a mug in front of each of us. "I'm Polly, and I'll be your server tonight. Would you like to hear the specials?"

Will smiled up at her. "Oh, I don't think that's necessary, is it Syd?"

I shook my head and held the menu out. "I'll have a DuBarry burger, medium-rare, extra cheddar, no onion, and a side order of sweet potato fries."

"Make that two, only I want my burger well done."

Polly scribbled the order down, tucked the empty tray under one arm, grabbed our menus, and hurried off to the kitchen. Once she was out of earshot, Will leaned back in his seat and tented his fingers beneath his chin.

"Okay, Syd. Time to fess up. You were at the gym checking out Petra's alibi?"

I gave a careful glance around, then leaned in closer to Will. In a low tone, I said, "Petra was there that morning. She was supposed to take the five thirty Zumba class, but it was canceled, so she took the seven thirty one instead."

Will frowned. "Yeah, we know that. Petra told us that when she gave her statement."

"How did she account for her time between five thirty AM and seven thirty?"

Will grimaced. "That's where Bennington got a little rough with her, and she clammed up. Said she didn't have to give us any more information unless we were charging her with something, and she'd be sure to have her lawyer present—why are you grinning?"

"No reason. That just sounds like her. Kat and I had a nice little chat with her as well. She stopped by the diner to tell everyone that now that she's in control of Littleton's money, she's not planning on raising the rents."

"That's good news, right?"

"Yeah, for the stores. The shelter's not out of danger yet—but that's another story." I leaned forward. "It doesn't surprise me she clammed up around Bennington. He's got the personality of a wet dishrag. On second thought, scratch that. A dishrag's got more pizzazz." I tapped my finger impatiently on the table. "You should get a statement from Dorrie Cavanaugh. She claims that she saw Petra Littleton in back of the gym around the time Littleton was killed. She feigned a stomachache to go outside and make a phone call."

Will's eyes slitted. "Did Dorrie mention a time?"

"She wasn't certain, but she believes it was somewhere around five thirty. She was with the masseuse shortly before that. So . . ." I sat back in my chair. "It doesn't look as if she could have done it."

Will drummed his fingers on the tabletop. "Probably not. Of course, the gym is close to the gallery, and she's in good shape, but . . . we can get the phone records. If she was talking on her phone anywhere between five and six AM, she's in the clear." He lifted his head and grinned at me. "Well, what do you know? You're pretty helpful after all, Syd."

"Thanks—I think." I let out a sigh. "I haven't done myself any favors by eliminating Petra. It will move Kat further up the list, am I right?"

He reached across the table and grabbed both my hands in his. "Remember what I said, Syd. I won't let Kat be railroaded for something she didn't do."

I didn't pull my hands away but rather leaned over a bit closer. "What about Trey? He owed his stepfather a huge debt. Are you absolutely certain he couldn't have done it?"

Will released my hands and reached into his pocket. He pulled out his cell. "100 percent. See?" He fiddled with the phone and then passed it over to me. I looked at the screen. On it was a photograph of Trey Devine, standing on what appeared to be a golf course, surrounded by a group of men. The time and date stamp read six AM on the morning of the murder.

"And before you ask, we checked out the photo. It hasn't been tampered with."

"Great," I murmured. "We're running out of suspects. Maybe Littleton named someone in that diary of his. Any luck with finding it?"

"Unfortunately, no. We went through that office with a fine-tooth comb, too. It's either very well hidden, or . . ."

"Or Littleton's killer took it," I finished. I slumped back in my seat and crossed my arms over my chest. "We should never have sold our house," I muttered.

He stared at me. "Why do you say that?"

"Because if we hadn't, Kat would probably still be living there, and I'd have moved in with her instead of Leila. Then I could have given her an alibi for the morning of Littleton's death."

He reached out and grasped my hand. "You told me that you didn't want Kat around when you saw Littleton. That's why you left so early. Think about it. If you'd been living with Kat, you'd have done the same thing, and you'd never have known if she was still in her room or not."

I scowled. I didn't want to admit he was right.

He touched my hand lightly. "Can you trust me to take care of this and watch out for you and Kat? Please?"

I was spared answering because Polly appeared just then, carrying a tray on which rested two fantastic-smelling burgers and a platter heaped with golden-brown sweet potato fries. "Who's got the medium rare?" she asked with a big smile.

I raised my hand, and she set the plate in front of me. The burger looked extremely delicious, but my ravenous appetite had vanished. I picked it up and took a bite. The ground beef, expertly seasoned, tasted like sawdust in my mouth.

There was a third party involved in Littleton's death—I was certain of it. And unless I could figure out who that was, and soon, I had a feeling my sister would soon be wearing an orange jumpsuit—and orange is so not her color.

Chapter Nineteen

It was a little before eleven PM when I finally pulled into my driveway. I let myself in the front door, switched on the table lamp, and flopped down on the sofa. I leaned my head back against the cushions. My head was pounding, mostly from frustration. For every two steps I thought I took forward, I ended up three steps behind.

I felt something soft brush against my ankles, and I looked down to see two bright-green eyes gazing back at me. Toby's head was cocked, and his tail twitched behind him. He reached up and put his paw on my knee—his way, no doubt, of asking, *rough night?*

"You have no idea." I reached down and gave him a scratch behind his ears. He immediately rolled over on his back, four paws in the air. I leaned over and trailed my fingers up and down his belly. He squinched his eyes closed and purred softly. "It doesn't take much to make you happy, does it?" I asked softly. "Humans should be as easily satisfied."

He opened one eye as if to say, *You betcha.*

I petted him for a few more minutes, and then I rose and stretched. Toby eased one eye open and looked at me.

"Time for bed, Toby," I said. "Although to be honest, I don't feel sleepy."

I walked down the hall and into my bedroom, Toby close behind me. I stripped off my sweats, crawled into my pj's, and hurried into the bathroom to brush my teeth and splash some water on my face before returning to the bedroom. Toby was nowhere to be seen, but a second later I spotted him, curled up in a ball underneath my desk. I pulled the chair out and eased myself into it, then cast an eye at the whiteboard propped up across from me.

"Well, I've all but cleared Petra," I announced. "And as for Trey and Colin, well, they've both got solid alibis and eyewitnesses. Someone else is involved here—but who could it be?"

I heard a slight rustling sound underneath my desk, and I bent over to look. Toby was lying on his side, his paws curled around a slip of yellow paper. I recognized it immediately. It was the note from the crime scene. I'd stashed it in my desk drawer, but apparently that hadn't stopped Toby from somehow pilfering it.

"Hey, buddy," I said. "What have you got there?"

Toby lifted his head, cocked it, and pressed his treasure closer to his chest.

I pointed to the scrap of paper he held tightly in his claws. "Hey, Tobes. How about you give that back to me?"

I reached toward the paper, but Toby wriggled back, his claws digging more tightly into his prize. "Ow-owrr?"

Hmm, looked as if a trade might be in order. I opened the middle drawer of my desk and whipped out the small bag of cat treats I'd stashed inside. I shook a few out into my palm and bent toward Toby once again. I extended my hand, just close enough to his face so he could smell the liver-and-chicken treats.

"How about a trade?" I said in a coaxing tone. "These treats for your prize?"

Toby's eyes narrowed, and his ears flicked, as if he were trying to decide. In the end, liver and chicken won out over paper. He released the scrap and nudged his nose into my palm. I set the treats down on the rug near the bed, and he trotted happily over to them while I dived under the desk to retrieve the soggy slip of paper. I held it gingerly by its edges. It looked as if it would crumble into dust at any second.

Toby glanced up from his nosh to look at me.

"You led me to this, didn't you," I murmured. "You must have had some reason. This is a clue, isn't it? A clue to the identity of Littleton's killer?"

Toby looked at me, blinked again, and then returned to scarfing down his treat.

I turned back to the paper and looked at it. Toby had certainly had fun with it; the paper was torn almost halfway down the middle. I picked it up, and the paper split into two pieces. I bent to snatch them up and laid them side by side on the desk. One piece said Kahn, the other Lee.

"Ow-owrr," said Toby.

"Yes, thank you, now I've got two pieces . . ." I stopped as a sudden thought occurred to me. I pulled my laptop over and turned it on. When Leila had typed Kahn Lee into the search engine, she'd gotten over nine hundred thousand results. But . . . what if it wasn't one person's name but two separate names? I called up Google and typed in "Kahn" and hit Enter.

Over forty-four million hits. Great. Obviously some narrowing down—check that, a great deal of narrowing down—had to be done. I typed in "Kahn—North Carolina—art gallery" and then hit Enter again. Most of the hits were for a sculptor, Ian Kahn, who had a studio in Winston-Salem. I clicked on his main website and read the bio. Kahn was reputed to be one of the leading sculptors in the world, his specialty being porcelain. His works were featured in over forty international museums, including the Metropolitan Museum of Art in New York City and the Vatican Museum. I clicked on the tab that said "Gallery" and spent several minutes looking at photographs of some of his works, which were undeniably beautiful. One of an Indian woman kneeling before a waterfall in a rock was especially beautiful, with its tones of amber and green. He specialized in porcelain works, but there were a few glass ones as well, some statues and paperweights. Precious few photos of those, though.

A bit farther down the page was a link for the North Carolina Arts Council. I clicked on that and got a listing of everything you wanted to know about the arts in North

Carolina but were afraid to ask. There were groupings of various arts councils, galleries, and individual artists. I scrolled down the listing slowly. Some of the larger galleries I was familiar with, but there were a ton of small ones I'd never heard of. The Brush and Canvas was listed in the middle of the pack, naming both Trowbridge Littleton and Colin Murphy as "Managing Directors." I scrolled down a few more, hoping that something would just jump out at me—and then one did.

Chatsworth Studios
Aamir Lee
Artist
130 N Chatham Ave
Prady, NC
chatsworthstudios.com

Hmm. Prady was a small town known primarily for being an artists' community, about five minutes away from Winston-Salem. Coincidence? Or something more? I peered again at the paper. There was a slightly curved mark after Lee—I'd initially thought it might just have been a careless mark, but it could be a *C*. *C* for Chatsworth Studios?

I sighed. "I'm grabbing at straws, right? But . . . I can't help but feel there might be something there. I think the first thing I should do tomorrow is get over to The Brush and Canvas, see if they know anything about either Ian Kahn or this Aamir Lee, or if they've heard of the Chatsworth

Studios and then take it from there." I glanced down at Toby. "What do you think?"

Toby looked at me solemnly. "Yowl," he said.

I smiled. "I'm glad we agree."

*   *   *

"Okay, so . . . tell me again what we're supposed to be doing here?"

It was lunchtime, and I'd talked Leila into meeting me in front of The Brush and Canvas for, as I had put it, some undercover work. I had also, of course, brought bribery: Kona-blend cappuccinos for both of us and one of Dayna's delicious caramel scones for Leila. I sipped my coffee as Leila bit hungrily into the scone.

"I'm on a fishing expedition, and I thought it might be easier to find out the information if you did it on the pretext of writing an article."

Leila eyed me over the rim of her Styrofoam cup. "You did, huh? What sort of article?"

"I don't know . . . a tribute to Littleton and his contributions to the Deer Park community? After all, this is your bailiwick, not mine." I motioned to the camera I had slung around my neck. "I'm just your humble assistant, after all."

She shook her head. "An article on Littleton is actually not a half-bad idea. I'm on freelance this week, and I need something to turn in. Am I supposed to be asking about anything in particular?"

"The types of exhibits, the artists, if there are any North Carolina artists featured, you know . . . like that."

Leila's eyes narrowed. "Uh-huh. Am I supposed to be asking about any North Carolina artist in particular?"

I chuckled. "That would be too obvious. But asking if they've ever featured sculptors wouldn't be a bad idea."

Leila finished her scone, wiped her fingers on a napkin, and then we entered the gallery. I'd never been in the showroom before, so I took a minute to just survey my surroundings. Colorful paintings of all types hung on the walls, along with some framed black-and-white photos. There were pinpoint spotlights set into the ceiling at different vantage points to ensure the artwork took center stage. White Formica blocks showcased bronze sculptures and a few pieces of ceramic art. A few glass pieces were scattered about, but I didn't see any porcelain, Kahn's preferred medium, anywhere. Over against the far wall sat a large wooden counter that looked to double as a desk. A young man sat behind it, twirling a pencil between his fingers. Kevin "Trey" Devine looked more bored than anything else. His head was bent, studying some sort of ledger, but as we approached, he snapped it shut, rose from his chair, and extended a hand.

"Welcome to The Brush and Canvas," he said. "Are you ladies looking for anything in particular?"

Leila reached into her tote and removed her press ID. Trey's expression, formerly friendly, now morphed into one of puzzlement. "You're a reporter?"

"Yes. I'd hoped to speak with either Mrs. Littleton or Mr. Colin Murphy, if either of them is around."

"My mother is in Durham visiting my aunt, and Mr. Murphy is in South Carolina on a buying trip."

"I see. So you must be Petra Littleton's son?"

"Yes. Kevin Devine, but most everyone calls me Trey." The frown deepened, cutting a sharp *V* in the middle of his smooth forehead. "Why exactly did you want to speak with them?"

"I'm doing an article on Trowbridge Littleton's contribution to the Deer Park business community," Leila said with a wide smile. "So of course we want to focus on the gallery. I take it you're in charge while they're away?"

"For the moment," he said, not without a trace of bitterness. "I imagine that will change shortly, though. You are aware that Mr. Murphy is in full charge now?"

Leila nodded. "We'd heard something along those lines. Does that mean you won't be staying on?"

He cleared his throat. "When my stepfather ran the gallery, I had a good reason for working here. That died along with him, and frankly this sort of work isn't my cup of tea, although I admit it hasn't been half as bad as I thought it would be. To tell the truth, I ended up enjoying it."

"Of course, and why wouldn't you?" Leila spread her arms wide. "Look at all this beautiful art! I can't imagine a more perfect job than to be surrounded by this beauty all day."

Trey glanced around, and his nose wrinkled slightly. "I used to think my stepfather had a cakewalk here, but I'm finding out that this business isn't as easy as it looks. It's a tricky thing to come up with just the right artists to showcase as well as the perfect blend of pieces. My stepfather tried to appeal to several different markets, as you can tell. There's something to appeal to the true connoisseur as well as the person on a budget—you know, the one who just wants something nice to hang over their sofa."

"Like us," Leila laughed.

"Exactly. My stepfather had many contacts in the art world. There are some beautiful pieces on display here and for sale. They appeal to every budget, every type of taste. For example . . ." He pointed toward a painting on a far wall that to me just looked like blobs of color all mashed together. "That's an Engledrumm. He's a new Impressionist painter who's been taking the art world by storm. Some of his paintings sell upwards of two hundred thousand."

We both let out a collective gasp. "Two hundred *thousand dollars*?" I asked.

"Oh yes. I saw one go for almost a million once at an auction."

I decided that an Engledrumm was definitely out of my price range. I raised the camera, snapped a picture of it. "I don't suppose you have anything more moderately priced?"

"Not of his. But we do carry some landscapes by North Carolina painters just starting out that are quite good and sell for far less." He pointed to one of a waterfall carved into a rock, with two eagles soaring overhead. "That was done by Nancy Lampman. She operates out of a small studio in Raleigh, and she's quite good. You can get that one for one hundred fifty."

I dutifully snapped a photo while Trey described some other paintings. When he paused for a breath, I asked, "I understand that the gallery also showcases sculptures?"

He nodded. "Oh yes, we have quite a few." He pointed to a small pedestal on which stood a bust of a woman. "That's a likeness of Diana, goddess of the hunt. It was done by Milo Titzman. He's another local artist, out of Durham." He walked over and tapped a finger against Diana's nose. "Black marble, very durable."

"You sound so knowledgeable," I remarked. "I can't believe you wouldn't want to make a career out of this."

"I might have, if circumstances were different," he murmured. He glanced around. The only other customer in the shop was an elderly woman at the far end, so he leaned into us and said in a low tone, "Off the record? I believe Mr. Murphy is going to close up the gallery shortly. He's expressed a definite interest in moving on."

Leila and I exchanged a quick glance, and I looked at Trey with what I hoped came off as wide-eyed astonishment. "You're kidding! I thought he loved this place."

Trey shrugged. "He used to, and then he and my step-father got to arguing. I guess it stopped being fun for Colin, and the gallery must hold bad memories for him. He wants to make a fresh start."

"I had no idea." I leaned my elbow on the counter and propped my chin in my hand. "What on earth did they argue about?"

He gave another swift glance around before answering. "You didn't hear this from me, but . . . Colin managed to connect with a famous artist—a really famous one—and got exclusive commissions."

"And that annoyed your stepfather?"

"Not at first."

He waggled his finger, indicating we were to follow him. We walked over to a small case covered with a black sheet. Trey lifted the covering, and we both gasped. Inside was a beautiful sculpture of an Indian woman kneeling in front of a waterfall. It was so lifelike, you could almost hear the water running, and I recognized it instantly. I looked at Trey. "It—is this a Kahn sculpture?"

He fairly beamed with pride. "Yes, it is. One of several sculptures we obtained the exclusive rights to show and sell, right before Kahn's untimely death."

Now we were getting somewhere! I leaned in for a closer look. The sculpture certainly was exquisite. I raised the camera and took a picture. "Are you certain it's a genuine Kahn?"

"Oh yes. There aren't many artists who could duplicate that lifelike style. And besides . . ." He pointed to the sculpture. "See that small mark there?"

We both leaned in and squinted. The mark he indicated was barely visible. "Looks like an inverted K," I said.

"That's Kahn's signature. We wouldn't touch it unless it was genuine."

"I see." I glanced around the room. "There are others, you say?"

"We had three in all. Two have been sold. I believe a few more might be coming in, but I don't have all the details."

My heart was hammering so loudly, I was certain it could be heard back in New York. "Is this what your stepfather and Colin Murphy argued over? Selling Kahn's artwork?"

He nodded. "I'm not quite sure what set Bridge off, but he came in one day and he was livid. Made me take all the Kahns and put them in the storeroom. Of course, once he passed, Murphy made me drag 'em out again."

"What a shame." I glanced around. "What about an artist named Lee? Do you carry any of his works?"

He pointed to a small framed painting on the far wall. "I do have an Annie Lee. She does animals and still life."

"Actually, I meant Aamir Lee. He's a relatively new artist, out of Prady. The Chatsworth Studios, I believe."

"Definitely nothing by Aamir Lee." He tapped his chin with his finger. "That studio name seems familiar. Just one second."

He moved off toward the desk, and Leila and I followed. There was a ledger open, and he was running his finger down a list. "Ah, here it is," he cried. "Chatsworth Studios. Veronica Martin, proprietor. I think perhaps either my stepfather or Colin might have dealt with this place, but as to what they picked up, I couldn't say. If you'd like to leave your name and number, I can check with Colin when he returns." He pushed a pad and a pen toward me. I scribbled quickly on it and pushed it back, then looked over at Leila. "Are we done here?"

"Oh yes," Leila said brightly. "I think I've gotten everything I need."

"Excellent," Trey said with a wide smile. "When will this article appear? I'd like to tell my mother about it."

"I'll write it up when I get back to the office, and once my editor schedules a date, I'll let you know," she said. She glanced at her watch. "Sorry, we've got to run. It was a pleasure."

"Same here. Come back anytime."

Once we were out on the street, I turned to my friend. "What are you doing tomorrow?"

"I'm supposed to be off." Her eyes narrowed. "Why?"

"Oh, nothing much. Maybe a little field trip to Prady."

"Actually, that doesn't sound half bad. I wouldn't mind checking out some of those craft shops there. One of the girls in the office got a beautiful hand-painted scarf that's just divine." She shifted her tote bag on her arm. "What did you think of Junior?"

"He wasn't as bad as I thought he'd be," I confessed. "But I'm still not completely ruling him out, in spite of his alibi."

"Then why'd you leave your name and number with him?"

I gave her a wide smile. "I didn't. I wrote down Mildred Hanratty's. She never wears her hearing aid, so if he calls, she won't understand a word he says anyway."

Chapter Twenty

I was walking down a street, shrouded in fog. In one hand I held a glass paperweight, in the other, the note that I'd found in Littleton's office—or rather the note that Toby had found. Suddenly, a dark figure in a cape jumped out at me from the mist—Trey Littleton! He loomed before me, then threw back his head and let out a loud laugh.

"Hah—you'll never pin that murder on me. I've got a good alibi. I was out on the golf course with dozens of witnesses."

"Nor me." A slim figure came at me from the left—Petra, dressed in a blood-red dress with a matching cape that swirled around her ankles. She pointed a finger at me. "I was on the phone when my husband was killed. I'm totally innocent."

"And I wasn't in the area either." I whirled around to face Colin Murphy. The edge of one lip curled sardonically. "Best alibi in the world—in an airplane, twenty thousand feet above the ground. Virtually impossible for me to kill him."

"Or me," said Trey.

"Or me," chimed in Petra. Then they all joined hands and chorused, "But it's not impossible for a third party to have killed Bridge. Not at all."

Trey suddenly turned toward me and stared right into my eyes. "But try to prove it," he whispered. Then he leaned over, stuck out his tongue, and licked my cheek!

"What the . . . ?" My eyes flew open, and I stared right into Toby's green eyes.

"Merow," he said. Then his tongue darted out and scraped across the bottom of my chin.

I reached up to pet him on the head. "You rascal. Thank God that was only a dream—or should I say nightmare?" But one fact I definitely agreed with. It would certainly have been possible for a third person to have killed Littleton. But how to find that out?

I propped myself up on one elbow and looked at Toby.

I tapped at my gut. "There's some connection between Kahn and that artist Lee from the Chatsworth Studios—I feel it right here."

Toby cocked his head and blinked.

I laughed and pulled him onto my lap. I rubbed him behind his ears. "Well, today I've got the day off, so Leila and I are going to Prady to do a little digging. I'm not exactly sure what we're digging for, but maybe we'll get to the bottom of everything—wouldn't that be great! It would certainly take that Bennington down a peg—and show Will just how helpful I can be at the same time, right?"

Toby sat up and gave his head a vigorous shake.

I ran a hand through my hair. "I just feel like there's something I'm missing, some little detail that will help me put these puzzle pieces together. I'm hoping that this little field trip might clear my muddled brain."

My cell jangled, and we both jumped. Toby teetered on my lap like a leaf in a windstorm and dug his claws into my comforter. I placed one hand on his back to steady him, reached for my phone, and glanced at the caller ID. "Relax, it's Leila," I told the cat. "She said she'd call this morning to let me know what time to pick her up."

"I am so sorry," Leila said after we'd exchanged good-mornings. "I can't take that half day. Janet Harkinson called in sick, so my editor wants me to cover the luncheon event at the Archaeological Association."

"Really? I didn't know Deer Park had an Archaeological Association?"

"We don't. It's in Morganton." She let out a long, drawn-out sigh. "That means I have a lovely three-hour drive up and back with Jim Wantrobski to look forward to."

"Wantrobski, huh? The guy from the funeral service who was giving you the goo-goo eyes?"

"Stop, he wasn't giving me goo-goo or any other kind of eyes. He's going along as photographer."

"Well, isn't he the talented fellow?" I chuckled. "I bet he didn't protest this assignment too much."

"Of course not, since he's the one who suggested my name as substitute. And before you say a word, it's because he knows I'm a damn good reporter."

I winked at Toby. "Sure it is."

"I'll gloss over that remark. Anyway, if you want to wait until tomorrow, I can take a half day for sure."

"No. I don't want to wait. I'll be fine going by myself."

"You're so impatient, Nancy Drew. Oh, wait, I almost forgot. Just for kicks, I asked our arts editor if he'd ever heard of that Ian Kahn fellow. Turns out he has. He was surprised, though, to hear that The Brush and Canvas had gotten hold of some of his sculptures."

"He was? Why?"

"He was under the impression that all the uncommissioned pieces of Kahn's were handled through his own gallery in Winston-Salem. He wasn't 100 percent certain, of course, but as long as you're headed there, it's worth checking out."

"It sure is. I might only charge you half a pizza and one bottle of wine now for bugging out on me. Oh, and my best to Jim."

"Smarty-pants."

I hung up the phone and looked at Toby. "It's a sign," I said.

Toby looked at me, then at my phone, then back to me and raised a paw. "Ow-owr."

"Okay, okay. You're right. I don't believe in signs. But if I did . . . this would be a good one."

*   *   *

Two hours later, I was on my way to Prady. Toby had whined and meowed when he saw me put the picnic basket into the back seat of the Jeep, but I'd given him a treat and told him he'd be much more comfortable waiting for me at home. I called Kat at the shelter to check in; she informed me that Petra had made good on her promise to stop by. They'd given her the royal tour and shown her all the puppies available for adoption. Petra had immediately bonded with Jonesy, a rescued bichon frise. "I waived all the paperwork, of course," Kat added. "Petra sailed out of here a happy camper with Jonesy snuggled in her arms." She let out a sigh. "I just hope that her favorable experience here might help to tip the scales in the shelter's favor."

"I hope so too," I said, thinking if today went the way I hoped, everything would be rosy and peachy-keen once again.

I made the turn off of I-40 onto NC-86. Twenty minutes later, I turned off at the exit for Prady. Another fifteen minutes and I was in the heart of the small town, the shopping district. I programmed North Chatham Avenue into my GPS, and a few minutes later, I eased my car into a parking spot in front of what looked to be a rather quaint gift shop. I parked and went to peer in the window and ultimately could not resist going inside. The proprietor, a slender young woman with pink-tinted hair wearing a multicolored caftan, gave me a big smile as I came inside.

"Good morning," she called out in a singsong voice. "I'm Emmie Bowden. Your first visit to the Eclectic Butterfly?"

"My first visit to Prady in general," I admitted. "I recently relocated to this area from New York. I'm—ah—a big art lover, and I heard that Prady is the place for young artists."

"That we are." Her head bobbed up and down, and her gelled pink spikes swayed slightly. She plucked at her caftan. "These are made by a young lady, Hilary Anderson. She tie-dyes the materials herself—all her own designs." She made a wide sweep with her arm. "And my shelves are full of ceramics and figurines and jewelry made by local artisans. Got a big selection here."

I paused to finger a gaily painted ceramic elephant. "I'm interested in sculpture—glass, primarily."

Emmie frowned. "You mean like paperweights?" She motioned toward a glass case. "I've got lots of nice ones—some with flowers inside, others have etchings of animals. Here's a nice one." She reached into the case and pulled out a lavender-tinted sphere with a butterfly etched on it. "Only seventy dollars. A bargain."

"It is lovely, but I'm interested in work by two particular artists. Aamir Lee or Ian Kahn?"

Emmie let out a low whistle. "Kahn, huh? Sorry, you won't find anything by him here. The commission on one sale of his alone would pay my rent for a year. Who was the other artist again?"

"Aamir Lee?"

Emmie's brows drew together, making a wrinkle in the middle of her forehead. "I'm not familiar with that name. What medium does he work in?"

"Truthfully? I'm not sure. Glass or porcelain, I think."

"Hmm. Well then, I suggest you try the Chatsworth Studios. They're just up the block. They deal with all the up-and-coming artists around here—if anyone knows, it's them."

"Thanks." And then, partly because I felt guilty for picking her brain and partly because I really liked it, I purchased a silver butterfly on a matching chain. Leila's birthday was coming up, and I figured she'd love it. After a slight deliberation, I purchased a silver ladybug necklace for myself. After all, ladybugs were good luck symbols, right? And I could sure use some of that now. I clasped the chain around my neck, stowed Leila's gift in my trunk, and headed in the direction of Chatsworth Studios. It was located two blocks down, in an old yellow brick edifice enhanced with dark-magenta awnings and wrought-iron décor. There was a wood-carved sign on the door that read,

Chatsworth Studios
Open 9–7 Sunday through Tuesday
Open 9–8 Thursday through Saturday
Private Showings by Appointment Only

And then below, in much smaller lettering: *closed Wednesdays.*

And today was Wednesday! Drat!

I fingered the charm around my neck. So much for my "sign" and for ladybugs being portents of good luck. My stomach rumbled, but I was hardly in the mood for the crisp watermelon salad and cream cheese on date-nut bread I'd made and stowed away in my picnic basket. After my long drive and my disappointment (although it was my own fault—if I'd been a really good detective, I'd have called ahead), I craved something much more substantial.

I looked around and saw a sign diagonally across that read: "The Pulled Pork."

"Sounds perfect," I muttered, making my way across the street. The fragrant aroma of pork mixed with heady barbecue sauce hit me the moment I walked in the door. A young boy in jeans and a plaid short-sleeved shirt, white apron knotted loosely around his waist, hurried up to me.

"Table or to go?" he asked.

I glanced around. A few tables were filled, and the patrons at them were eating hungrily. My stomach rumbled again. "Table," I said. He led me over to one in front of the large picture window and handed me a laminated menu. "The lunch special's the best deal," he said, inclining his head toward the blackboard. "It comes with your choice of cola or sweet tea."

I glanced at the blackboard, whose sign proclaimed: "Today's Special: *Pulled pork or pulled chicken on a kaiser roll, sweet potato fries, and coleslaw—jes' like yer momma used to make.*"

"Sounds good," I said. "I'll have the pulled pork with sweet tea, please. Oh, and you can hold the coleslaw?"

He scribbled my order down on a pad. "No problem. Would you like to substitute potato or macaroni salad for the slaw instead?"

"Macaroni salad, please."

He smiled and withdrew, returning in a few seconds with a large glass of sweet tea, which he set in front of me. "Your order will be out in a few minutes." He eased one hip against the edge of the table. "You a tourist?"

I shook my head. "Oh, no. I live over in Deer Park."

His eyebrow shot up. "Whatcha doing out here?" As fast as the question came off his lips, he answered it. "Wait, don't tell me. You must be interested in art."

"Yes. I came out hoping to have a look at the Chatsworth Studios. I didn't realize they were closed today."

"Oh, Chatsworth, eh?" He seemed impressed. "Any artist in particular? They represent quite a few good ones and some new up-and-coming ones, too."

"Mm-hm. I was hoping to find something by Ian Kahn."

"Oh-ho, a Kahn fan, eh? Good luck with that," he laughed.

"How about Aamir Lee. Have you heard of him?"

The woman at the opposite table said, "Her."

I swung my gaze to the woman. "It's a woman? The notice said Aamir, so I assumed . . ."

The woman licked barbecue from her fingers and smiled. "That name gets misprinted all the time. It's Aamira."

"I stand corrected," I said. "She's a sculptor, correct? Or does she work in other mediums?"

"An occasional painting, but mainly the sculptures—brass, plaster, bronze cast, glass." She cocked her head at me. "You don't seem to know too much about her."

I held up both hands. "Guilty," I admitted. "I'm just starting to build a collection, and I've heard good things about Aamira Lee. I heard that Chatsworth Studios show-cases her work, and I was hoping to take a look—maybe invest in a piece."

"Hmm. Well, I don't usually make a practice of opening on Wednesday, but I'm also a firm believer in fostering a newbie's art appreciation. So I'm going to make an exception." She held out her hand. "Today's your lucky day, Ms.—"

"You can call me Sydney."

"Okay, Sydney. I'm Veronica Martin, the owner of Chatsworth Studios. Once you finish your barbecue, I'll take you over to the studio. Give you a private showing. Sound good?"

My hand reached up and fingered the ladybug around my neck. "I'd appreciate that, Ms. Martin. I'd appreciate that very much."

*   *   *

I finished my barbecue, paid my bill, and then Veronica Martin and I walked back over to the gallery. Veronica fiddled with the alarm keypad and then unlocked the door and switched on the lights. The Chatsworth Studios had a similar setup to The Brush and Canvas. Beautiful paintings of all shapes and sizes dotted the cream-colored walls, and large Formica blocks in various colors showcased sculptures done in a variety of mediums.

I turned to Veronica. "This is a lovely gallery."

"Thanks." She gave a swift glance around the studio. "I won't lie—this place could use a bit of an overhaul, though. We've been around a long time." She dug her toe into the beige shag carpeting. "This carpet has seen better days. I'd love to replace it with something in a soft mauve, but thick shag carpeting is through the roof . . . oh well. Someday."

She inclined her head toward the far wall. "You were interested in Aamira Lee? That's one of her latest, over there."

I walked over to the painting Veronica indicated. It was a portrait of a young mother with two small children. The colors were so vivid and the faces so lifelike, I half expected to hear the woman speak or the children giggle. "Beautiful," I murmured. "She's very talented."

Veronica gave me a wide smile. "You haven't seen anything yet. Follow me."

I followed Veronica down a short hallway and through a curtained alcove into an even bigger room. Sculptures were everywhere—on the floor, on large ceramic blocks, on low glass counters, lit by soft overhead lights. She led me across the room to a small area cordoned off by a beautiful Chinese-style floor screen. I couldn't help but admire the sculpture of two geisha girls that stood on a low table just to the screen's left.

"Wow. Aamira Lee?"

"Yep. But the real beauty lies behind the screen."

Veronica motioned for me to follow her. I stepped behind the screen, and my breath caught in my throat. On different ceramic blocks and low tables rested every type of glass sculpture imaginable. Birds, dogs, cats, trees, flowers, people in various poses, all done in vibrant colors. Off to the far left was another table full of beautiful colored glass spheres. The overhead lights made them twinkle like so many jewels.

"Wow!" was all I could say. "She did all these?"

Veronica nodded. "Beautiful, no? Mark my words, she's going to be famous someday. You'd be smart to get in on the ground floor—pick up something while it's relatively cheap as an investment piece." She picked up a small statue of a hummingbird poised over a flower. "This is a relatively inexpensive one—two hundred."

"It's beautiful." I leaned in closer to examine it. Near the base was a mark that looked like a tiny inverted comma—like the mark that had been on the note Toby had found. I pointed at it. "What's that?"

"Her signature. That's how you know you have a genuine Lee."

"So you really think she's going to be famous? As famous as Ian Kahn?"

"No one's that famous—except maybe Michelangelo or van Gogh," laughed Veronica. "It's a pity about that accident—Kahn had a bright future in front of him."

"You don't have any of his pieces?"

She shook her head. "If only. No, he's handled exclusively at his own gallery, as far as I know."

"I imagine that you work with dealers from other galleries, right? Or auction houses?" I reached into my shoulder bag and pulled out the photo of Littleton I'd clipped from the paper. "Have you ever seen him?"

Veronica frowned at the picture. "He does look familiar, but I can't quite place him . . ."

At that moment, the bell above the door tinkled, and a few minutes later, a tall, thin man dressed in black jeans and a black T-shirt poked his head inside the room. "Ronnie! I thought I saw a light on. Why is the gallery open?"

"Prospective buyer. I couldn't resist." Veronica jerked her thumb in my direction. "This is my brother, Ronald Martin." She grinned at my puzzled look. "Our parents were overly fond of the name."

"They called us both Ronnie—it got very confusing after a bit." Ronald chuckled. "Folks around here refer to us as the Ronnies instead of the Martins."

Veronica smiled at her brother. "Sydney here is from Deer Park. She's interested in acquiring something by Aamira Lee."

"You are?" He leaned in closer to me. "Good choice. Aamira's one of our best. She's going to be famous someday—and us too for discovering her." Ronnie's joyful expression sobered. "If she can get her head out of the clouds, that is."

"Now Ronnie," Veronica chided her brother. She turned to me. "Aamira's work is getting noticed, and she's after having her head turned by some folks, but . . . in the end she'll come around. She'll realize she should stay loyal to the ones who discovered her in the first place." Veronica waved Littleton's photo under her brother's nose. "He look familiar to you?"

Ron leaned over, peered at the picture. "Oh yeah, I remember him. He was here a few weeks ago. Odd duck, but he knows his art." He glanced over at me. "Friend of yours?"

"Of sorts," I said carefully. "You said he was in here?"

"Yes, about two weeks ago. He was interested in a new painter of ours—Hayley Plumm. She does very avant-garde paintings. He wanted to discuss a possible joint showing." His hand reached up and rubbed absently at the back of his neck. "He sure forgot about that fast enough once he saw . . ." Ronald stopped and snapped his fingers. "Maybe it's better to just show you."

Ronnie vanished, returning in a few moments with a piece he set down on top of a glass case. I inhaled my breath sharply. The beautiful amber-and-green piece depicting a waterfall was an exact replica of the one by Ian Kahn I'd seen at The Brush and Canvas!

I looked at both of them sharply. "I thought you said you didn't carry Kahns?"

Veronica drew herself up. "We don't. This piece was done by Aamira Lee." She cocked her head at me. "Why did you think it was a Kahn?"

"I saw something similar to this in another gallery recently," I said carefully. "The manager said it was a Kahn." I pointed at the sculpture. "Trust me, this could be its twin."

Veronica frowned. "Hmm. Maybe that explains it. Your friend seemed to get a bit agitated when we told him that piece was the work of a local artist. He wanted—no, demanded—to know more about her. He got quite annoyed when we told him we have a strict 'no information' policy on the artists who are on exclusive contract with us. And when I mentioned that he was the second person to come in within the last three months to inquire about her work, well, he got so red in the face, I thought he might have a stroke in front of me."

My head snapped up. "The second? Who was the first?"

"A woman. She was in here, oh, about two months ago and saw another piece Aamira had made, and she was quite taken with it. She wanted us to give out Aamira's address as well, but we told her the same thing."

"I see. Do you still have the piece that the woman was interested in?"

"No, she purchased it. But there's a similar one, right here." Veronica pointed to a low table in the corner. The paperweight was indeed ornate, and it depicted a silvery moon over a small town against a midnight-blue sky. The town buildings looked so lifelike, I half expected someone to exit one of them any second. As I stared at the paperweight, that niggling feeling came over me again. I'd seen this piece somewhere before—where?

I tore my gaze away from the glass piece and asked, "Did this woman leave her name?"

"No. When we refused to give out any information about the artist, she stormed out. She hasn't been back since, thank God." Veronica waved her hand in front of her face. "We don't need her type around here."

"I don't suppose you could describe her?"

Veronica's mouth puckered as she thought. "About five-seven, dark hair, in her fifties but well preserved—you know, the type that looks forty? She had on a black pantsuit with a teal blouse. Oh—and a Dooney and Bourke handbag. I never forget a Dooney and Bourke." She paused. "And a killer ring on her pinky finger. I thought it was a diamond, but she said it was her birthstone. White topaz."

"I see." I glanced at my watch and started edging toward the door. "I've got to get going. I just remembered I have another appointment I can't miss."

Out on the street, I exhaled a deep breath. The pieces were falling into place now, even more so after Veronica's spot-on description, right down to the distinctive pinky ring. Now I was certain I knew who the mysterious third party was. Natalie Helms.

Chapter Twenty-One

I stood for a moment in front of the studio, debating my next move. Littleton had come here to inquire about one artist and had ended up with questions about another. The Lee sculpture had been a twin to the one I'd seen at The Brush and Canvas, the one that Trey touted was a Kahn original. I pressed a hand to my forehead, reviewing all the facts in my mind. Natalie Helms had worked as an art historian for a large museum; she visited galleries and shows quite frequently and took on small pieces on consignment for her bookshop. She knew her art—that was certain. By her own admission, she'd been friendly with Bridge at one time, but that relationship seemed to nose-dive after his marriage to Petra. She'd also known Colin Murphy and had recommended him to Littleton as a partner in his gallery. And she'd been spending money like crazy lately. I wasn't buying her story of inheriting a small stipend.

If the idea germinating in the back of my mind was true, Natalie's sudden wealth went a lot deeper than that. I pulled my phone out of my pocket, intending to call Will, but my fingers hesitated over the keypad.

All I had right now was a theory. A good one, but just a theory. I really had no proof. I couldn't call Will out here on what might end up as a wild-goose chase. I had to be sure.

But how to get proof?

I pulled the phone back out and dialed Leila's number. The call went straight to her voice mail. I left a message, asking her if she could ask her art editor if he had any contact information for Aamira Lee. After a brief hesitation, I asked if she could find out if Natalie Helms had ever displayed any of Lee's pieces in her shop. I hung up, still feeling unsettled. There was no telling when Leila might be able to get back to me.

I caught sight of a small café nestled in between a bookstore and a jewelry store. I crossed over to the café, pushed open the door, stepped inside, and was immediately assailed by about five different fragrant aromas of coffee. The line was pretty long. I got on the end of it and watched as the people came away from the counter with their food: regular coffees, iced coffees, cappuccinos, and an array of tempting baked goods. I ordered a caramel cappuccino and an apple popover, and once I was served, took my tray to a small table all the way in the back of the store. I took a long, fortifying sip of coffee, a bite of the popover (which was excellent, by the way), and then whipped out my smartphone. I called up Google, typed Aamira Lee into the search engine, and hit Enter.

Aamira did have a small website, but the information on it was sketchy at best. There were a few photos of glass pieces, more of bronze ones. There was no photograph of the artist, and the only contact information to arrange a viewing of the pieces or a showing was for Chatsworth Studios.

Undaunted, I called up Whitepages and plugged in "Aamira Lee—Prady, North Carolina" and hit enter. No exact match came up, but there were two possibles: an Imerie Lee in Douglastown and an Amiera Lee in Raleigh. I tried again, this time typing in "A Lee." This time the amount of hits was staggering—several hundred in the entire state! I let out a moan of frustration.

The old man seated across from me glanced up. "You sound pretty disgusted," he remarked.

"I guess I do. I'm trying to locate an artist, and I'm not having much luck."

"An artist, eh? Local?"

"As far as I know. She's supposed to live in Prady."

He pushed his glasses up on his beak-shaped nose and leaned forward. "Did you check over at Chatsworth Studios? They handle most of the local artists around here."

"I did that already. They told me they don't give out information on artists who are under contract to them."

"Humph," he snorted. "Then you must have been asking about that Aamira Lee."

I stared at him. "Yes, I was. How did you know?"

"Because that girl's got more talent than the law allows. She's going places, and the Ronnies are bound and

264

determined to go along for the ride." He held out his hand. "Sorry, I didn't mean to be rude. I'm Bud Granville. I've lived here all my life, so there's very little about this town I don't know."

"You know the artist, then?"

He nodded. "Charley's lived here all her life."

"Charley?"

"Her name's Charlotte Potts, but everyone calls her Charley. Aamira Lee, that's a name the Ronnies made up. They thought she'd sell more paintings and sculptures if her name sounded more exotic." He reached up to scratch at his sideburns. "Can you imagine that?"

Having a marketing background, I certainly could. "It's all perception," I said. I typed in "Charlotte Potts," hit the Enter key. "How many people around here know Charlotte is Aamira?"

"Most all the old-timers. Not many others. The Ronnies are rabid to keep her identity secret from other art dealers who might steal her away, and customers who want to approach her direct and cut out their commission. Can you say paranoid?" he asked with a chuckle.

"Was anyone else here recently inquiring about her?"

He shrugged. "Not as I know of, but of course that's not to say there couldn't have been." He leaned forward. "To tell you the truth, I'm a little worried about Charley. She's been acting kinda weird lately. I think her new friends are putting ideas in her head."

"Her new friends?"

"Last time I saw her, she said that she'd gotten in with some broker on the sly, and she was gonna make a pile of money and blow this town. I told her she'd better be careful. If the Ronnies got wind of that, heck, they'd dump her, and there would go any chance she had at an art career, not to mention they'd probably sue her for everything she has—not that Charley has a heck of a lot. Her parents died when she was ten, and her aunt who raised her died last year. All Charley has is her chicken farm and her art. She doesn't have much schooling, and at times she can be a bit slow, to put it kindly. She has no parental figure to advise her. Like I said, I'd hate to see her get in trouble."

"So would I," I said, and I meant it. "I think you might be onto something, Bud. I think this person is taking advantage of Charley, and she could be setting her up for a big fall. I'd sure like to help her—if I could find her."

He regarded me thoughtfully. "Just what's your interest in all this, might I ask? I have the feeling it's not entirely fueled by a passion for art."

"It's not," I admitted. I had the feeling Bud would settle for nothing less than the truth, so I told him all about Littleton's death, and about his hatred of the shelter, and about Kat being pegged as a potential suspect. "So you see," I finished, "I want to help clear my sister's name and find the real killer. If it's who I suspect, then Charley might have bitten off a bit more than she can chew, and she could be in real danger."

Bud gave me a hard look, almost as if he were trying to determine if I were sincere or not. At last, he gave a quick nod. "I believe you," he said. "You seem like a square shooter to me, little lady. I think you do have Charley's best interest at heart, and who could blame you for wantin' to clear your sister? Got a pad or a pen?"

I held up my phone. "Better than that. I've got the notes feature on my smartphone."

He chuckled. "I got to get me one of those one day," he said. "Okay, Charley's chicken farm is out in the sticks, a little shack set back in the woods. It's about an hour and a half from here. Take I-10 all the way to the Douganville exit, and when you get off, make a left. About a mile up, you'll see a dirt road. The marker still says Alvin's Alley, but they renamed the road about two years ago. Follow that as far as you can go."

I slid my phone back into my jacket pocket. "Thank you so much, Mr. Granville."

"You come back, let me know how you make out, you hear?" Bud glanced down at my kitten-heeled shoes. "And if I were you, I'd stop over at the Kmart and get a pair of good sneakers. Lots of mud out there."

*　　*　　*

Twenty minutes and a new pair of sneakers later, I was driving down I-10. A large sign read "Douganville: 5 miles," so I figured it wouldn't be long now. There was no denying the jazzed-up feeling pulsing through my veins. I was onto something, all right. Something I hadn't expected when I'd started out on this quest. And if I was right . . .

I got off the exit and in my haste made a right instead of the left Bud Granville had told me. I looped back, made the correction, and then leaned forward, my eyes peeled for Alvin's Alley. About a quarter of the way down, I heard a soft scratching sound. It seemed to be coming from the picnic basket that I'd forgotten all about.

"Fudge," I cried. I pulled over to the side of the road and twisted around in my seat. It was possible some small animal might have gotten inside and eaten the lunch I'd prepared for myself. I reached out, grasped the basket by the handle, and lifted. Wow, was that heavy! What had gotten in here, a raccoon? I set the basket back on the seat with a *thunk* and heard a soft "Merow."

"Oh no. Don't tell me . . ."

The basket top suddenly opened, and up popped Toby's head! He swiveled around, looking left to right, and then his green gaze settled on me. With one fluid motion, he was out of the basket and hopped into the passenger seat, where he turned around twice before settling back, forepaws extended in front of him. He cocked his head. "Merow."

"You rascal! You snuck in the basket." I reached out and gave his head a pat. "I guess you really didn't want to be alone, huh? Okay, pal. You get to go on this adventure with me. Who knows, we might be calling Will and giving him the solution to Littleton's murder before dinnertime. Wouldn't that be nice? We could have Bennington eating crow."

Toby's ears flicked forward at the words "dinner" and "crow." Then he settled himself on the seat, laid his head on his paws, and closed his eyes, probably to dream of a nice fish dinner. I started up the car again and pulled back onto the dirt road. Truthfully, the area appeared so deserted, I was glad of the company—even if it was of the four-footed variety.

* * *

The tiny sign for Alvin's Alley loomed up out of nowhere; if it hadn't been for Toby's sharp meow, I surely would have missed the turnoff. "You're a good copilot," I told the cat as I braked fast and then swung onto the rutted dirt road. For a good fifteen minutes, I felt as if I were driving through the enchanted forest in Disney's *Snow White*. All I saw were trees, shrubs, and low-hanging branches. A few birds skittered past, and Toby immediately put his paws on the dash and made chittering noises in his throat. I took one hand from the steering wheel and gently nudged him back onto the seat.

"If you want to ride up here," I said in a stern tone, "you have to obey the rules."

Toby cast me a somewhat baleful look, then stretched out on the seat and put his head on his paws, casting a wary eye toward the sky.

Another five miles or so down the road, I could see a small clearing. A wooden house squatted there, its paint worn off by years of rain, heat, and humidity. A few of the roof shingles dangled precariously, and I could see that a few of the steps leading up to the front door were broken. Adjoining the house were two smaller, equally rundown buildings. I noticed a large clump of bushes off to the left. I pulled in behind it, and then, after making sure to crack my window, I switched off the motor, pocketed the keys, and looked at Toby.

"You stay here, okay. I shouldn't be long . . . I hope."

I exited the car and stood for a moment. Everything was quiet—maybe a bit too quiet. There was no sign of another vehicle parked anywhere, so it was possible Charley was out somewhere. I walked slowly up the pathway and up the short flight of steps to the front porch. I walked over to the grimy window and peered inside. I could see a sofa, two chairs, a table with a lamp, and an old-style television set. No signs of life, though. I walked over to the door. There was no bell, so I made a fist and knocked. "Hello," I called. "Charlotte Potts? Anyone home?"

No answer. I tried the doorknob. Locked. Damn.

I stood for a minute, debating. My eye fell on the two adjacent buildings, and I ambled over that way. As I approached the smaller one, a faint sound reached my ears. Chickens clucking. I walked up to the door and pushed it open a crack, then stepped back as the smell hit my nostrils. A quick glance inside revealed row upon row of chickens in cages. I shut the door and turned toward the larger building. As I approached, I saw that the door was slightly ajar. I walked over and gave it a tentative push. It creaked inward on rusty hinges, and I stepped over the threshold. It took my eyes a few minutes to adjust to the lower level of light, and then I gazed about, biting back a gasp of astonishment.

The shed was full of floor-to-ceiling shelves filled with all different types of sculptures. They were all delicate, exquisite, beautiful . . . and they all looked amazingly like the photos of ones done by Kahn I'd seen on his website. I doubted Kahn himself, if he were alive, would be able to tell the difference. I felt a sudden surge of anger. The girl was truly talented, and Natalie was exploiting that talent. I whipped out my phone, took a few pictures. A low table in the far corner was covered with a white sheet. I moved closer and was just about to lift the edge for a peek when I heard voices. I looked around for a hiding place, saw a small table off to the far side. It had a white tablecloth across it that reached down to the floor. Without any hesitation, I curled myself into a tight ball and rolled underneath the table, not a moment too soon. I peeped out from around the corner of the tablecloth and saw two figures framed in the doorway. They were both women: The first was tall and angular, with a mass of stick-straight red-gold hair and black-rimmed glasses perched atop an aquiline nose. This, I assumed, was Charley Potts. The other figure was a familiar one I recognized almost instantly. Natalie Helms.

"Don't argue with me, Charlotte," Natalie snapped. "I'm telling you, we need all the sculptures and glass paperweights—everything you have ready—today."

"You told me I had another month," Charley protested. Her voice was a high, nasal tone, one that would surely grate on someone's nerves if they had to listen to it for too long. "I don't have half of what you want ready."

"It doesn't matter," Natalie said in a gruff tone. "We—ah—our plans have changed. We don't have as much time here as originally planned. We'll just have to make do with what you have."

"Okay." A note of suspicion crept into her voice. "You got my money?"

"Of course." I saw Natalie's hand dip into her tote and remove a long white envelope. "Just as we promised. Five thousand dollars, payment in full."

The girl's face lit up. "Five thousand! Golly! That's two thousand more than you originally said!"

"Yes, well . . . you've done such a good job. We thought you deserved a bonus." Natalie patted her bag. "There are some papers you need to sign, dear. Papers of authenticity. Make sure you put that pen name on them, as we discussed."

Her tone turned pouty. "I still don't see why I can't put my own name on 'em. Or the name the Ronnies made up for me."

"I told you why, dear," Natalie said smoothly. "It's unfortunate, but art is still mostly a man's domain. And Ian Kahn is a good, strong name."

"Well . . . okay. I guess you know best." Charley let out a sigh. "We might as well go on over to the house and settle things."

"Excellent. The van will be here shortly."

I heard footsteps slowly shuffle off, but I waited a good ten minutes before I emerged from my hiding place. I shook my head. Bud Granville had said Charley was a bit on the "slow" side. I had an idea that Charley Potts had no clue she was committing forgery, although if it had been me, the idea of "commissioned copies" would have raised a huge red flag. I was also pretty sure five thousand dollars wasn't even 0.1 percent of what Natalie was actually getting for them. And she wasn't alone in her slick scheme, either. I'd have been willing to bet every cent in my bank account that her partner in crime was none other than her "friend" Colin Murphy.

I exited the barn and made my way slowly forward, hugging the building. I wanted to remain in the shadows just in case Charley or Natalie happened to look out the window. I was about to make a break toward the area where I'd hidden my car when I stole a glance over at the house. There was an open window facing me, and I could see two figures moving around inside. I could hear both Kat and Will citing my inner curiosity as my inner Nancy Drew kicked in. Throwing any last vestiges of caution I possessed to the proverbial wind, I crept up onto the porch and flattened myself against the side of the house. I dropped to my hands and knees and crawled over to the window, then slowly raised myself so I could peep in. The first thing I saw was a small refrigerator and then a gas stove—the kitchen, no doubt. Charley was seated at a long table, Natalie right next to her. There was a stack of papers in front of Charley. She had a pen in her hand, and she appeared to be reading one. I heard Natalie say in a sharp tone, "You know what it says, Charlotte. Just sign."

Charley's head shot up, and she shot Natalie a somewhat dazed look. She opened her mouth to speak and then apparently thought better of it. She shrugged, and then her pen started to move across the paper. My eyes darted quickly around the small kitchen, finally coming to rest on a tote bag sprawled on a chair just to the left of the window. My eyes widened as they fastened on an object that was sticking out of the top of the tote—it appeared to be the edge of a brown leather book with a ripped edge. I pressed closer, trying to get a better look. I could make out two initials on the cover of the book. One was partially obscured by the edge of a scarf sticking up, but I was pretty sure the other one was an *L*. An *L* for Littleton. That had to be the missing diary! I stood up and took a step backward, stepping on a loose board that let out a loud creak! "Darn," I muttered.

Inside the house, I heard a chair scrape back. "What was that noise?" I heard Natalie ask.

I didn't wait to hear more. I fairly flew off the porch and started to run toward the bushes where my car was parked. As I ran, I whipped out my cell, intending to call Will, but when I went to turn it on—nothing. Damn, no reception here in the sticks. It would have to wait until I got a bit farther out.

I was almost at the spot where my car was hidden when I heard a door bang open behind me and a woman's sharp cry.

"Well, well. Seems we've got company!"

I broke into a run. I glanced over my shoulder and saw Natalie, her face contorted in an expression of hatred, coming after me, her hands balled into fists. I sped up, my sneakered feet fairly flying over the gravel. Finally, I reached my car and hopped inside. Toby glanced up sleepily from his position on the front seat, then lifted his head as I switched on the ignition and slammed the car into reverse.

"Hang on, boy," I told him. "We've got to burn rubber and get Will and Bennington down here ASAP."

I backed up and made a sharp turn, my fender just narrowly missing Natalie, who was screaming at me to stop the car. "Not on your life," I yelled out the window. I pressed my foot down hard on the accelerator, and my car shot forward, racing back down the dirt road. I had to hand it to them: on paper, it was the perfect murder. Who would suspect Natalie? I surely hadn't. She had no viable motive for wanting Littleton dead, and Colin Murphy had given himself the perfect alibi.

I stole a quick glance at Toby. "Won't Bennington's face be red?" I asked the cat. I glanced in my rearview mirror. No other car was in sight, which I thought was odd. I'd fully expected Natalie to give chase. I reached into my pocket for my phone and switched it on. Thankfully, it was working now. I dialed Will's number, but it went straight to voice mail. I didn't hesitate. I left a message, hitting the highlights, and ended with my location and the fact I was headed back to Deer Park. "Please get here as fast as you can. I think Natalie and Colin are in the process of skipping with the evidence." I slid my phone back into my pocket and smiled at Toby. "Don't worry. Once we get on the highway, it's full speed ahead to Deer Park. We won't let them get away with this—uh oh." I was only a few feet away from the turnoff to the main highway. Another vehicle was there: a large white van, just slowing down to make the turn onto the narrow dirt road. I gunned the engine and sped past, but I couldn't resist a quick glance over my shoulder at the astonished face of the van's driver . . . Colin Murphy.

Chapter Twenty-Two

I pressed down hard on the accelerator, and my convertible shot down the road. Toby let out a sharp yowl and dug his claws deep into the leather upholstery. "Hang on, boy," I muttered. "This is life or death, for real."

I glanced into my rearview mirror, and my heart sank right down to my toes as I saw the van negotiate a sharp U-turn and come barreling after me. It wasn't five minutes later that the vehicle came abreast of mine and slammed its front bumper into the rear end of my car. The force of the impact thrust me forward onto the steering wheel, and for a brief moment, I lost control of my car as it fishtailed down the middle of the narrow road. After a minute, though, I was in control again. I saw the van gear up for another hit, and I reflexively pushed down hard on the accelerator. I snuck a quick peek at the speedometer as my car fairly flew down the road. Fifty, sixty, seventy miles per hour—way too fast on this narrow little road with all its twists and turns. I eased my foot off and edged it onto the brake at the same moment Colin sent the van rocketing forward and into my rear bumper a second time. This time I swerved dangerously close to the shoulder of the road, sending a shock of gravel pebbles up onto my windshield.

I straightened out again, then once again stomped down hard on the accelerator. I was flying down the road at a brisk eighty miles per hour, and the van was keeping a steady pace with me. I figured Colin's next move would be to creep up next to me and run me right off the road. At the speed I was going, that would spell inevitable disaster, unless . . .

I spied an indentation in the road just ahead. A grassy rutted trail that looked as if it led into a thicket of woods and swamp. Breathing a prayer, I gave the wheel a sharp tug and aimed for it. There was a thud and a crunch as tires met gravel, and then I was bouncing down the rutted trail. I lifted my eyes from the road just long enough to glance in the rearview mirror.

The van was right behind me.

Toby let out a *merow* and then dived under the dashboard. I didn't blame him. I wished I could dive under there myself.

Branches and vines slapped at my windshield as I bumped along the road. Soggy grass turned to mud and then to marshy swampland as I plowed along. The trail I'd initially followed was slowly disintegrating. Another glance in my rearview mirror told me that Colin apparently had no intention of giving up the chase.

Toby had crawled back up onto the seat and was leaning his head against the passenger window. Suddenly, his ears flicked forward. His paw swatted against the window. "Merow! Ow-owrr!"

"What's wrong, boy?" I slowed down a bit, peered out the window, and then I saw what had attracted his attention. A short trail, off to one side. And in the distance, what looked like the chimney of a house!

"Good boy," I praised the cat. "Now hang on."

I gave the wheel a sharp turn and veered to the right, then gunned the engine and shot down the trail as the van whizzed past in the other direction. I made my way slowly down the tiny trail, which was more mud than anything else. Halfway down, the convertible's tires got mired in a rut. After about ten minutes of rocking and spinning my wheels, I opened the door and hopped out—and sank ankle-deep into mud. Toby hopped onto the driver's seat and looked out, his nose wrinkling at the sight of all that mud.

"Stay in the car, Toby," I directed the cat. I shut the door and stood for a minute to get my bearings. The building was visible now, and I could see that it was a cabin similar to the one Charlotte Potts lived in. Mentally blessing Bud Granville for his advice on my choice of footwear, I started to plod down the muddy trail toward the building. I was almost there when I stiffened. Had I heard the faint buzz of a motor? The sound wasn't repeated, and I shuffled forward. As I walked up the rickety steps, I heard an unmistakable click. I whirled and looked straight into the barrel of a .45 revolver, held in the hand of Colin Murphy!

279

"I told Natalie you were a meddling pest, especially after you asked about Kahn Lee," he muttered. "She dismissed you, until you asked her the same thing. We knew we had to settle up and get out of here as fast as we could. When I returned to the studio today and Trey told me about the reporter and photographer, I knew we had to make our move now."

"How—how on earth did you get here?" I sputtered.

He laughed. "I grew up in this area. I know all the backroads. When you turned off, I just kept going straight to the paved road that was up ahead. I figured you were headed here—it's the only building for miles, unfortunately for you." He waved the gun. "Now get inside."

I pushed the door open and walked inside, being careful to duck my head against the low ceiling. The cabin was old, and it was apparent that it was abandoned and in complete disrepair. Rotting, fallen beams were everywhere. All it would take was one match, I thought, and this place would go up like a firebomb. My blood turned to ice. Was that what he planned to do? Burn me alive?

"Keep moving," said Colin.

"Wh-what are you going to do?" I asked.

"Well, we'd planned to milk this venture for another few weeks, but now, thanks to your meddling, we're going to have to cut our little sideline short," he said. "The sculptures we'll pick up from Charlotte Potts will net us a tidy sum, although not as much as we could have gotten over a few more weeks' time. By tonight we'll be on a plane bound for Dubai. The US doesn't have an extradition policy there as far as I know, and with the money we'll be collecting, we can live like kings."

I rubbed my sweaty palms against the sides of my pants. "So whose idea was it to kill Littleton? Yours or Natalie's?"

He chuckled. "Actually, it was a joint decision. Natalie and Bridge were quite an item back in the day, when she worked in Boston and he traveled there on buying trips. They eventually ended the romantic aspect, but they remained friendly until he married Petra. Natalie moved here after she got laid off and expected Bridge to continue to treat her like royalty, but those days were gone. He was going to raise her rent just like everyone else's."

"So she resented that."

He snorted. "That's putting it mildly. Natalie thought she was doing me a favor, recommending me to Bridge. At first I thought it might work out, but it wasn't long before I realized our partnership only worked as long as Bridge got his way. And seeing as he had the controlling interest, he always did. The guy was a complete control freak. He didn't want to change one thing, and he wasn't interested in chatting up any artist whose work he wasn't fond of."

"You were fed up, tired of playing second fiddle. You wanted to get out from under his thumb."

Colin let out deep breath. "If only Bridge hadn't visited Prady, looking for those Plumms—we might have gotten the extra few weeks we needed to amass a real fortune."

"Don't you feel bad in the least about involving that innocent girl in your scheme?" I cried.

"A good lawyer can get her off with a light sentence. She wasn't all that innocent. She was eager to take our money."

"I bet if she knew just how much the two of you were making on that artwork, she'd have injected the two of *you* with poison. Natalie is the one who did it, right?"

"Yes. One of her more brilliant ideas." Colin waved the gun at me. "A pity you had to go and meddle. It's too bad it's come to this, but . . . I'm afraid your time is up."

"You'll never get away with this," I said.

"I beg your pardon. I already have." He pulled a coil of rope out of the pocket of his jacket. "I'm going to tie you to that post, and then I'm going to start a little bonfire. Don't worry—I'm sure you'll be dead from smoke inhalation long before the flames get to you."

I twisted my head, looking frantically for some means of escape. It seemed as if there were none and then . . . I stepped backward, felt the floor give slightly. I looked down and saw that the floorboards in this section were practically rotted through. I glanced up and saw Colin coming closer. As he reached for the rope, he lowered the gun for a split second, and that was all the time I needed. I stomped down hard on the rotted section of floor, and the next instant I felt myself falling downward. Above me, I heard Colin's frustrated scream: "You'll never get away."

I landed with a plunk on the hard ground, and it took me a few minutes to catch my breath. I struggled to my feet, and a searing pain shot through my left ankle. I must have twisted it when I hit the ground. No time to baby it, though. I sniffed at the air as the acrid odor of burning wood reached my nostrils. He'd set fire to the cabin anyway! My head whipped every which way, looking for some sort of exit out of my prison.

But I couldn't see any. I rocked back on my heels as wet tears stung the corners of my eyes. Was this how it all ended?

"Meroow!"

I twisted my head around and rubbed at my eyes with both hands. Was I dreaming, or was that Toby squatting in the corner?

"Merooow," he said again, more urgently this time, his paw waving in the air.

And then I saw it, right behind him. A small opening, barely three feet wide. Some sort of tunnel? With Toby leading the way, I dove into the dark crawl space and hoped for the best.

I crawled along on my hands and knees. Toby stayed in front of me, tail swishing, and every now and then, the tip would hit me in the face. I wondered briefly just how far the tunnel might extend—it seemed to go on forever. Finally, though, we came to another opening. I saw a glimmer of the twilight sky above, and a blast of cool air slapped me in the face. I crawled upward, and a few minutes later found myself back outside, at the edge of the clearing. A blast of heat hit me square in the face, and I turned in that direction. I could see the house burning, and a little farther beyond, my car still sat where I'd left it. No sign of Colin's van, though. He must have taken off as soon as he'd struck the match.

I struggled to my feet, bit back a cry as I felt pain shoot through my injured ankle again, and then started to slowly limp toward my car. Halfway there, I heard a slight rustling in the bushes. I looked around for Toby, but the cat seemed to have vanished. "Toby?" I called in a hoarse whisper. "Where are you?"

A second later, the bushes parted, and Colin emerged, gun in hand. "I had a feeling we hadn't seen the last of you. And I just can't leave here with any loose ends hanging."

Suddenly, we both stiffened. Off in the distance— could it be? The faint whine of a police siren.

"How the heck?" Colin growled, then pointed the gun at me. "It doesn't matter. I know a back way through those woods. They'll never catch me. Good-bye, Ms. McCall."

He leveled the gun at my chest and then . . . he screamed in pain as Toby dropped out of a nearby tree, right onto his shoulder, and dug his sharp claws right into his neck.

"Owwww! Get this damn cat off me."

He reached up and tried to pull Toby off, but the cat hung on fast. In the meantime, I hobbled forward and snatched up the gun Colin had dropped. I made sure the safety was on, then I raised it and pointed it right at him.

The cat looked up, saw the gun in my hand, jumped off of Colin's shoulder, and trotted over to me. Colin lay on the ground, clutching at his neck and moaning.

A few minutes later, Will and Bennington burst into the clearing, guns drawn. Both of them stopped and stared when they saw me.

"Here's your killer," I said. "One of them, at least. The other one's back at Charley Potts's cabin with the forged sculptures."

Bennington pulled handcuffs out of his pocket and snapped them on Murphy's wrist. Will hurried over to me, gently took the gun from my trembling hands, and then enfolded me in his arms. "It's a good thing I checked my messages," he said gruffly. "You took some chance, Syd."

"Maybe," I said, looking up at him.

And then I fainted.

Chapter Twenty-Three

It was two days later, and I was lying on the couch in the living room, my bandaged ankle propped up on an ottoman. I'd been taken to the ER at Deer Park General, where I'd been treated for shock and a sprained ankle. Kat and Leila had come to get me, and Kat, after giving me the bear hug to end all bear hugs, had yelled at me nonstop for an hour about how I shouldn't have played detective. Leila, on the other hand, had busily taken notes, the result being the headline in this morning's paper: "Local Woman Instrumental in Bringing Trowbridge Littleton's Murderer to Justice."

Kat came in, balancing a breakfast tray, which she set down in front of me. "Scrambled eggs, whole wheat toast with jam, and three slices of nice, crisp bacon. Your favorite breakfast."

"Wow." I picked up a slice of bacon, broke it in half, and shoved a piece in my mouth. "Delicious. Maybe I should track killers down every day."

"Don't be smug." Kat looked at me anxiously. "The doctor said you have to stay off your feet for at least a week."

I hung my head, feeling contrite. "Yeah, I am sorry about that."

"You should be," Kat said. She was trying to sound stern but was failing miserably. "After all, I need my new publicity director all in one piece. While you were out chasing down Colin and Natalie, Petra called a meeting with the mayor. Apparently, she was pretty high on the shelter after her positive adoption experience. She went on and on about how well the facility was kept and the excellent care we give our animals. And of course, she couldn't stop talking about Jonesy and how lucky she was that she found him."

I pressed a hand to my head. "Well, gee. Who'd have ever thunk that?"

"Not me," Kat said with a deep chuckle. "Anyway, to make a long story short, Petra proposed another long-term lease on the shelter building . . . at a 20 percent *lower* rental fee than the previous deal!"

"Oh my God!" I squealed, and then suspicion settled in. "Wait a sec. What happened to the tenant who was willing to pay double or triple the rent for that space?"

"That's the best part. Thanks to you, Petra could afford to be generous with the shelter deal!"

I furrowed my brow. "Thanks to me? I don't get it. Why me?"

Kat's grin stretched from ear to ear. "Because of your detective work, another property became available—a property much better suited to this new vendor."

"What property is—oh, wait. You mean Natalie's bookstore?"

"None other. Natalie certainly won't be using it now. Petra rented it to Crowden's at a 45 percent increase over what Natalie was paying."

My eyes popped. "Crowden's? The bookstore chain? Wow!" I sank back against the cushions. "Talk about a match made in heaven."

"And that's not all," Kat said, eyes twinkling. "Petra also made a very large donation to the shelter in Jonesy's name—very large. She said she plans to make a similar one each year, so now our budget can justify hiring a publicity director full time." Her smile widened. "All you have to do is work your tail off to validate your position."

"Oh my gosh," I said blissfully. "I can do that."

"Of course you can." Kat reached out and patted my hand. "Just do me a favor, and promise me you will never put yourself in danger like that again."

"Well, that should be easy." I grinned at her. "I have no intention of finding any more dead bodies or chasing down any more murderers—at least not in the foreseeable future."

Kat frowned. "What about the *un*foreseeable future?"

Thankfully, the doorbell rang just then. Kat made an exasperated noise and then got up to answer, returning a few seconds later with Will in tow. He held a bouquet of carnations and pansies—my favorite flowers—in his hand. He set it down on the coffee table and offered me a lopsided grin.

"Hey there, Sherlock. How are you feeling today?"

"Better. I'm sorry I was such a wuss and fainted."

"Under the circumstances, I think we can forgive you," he said with a chuckle. "Oh, and by the way, congrats. Kat tells me your job is permanent now."

I shifted on the couch. "What happened to Natalie? Leila's account doesn't say much other than that the criminals were arrested."

"We got her leaving Charley Potts's house. She knocked the poor girl out and was going to take off in her pickup. She was going to cheat her out of everything too. We found the cashier's check made out to Charlotte Potts in her bag." He shook his head. "Of course she's placing the blame on Murphy, and Murphy insists it was all Natalie's idea. No honor among thieves with those two," he chuckled.

"Yeah, well, the one I feel sorry for is Charley Potts. She's rather an innocent victim."

"Well, on some level she must have known that what she was doing was wrong. But we figure if we offer her immunity on a forgery charge in exchange for her testimony against those two, justice will have been served."

"Thank goodness." I leaned back against the pillows. "So did they explain why and how they did it?"

"Yep." Will leaned back in the chair and laced his fingers behind his neck. "As you know, Natalie and Littleton were an item back in the day, but their love affair had run its course, and now their friendship was tenuous at best. Not the case with Natalie and Colin Murphy. Natalie recommended Colin to Bridge, half because she had a crush on him and half because she thought his knowledge of art might pay off one day.

"Natalie happened to go to the Chatsworth Studios one day looking for some artwork to sell in her shop, and she came across a sculpture that she was certain was a Kahn. She was shocked when the Martins told her that Aamira Lee had done it and immediately set about tracking the woman down. Once she did, she noticed that Charley wasn't very well educated, so it was a simple matter for her to convince the girl to make what she called 'commissioned copies.' She showed her different photographs of Kahn pieces, and Charley duplicated them, right down to the signature. Once she had Charley nailed down, she went to Colin with her scheme. Colin was more than willing to go along with it, because he was having difficulties with Bridge. He saw his chance to make a break, make enough money to get a fresh start. They planned to sell as many sculptures and paperweights as they could at sky-high prices, take the money, and flee the country."

"But Littleton found out about it," I said. "The Ronnies said he was at their studio and saw the sculpture of the Indian woman—the same one that his gallery was touting as an exclusive."

Will nodded. "That was the part Colin and Natalie hadn't counted on. It didn't take long for him to put two and two together, especially once he saw that paperweight. He'd remembered seeing the exact same one in Natalie's office, so now he knew the two of 'em were in on it together. He was furious—he confronted Colin, told him that he would not have his gallery's reputation ruined, and told him to get out. Natalie met him at the food court and tried to reason with him, but he was having none of it."

"Ah, so it was Natalie Leila saw, not Grace." I nodded. "I get that. They have similar builds, and their hair is the same color. At a distance, you could mistake one for the other, and Natalie does have a coral sweater similar to Grace's."

"Littleton gave Natalie thirty days to give up her lease and get out of Deer Park, or he was pressing charges. In the meantime, Colin had gotten nervous and searched Bridge's office. He'd mentioned to Colin that he'd planned to leave him the gallery in his will, so when Colin saw the appointment calendar with his lawyer's name on it, he figured out what Littleton planned to do. Colin panicked and called Natalie, who hit upon the plan to inject him with the poison. Years ago, she'd been a nurse's aide. She made the plane reservation for Colin so that he'd have an airtight alibi, and she was pretty sure no one would suspect her—after all, she was about the only shopkeeper who didn't have an issue with Littleton."

"Which in itself should have raised a red flag," I remarked. "And it's true—who would ever have suspected Natalie? She's so innocent looking."

"Yeah, like Lucretia Borgia. She snuck up behind him and jabbed him in the neck, then pushed him inside and slammed the door . . . She knew the dose she'd given him would act quickly and he'd be unable to get out and call for help. Colin had told her where the diary was, but when she went to get it, she found out that Littleton had moved it. She found it, though, and left only minutes before you and Kat came in."

"Thank God we missed her." I suppressed a shudder. "Well . . . all's well that ends well, I guess." I cocked my head at him. "One thing puzzles me. I know you said you got my message, but how did you know my exact location?"

His lips curved upward. "You still had your phone on, and you've got GPS on it."

"I owe Leila for that. She suggested I get it."

Will's hand folded over mine. "You were lucky, though, Syd."

"How so?"

"Ow-owrr."

Toby made a flying leap from the floor onto my lap. I petted him and grinned at Will. "Luck in feline form. It was really quite a sight, Toby dropping right down on Murphy like that. If he hadn't . . ."

Will reached out to stroke the cat's head as well. "If he hadn't . . . well, let's not think about that."

"You're right. I should be thinking of something much more pleasant, like our next cat café event." I shot him a teasing glance. "Are you interested? Cats make wonderful companions, and they're great low-maintenance pets for working people."

"I'll think about it. In the meantime . . ." He leaned in a little closer. "There's a little matter we need to resolve."

I widened my eyes. "There is?"

"Yep. Kat's officially off the hook for Littleton's murder. You do remember what you promised me if I got her off, right?"

"I remember. Technically, though, you didn't get Kat off. I did."

"We can debate that point over a dinner at Ferrulli's," he said softly. "With a nice merlot thrown in for good measure."

I lowered my lashes. "I think that could be arranged. When exactly would you want to do this?"

He moved in closer to me, so close I could smell the tangy scent of his aftershave. "I think as soon as possible. I don't trust you, Syd McCall. Now I'll never admit this—and especially not to Hank—but truth be told, you're not a half bad sleuth."

I goggled at him. "What? You're actually complimenting me? I'm flattered."

"You should be. Besides, if we wait much longer to go out and start getting reacquainted, you'll undoubtedly get yourself tangled up in another murder—and I'll have to rescue you again. So—what do you say? I'm off tonight. I can pick you up at six. Literally. I can carry you to my car."

"Not necessary," I laughed. "I have a cane that Kat got me."

"Perfect." A brief silence stretched between us. "And?" he finally prompted.

I made the sign of the cross over my chest. "I'll make the same promise to you that I did to Kat. No more investigating."

He eyed me. "You forget, I know all your tricks. You've got the toes on your good foot crossed, haven't you?"

"Have not." As I said the words, Toby let out a loud *merow*.

Will started to laugh. "Even that cat knows you're lying."

I shot Toby a look. "Squealer!" I turned back to Will and held up both hands. "Fine. I promise—no more sleuthing, at least not until my ankle's healed. Satisfied?"

"I guess I'll have to be—for now," he murmured. For a second, I thought he was going to kiss me, but he straightened, rose, and cleared his throat. "Until later, then."

"Until later."

After Will had let himself out, I lay back against the couch cushions. Toby jumped up onto my lap and lay looking at me, his green eyes wide. I stroked his head and sighed.

"I'm not sure where things might go with Will," I told the cat. "But one thing I do know. If—or when—he tries to kiss me, I'm going to let him. And . . . I might even kiss him back. What do you say to that?"

Toby looked at me for a long moment, then laid his head down on my lap and started to purr.

I chuckled and rubbed the top of his head. "I thought you might agree."

Acknowledgments

Thanks as always to my wonderful agent, Josh Getzler, who puts up with my e-mails and whining on a consistent basis! Thanks also to his lovely assistant, Danielle Burby, who gave me the idea for a story featuring a cat café at BEA two years ago! I would also like to thank my editor at Crooked Lane, Matt Martz, for his inspiration to center the series around a shelter, and also the editorial staff at Crooked Lane! They are amazing!

I want to thank all the writers who have appeared on ROCCO's blog for their friendship and support, and a special thanks to Liz Taranda at the Clifton Animal Shelter!

I would also like to thank all of my loyal readers who have followed my Nick and Nora series, and I hope that you enjoy this one! I wouldn't be here without you!

And a special PS to my buddy Cathy Collette: hardcover! Woo-hoo!